THE SECRET OF HADITHA

ANDREW VINCENT

CRANTHORPE
MILLNER
PUBLISHERS

First published by Cranthorpe Millner Publishers (2022)

ISBN 978-1-80378-039-9 (Paperback)

www.cranthorpemillner.com

Cranthorpe Millner Publishers

To

Lee,

This book is dedicated to my loving family, my wife
Sharon, my mum, dad and my two amazing boys Ben
and Adam, who all helped me through the dark times
during lockdown, in their own unique ways!

Best wishes

A

PROLOGUE
April 2009

John remembered that night so vividly it was like someone had slipped a pill into his whiskey. The smell of the dusty roads where he had been dropped, a few miles from the target; the taste of the dry air as he had paused to make sure he was following the correct co-ordinates; the fear in his blood stream, as he had contemplated what he might find underneath the desert below his feet.

He had managed to acquire some night vision equipment, by pulling in a favour at the nearest British base, and having been dropped off by his old mercenary informant, Mustafa, he had been confident that no one had followed him on the drive up. After that, it had simply been a matter of waiting, until the darkness of the early hours had given him enough cover to commence his first ever black-ops mission.

Designed to prevent accidental breaches by locals, and with no CCTV cameras or guards to negotiate, John had known the perimeter would offer little resistance, and he had quickly scaled the fence. Scanning the terrain on the other side, he had seen no immediate problems, so after checking his backpack for damage, he had started walking, beginning the two and a half mile hike up to the place where his informant had said he would find the secret of Haditha. As the terrain had grown steeper, he had considered how he might get a look inside. That had been the obvious challenge; without his first-hand account, the operation would ultimately be deemed a failure.

A sense of urgency had accompanied his first glimpse of the early morning sunlight breaking through the black night sky, and he had known that he needed to pick up his pace if he wanted to reach his destination before sunrise. After surveying the surrounding area, John had spotted a small building in the distance, guarded by two men, holding semi-automatic weapons. After calculating how far away he was from the building – more or less a thirty-second sprint – he had taken a moment to collect his thoughts, hiding behind one of a few small trees in the sandy wasteland.

Promptly turning on his night vision goggles, which had been slowly losing their effectiveness in the burgeoning daylight, he had managed to check out the remaining area. The area of the complex to the right of the main compound had been devoid of heat signatures, making it the perfect place for him to wait for an opportunity to sneak inside. Unfortunately, the small, dusty road to his left – the only entrance or exit for vehicles travelling to and from the compound – had been manned by two guards, armed with submachine guns and communications devices.

John had remained hidden behind his tree for a good few minutes, trying desperately to work out a sensible plan and then muster the courage to make his move. Neither the plan, nor the courage, had been forthcoming.

Eventually, after more thought and wasted time, he had removed his backpack; placed the night goggles inside, and removed his combat clothes and shoes, replacing them with standard army base footwear and slacks. Taking one last sip of water from his bottle, he had made a small hole in the ground to stash the rucksack, making sure his things were out of sight and recoverable upon his return.

Wary of being exposed by the sunlight, John had crouched low to reduce his risk of being seen, before making the short dash towards the complex. The two guards at the checkpoint had been pre-occupied with a truck arriving, and the other two guards had been out of sight after the first few metres. In one breath, John had made it to his next safe point, unseen and unheard. Leaning his aching body against the wall, he had realised then that there was no way back now; he had just well and truly taken the plunge into the deep-end.

Recovering his breath, he had glanced up to the skies, not sure whether he was looking for divine intervention or just for the bloody sun to stop coming up. Regardless, his prayers had gone unanswered; sitting there, John had watched the daylight break and the sun rain down over his body and the complex he was leaning up against.

In that moment he had realised that he still had no plan of how to gain access to the compound below, or even how to get himself out in one piece. Would he complete the mission? Or would he simply sit against the wall until he was eventually found, arrested or worse? In that moment, nothing had been certain.

CHAPTER ONE
February 2020

John was cooking dinner, embracing the calming monotony of family routine. He had no desire to return to his former life, far from it; he was enjoying living in the moment, and regularly congratulated himself on the decision he had made over a decade ago.

"Ethan! Ethan, get down 'ere. Dinner's ready in five," he shouted up the stairs. "If I have to shout you again, you'll lose the Xbox." Kids offered different problems, he thought to himself. Certainly less complex, but no less demanding.

While Ethan was hiding away upstairs, Amy was diligently laying the table and Wendy was finishing off some marking. John was happy to leave them be; he enjoyed the peace and quiet of cooking, it was his way of relaxing. That did not mean he was pleased with Ethan being stuck on that game again for over three hours, he just chose to let it slide, preferring instead to enjoy a moment of tranquillity before dinner.

"Dinner's ready, guys!" he announced, a couple of minutes before it actually was. He knew it would take at least two more attempts before Ethan would begrudgingly prize himself from his game. John hated

4

it; he hated everything it stood for: the guns, the violence... most of all, he hated the fact that Ethan was completely obsessed with it.

"Get down 'ere now, Ethan. I mean it pal, it's rude; your food's getting cold."

Amy had been quick to heed her dad's call to dinner, and was already tucking into a slice of garlic bread, eagerly anticipating the delivery of her pasta. Spaghetti Bolognese was John's signature dish, and his family loved it. Wendy was also at the table, trying desperately to avoid eye contact with her husband, fearing she would inevitably be dragged into the impending conflict.

"Calm down, John, come and eat yours," she whispered, sensing John's frustration building.

"Ethan, last chance..."

"I'm here, I'm here. Chill out, man. Ooh, Spag Bol. Pass the cheese will you, sis?"

John turned in his son's direction, ready to yell at him again, then stopped himself. Let it go, John, he said to himself. Let it go. Remember your blood pressure.

"John, come and eat yours, it's fantastic! So, how was school, Ethan?" Wendy asked, attempting to salvage their evening.

"Alright..." Ethan grunted.

This was the Cooper family routine: evening meal around the dinner table on Mondays, trying desperately to hang onto their own, self-inflicted family values. It seemed so much harder now that the kids were growing up.

John was a chef at the local hotel and worked evenings and weekends mostly, so Monday was his night off, hence the Spag Bol. Wendy was a primary school teacher and loved Mondays, because it meant she didn't have to cook, for once. 'Married to a chef that doesn't do any cooking!' she often joked with her friends.

"What's for pudding, Dad?" Ethan finally uttered, as he wolfed down his mountain of spaghetti,

"You haven't eaten that yet. Honestly, I spend two hours cooking and it takes you twenty seconds to demolish it. You can have pudding, but only after you've done your homework, okay?"

John glanced up at Ethan and gave his son a reassuring wink – a peace offering, designed to facilitate the return of calm to the household – before promptly spooning another dollop of Bolognese onto his plate. In that moment, during that transient passing of time, everything changed for the Cooper family forever.

"Kids, get under the table, now—"

Before John could even finish his sentence, two men, dressed all in black, smashed through the front door and stormed the kitchen.

"Everybody down!"

"Do as they say, kids, this won't last long."

"Correct, John. If you do as we say, no one'll get hurt. Now, where is it?"

"Where's what?"

"You know full well what, stop pissing about, otherwise my friend over there'll hurt your family."

His smaller, uglier looking accomplice had already moved across the kitchen and positioned himself next to Wendy and the kids. He was pointing a Russian Makarov pistol at Wendy's head.

"Careful guys, I mean it. If you hurt them, I'll hunt you down and kill you." John's tone could have cut through steel.

"I don't think you're in a position to make threats, do you? Now, tell me where it is, and we'll be gone."

"Who are you? Who sent you?"

"Hey, I'm asking the questions 'ere, now where's the rock?"

"Stay calm, Wendy," John said, ignoring the question, focusing his full attention on his wife. "This'll all be over soon, I promise."

The intruders glanced at one another, confused by John's response.

That glance was all the encouragement John needed; his window of opportunity. Diving towards the kitchen knife set opposite – the one his mother-in-law had bought them for their wedding that had never been used – he pulled out the carving knife and stabbed the invader in the stomach. The intruder's giant frame hit the wooden flooring, and in what seemed like one fluid motion, John kicked him in the chest and wrestled the gun out of his hands.

Before the other attacker had chance to react, John squeezed the trigger, shooting him twice in the stomach. The other intruder also fell to the ground, firing a couple of rounds skyward in the process, before landing in a heap right next to John's traumatised family. Wendy quickly snatched the gun from his hand and threw it across the floor in John's general direction.

"Right, listen up you two. You better start talking quick. Who sent you?"

"I don't know, honest," replied the first attacker, clutching his stomach.

"Well, maybe this'll jog your memory." John prodded his weapon into the man's open wound, ignoring the screams of pain. "I could let you live… I could… but I'm guessing you only have fifteen or twenty minutes left 'til you bleed out. So keep it short. My wife can phone you an ambulance, just as soon as you talk to me."

"What do you want to know?'

"Who sent you? What do you want? What rock?" John barked at the men. "You don't have much time, guys. Last chance, who sent you?"

Wendy was still underneath the dining room table clinging to her two children, who had not moved a muscle, seemingly frozen solid by what they had just witnessed.

"Time's ticking. Your friend over there looks in bad shape, so I suggest you start talking."

"All right… some guy on the internet hired us, okay? I don't know his name; he's paying us ten grand each to get this diamond from you, that's all I know. Now, please, phone us an ambulance."

"Name? What's the guy's name, and where's he from?" John persisted.

"I don't know, I swear! He just said get the rock. Now please, I'm dying…"

"Where are you from?"

"Moscow."

"Moscow? What the… what's the plan, then? What happens next?"

"What do you mean?"

"I mean, where's the drop off? When are you meeting? Come on, mate, you know what I want to know."

"I'm not sure. We were told to make contact again, when we got back to Russia, to arrange the drop off and

8

payment. That's everything I know, I swear. Please, I'm begging you, Petr is dying over there!"

"Oh, you're begging me now are you." John paused his interrogation, conscious that the man was in serious trouble, and bleeding heavily. "Okay, phone them, Wendy. Tell them we have two foreign men with critical wounds bleeding out on our kitchen floor, and tell them to send police too."

Wendy did as she was told, comforted by his calm authority, yet subconsciously wondering where the hell it had been during their twenty years of marriage.

"Here, press this on the wound to stop the bleeding," John said to the man with the knife wound. "What's your name?

"Michial," came the faint reply. "Thank you."

John turned his attention to Petr. Michial was right, his partner was in bad, bad shape. John tried to stem the flow of blood, but to no avail. They both needed an ambulance, fast. He continued to press on the man's wounds and tried to keep him conscious, until, to his relief, he heard the sound of an ambulance siren approaching.

Two paramedics, a man and a woman, entered the house through the front door, pausing in shock as they saw the carnage that had just unfolded.

"Blimey, what the hell happened here?"

"They broke in, but I managed to disarm them," John replied, as he comforted his wife and kids.

"What, both of them?"

"Yeah. I must have caught them off guard, I suppose. I served in the army, 4th Battalion, Parachute Regiment."

"As a chef!" Wendy exclaimed. "How the hell did you just do that?"

"Everyone gets basic combat training, honey, even the chefs," he assured her. "So, what's the prognosis, pal?" he asked one of the paramedics, trying desperately to direct the focus away from his heroic exploits.

"Well, erm, he's losing a lot of blood. We'll need to get him in asap. Help me lift him, will you?"

"Really? I'm not sure that's a good idea, mate."

"Err, yeah, you're right, sorry. Err, Susan? Give me a hand?"

"Don't you need to take a look at the other guy first?"

"Yes, will do. Let's just get this fella in the ambulance first, then I'll get to him."

While the paramedics struggled to lift Michial onto the stretcher, Wendy was frantically trying to get her husband's attention. A second ambulance had just turned up and Wendy was confused. "John? John, another ambulance is here, what's going on?" she whispered, out of earshot of the paramedics.

John took a closer look at the paramedics, who were busy treating the wounded man on his kitchen floor. Something seemed off. Real paramedics would never ask a bystander to help them lift their patient into an ambulance, and as far as he could recall, most of them did not usually conceal Walther PPK's in their waistbands.

"Stop there, don't move," John murmured menacingly, placing his own pistol against the back of the male paramedic's head. "Who are you? What's going on?"

"What do you mean, mate?"

"What're you doing, John?" Wendy whispered urgently.

"Shh, honey, trust me. You're not paramedics. The

real ones have just turned up, look."

Before John could decide what to do next, the decision was made for him. He heard a distinctive whooshing sound and instinctively ducked behind the island in the kitchen as a bullet whistled past his nose. Recovering quickly from the shock, he mustered the courage to poke his head out from behind his refuge, and immediately spotted the female 'paramedic' walking towards him, firing what looked like another Walther PPK.

Fearing for his family, John rolled out into the open and fired his pistol at her, shooting her three times. As she felt the full impact of the bullets striking her just above the heart, John fired another two shots, both directly into the back of the male 'paramedic', and watched in a state of slow motion as both imposters hit to the ground in unison.

He paused, listening for signs of life, but heard nothing, and promptly scrambled to his feet to assess the damage. It was carnage. Both paramedics lay dead on the floor, the two Russian intruder's lay dying, and there was blood soaking into every nook and cranny of their kitchen.

John turned to comfort his family, but before he could reach them, he was met by the fragmented, confused cries of his wife, calling his son's name.

"Ethan? Ethan! Ethan, no… talk to me. John? John, he's been shot… John, help… help him. Ethan!" she sobbed.

"Quick, Wendy, lift his head. Can you see the wound? Lift his head," John responded, trying to mask his panic. "I'll hold this on the wound, get the ambulance staff in here quick. Ethan hasn't got long;

he's bleeding too much…"

CHAPTER TWO

John's heart sank deep into the bowels of his body as the doctor approached.

"Mr and Mrs Cooper?" he asked.

"Yes," John replied, clutching his wife and daughter tightly as they sat huddled together on the hard, plastic hospital bench.

"My name is Mr Rubani, and I'm the doctor in charge of looking after Ethan. Firstly, I want you to know that we're doing everything we can for him, and that he is in a stable but critical condition."

"Critical?" Wendy sobbed.

"Yes, I'm afraid his condition is very serious. We decided that it was best to put him in an enforced coma; he has lost a lot of blood. He is stable now, and we have removed the bullet; fortunately, it missed all his vital organs. But, because of the blood loss, the next forty-eight hours are vital."

"Thanks, doctor. Can we see him?"

"Yes, of course. Nurse Maddock will take you in now, but please, only two people maximum at a time, and only for a few minutes. He needs to rest. I will update you as and when anything changes."

"Thank you, doctor," John and Wendy muttered in

sync.

"Follow me," nurse Maddock asserted, as she waved them towards the corridor. "This might be upsetting, but remember what the doctor said. Ethan's currently in a stable condition, so hold on to that for now."

John attempted to pull his girls up to their feet, conscious that their own strength had seemingly evaporated from their bodies. He felt the weight of their heads on each shoulder as he slowly trudged through the hospital. The walls seemed to be moving inwards and outwards, pushing him sideways as his eyes struggled to focus on the obstacles ahead of him. He even knocked Wendy into the wall at one point, as they manoeuvred around a hospital bed, but she didn't seem to notice.

Eventually, they reached Ethan's room. John could see him through the window; he was connected to various different machines and there were tubes everywhere, just like in a movie. That was what it felt like; this whole thing was like a scene from a movie to him. Amy fell even deeper into her dad's shoulder as she spotted her brother, and John wrestled to get her upright again.

"C'mon, Amy," he whispered. "Remember what the doctor said? He's in a stable condition. Now, how's about you and your mum go in there and give him all the love he needs to get better?"

As Amy clung tighter to her dad's jacket, Wendy pulled away slightly and looked up at her husband.

"It's okay, you and Amy go first, love. I'll wait outside. You heard what the doc said, we don't want to overcrowd him."

"Are you sure?"

"Yes, go on. Tell him we're here with him."

"Okay. You ready, sweetheart?"

Amy nodded, and the girls helped each other through the door as John watched through the window, his head spinning from the events of the last few hours.

What should he do now? Was his secret about to be exposed? How would his family cope? Who was after him, and why? Too many questions were circling his brain, and but worst of all, the guilt was beginning to eat away at him; the guilt that came with involving other people in his own problems. He had never wanted his family to come to any harm; that was the reason he had left it all behind in the first place. And now, his son was in hospital. Why had they come for him now, after all this time? He sighed. These were all questions for tomorrow. Today, he needed to be there for Wendy; for Amy, and most importantly, for Ethan.

"He just looks like he's sleeping," Wendy murmured, as she came back through the door. "Go on, you go and see him. After you've been in, you should take Amy home; get some rest. I'll stay the night with him."

"Not a chance. I'm staying too. We'll phone your dad and get him to come to the hospital, to take Amy back to theirs. God knows how I'm gonna tell him…"

John entered his son's ITU room, something he never expected he would have to do, and found Amy slouched in a chair. She was completely silent, staring up at her little brother with a shocked, frightened look on her face. Her expression had not changed since the two intruders had barged into their kitchen just a few hours earlier.

He looks like an angel, John thought, as he gazed at his son's face. Ethan's forehead was creased, as though deep in thought; contemplating; soft and untouched, just like he had been the first time John had seen him, here in this same hospital, nearly twelve years ago.

"Hey kiddo," John whispered. "I'm so sorry... for everything. I'm so sorry. It's all my fault. But I promise you... I promise I will find out who did this to us, and I will never ever let them near you again."

CHAPTER THREE

Wendy woke from a restless sleep, slumped in her chair, her left hand numb and tingling after being used as a pillow for the last three hours. The early morning sun was peeking through the hospital blinds, shining a torch on Ethan's beautiful face. All at once, it hit her. This was not some crazy dream… this was a harsh reality. Ethan had been shot, and somebody, somewhere, wanted them dead.

John was already around the corner at the local Starbucks, getting breakfast and coffee for them both. He had not slept a wink; he had been too busy organising for Amy to be collected, and recovering from the trauma of retelling the whole damn nightmare to his parents. It was the guilt, more than anything, that had kept him awake; the overwhelming sense that he had let his family down. He had spent the night reliving every second in his brain, trying desperately to understand why someone would want to harm them.

As he trudged back to the hospital, two lattes in hand, he knew he was about to face a barrage of questions: from the police… from MI5… but the most challenging to answer would be the questions from his wife. She deserved to know what was going on; he owed her that.

He might not be able to tell her who had attacked them, but he could reveal to her the secrets of his past, and explain the possible reasons behind the attack. At least then she would understand why this had happened, and the confusion that was no doubt engulfing her mind right now would be alleviated.

****

When John reached the hospital room, Wendy wasn't alone.

"Got us some breakfast, hun."

"John, this is DCI Littlehart and Sergeant… umm… Sergeant…?"

"Sergeant Muloy," the female officer reminded her, in a soft Mancunian accent.

DCI Littlehart was a tall, skinny, well-dressed cop; unshaven but well groomed. He had obviously been fast-tracked through the system, for he looked to be in his mid-thirties, and was certainly no older than forty.

"I'm sorry to intrude at a time like this, Mr Cooper, but in light of last night's events, I need to ask you a few questions, if I may?" His voice was calm and understanding, but there was a hint of suspicion in his tone.

"Of course," John replied. "But not here. Let's go somewhere away from my boy. Wendy, you stay with Ethan. I'll find a room where we can speak to the police."

"We'll need to speak with you as well, Mrs Cooper," the inspector interrupted.

"Yes, but not now. She needs to be here with Ethan, surely you can see that, mate?"

"Yes, of course," Sergeant Muloy intervened. "I have reserved a room for us just across the corridor. Would you like a drink, Mr Cooper?" she added, as she escorted John out of the room.

"No, thanks, I've already got a coffee. See you soon, love. Stay strong, okay? I love you."

John and the two officers swiftly left the room, and Wendy found herself alone again.

"It's okay, little man. You can rest again now. Daddy is sorting it all out," she muttered, more to herself than her son, she realised.

As she sat there, staring at Ethan's unmoving body, trying to ignore the images that kept invading her brain, she focused on the two questions that had been eating away at her since her son had been shot. Who had tried to kill them? And why? John was a chef; it wasn't exactly a dubious occupation. Yes, he was a powerful, imposing looking man; tall, dark and handsome; sharp as anyone she had ever known, but he was friendly and well-liked. He had no quarrel with anyone. Then there was the matter of the diamond. What diamond were they after? As far as she knew, they did not own any diamonds, apart from the one in her engagement ring, but that was only small, and nearly twenty years old. It couldn't be worth more than a grand at most.

"Stop it, Wendy," she muttered out loud to herself. "You'll drive yourself mad!" She turned back to her son, and laid her hand on his wrinkled forehead. "Let me concentrate on you, sweetheart. Daddy will sort the rest."

CHAPTER FOUR

John sat across from DCI Littlehart and Sergeant Muloy, in a room barely big enough to fit them all in.

"Sorry about the tight space," Sergeant Muloy began, smiling apologetically. In her late twenties, the sergeant was a petite woman, with long, straight, dark hair, bold blue eyes and a kind face.

"The sergeant and I will be leading your case, Mr Cooper," the inspector continued, getting straight to the point. "We need you to help us understand what went down last night."

"Anything I can do, detective."

"Great. Let's start with your associates. Do you know anyone who would want to harm you or your family, Mr Cooper?"

"No, absolutely not. I'm just a chef; I have no enemies; no problems. My life is usually fairly boring, to be honest," John answered, already establishing a defensive position. "Do you think this was a robbery gone wrong, detective?"

"At this stage, we're not ruling anything out, Mr Cooper. How about you tell me what happened, in your own words?"

"Well, we were eating dinner, it must have been

about half six. Suddenly, two men barged through the front door, holding guns and demanding that I give them some diamond or other—"

"What diamond would that be, Mr Cooper?" Sergeant Muloy interrupted.

"I've honestly no idea. I don't own any diamonds, why would I? We live a very modest life, on a Head Chef's wage. If I had a great big diamond in the house, don't you think I'd have sold it by now, Sergeant?"

"Please, call me Lucy, Mr Cooper," the sergeant responded, trying to diffuse the tension. "So, you've never seen these men before?"

"Nope. Never. They had Russian accents, I know that much, and when I quizzed them, they said they were just over here to do this job and then had orders to get straight back to Moscow."

"Who hired them?"

"You tell me, detective," John replied. "They said some guy off the internet contacted them, and offered them ten grand a piece to steal this diamond thing. They didn't give names or nothing. Mind you, I only had five minutes with them. Have they said anything else to you? Where are they now?"

"Petr Karakov died on arrival last night, and his accomplice, Michial Rebrov, is still in a coma. So no, we haven't been able to speak with them."

"Where is he? Is he in this hospital?" John enquired, becoming increasingly agitated. "You need to wake him up and get him talking for Christ's sake."

"Not possible, I'm afraid, Mr Cooper. He is currently on a life support machine."

"So you see, Mr Cooper, you have put three bodies in the morgue, and one in intensive care, not to mention your son—"

"I am well aware of my son's condition, detective! And if you think you are gonna come in here and give me a hard time, you can think again, I'm not having it, I've got enough shit on my plate already pal!"

The detective raised his hands, his palms facing John. "Apologies. I didn't mean to offend. We're on the same side here, so let's calm things down a couple of notches, okay?"

John nodded brusquely.

"Why don't we try something else," Lucy suggested. "Have you ever been to Russia, John? Any connections at all?"

John paused for a moment, before replying with a firm, "No."

"What about your time in the army? Did you come into contact with any Russians then?"

"No. I was a chef, not on the front line; didn't serve too many Russians sticky toffee pudding, I'm afraid."

"You served in Afghanistan from 2001 to 2005, and then in Iraq from 2005 to 2009, is that correct, John?"

"Yes."

"Why did you leave?"

"Jesus, what's this got to do with anything?"

"Answer the question, please, John."

"I guess I was fed up with not being home. I missed my family; Amy was nearly five, and she barely knew who I was, so when Ethan came along, I decided I wanted to be a proper part of his life. Jesus, I feel like I'm the one under suspicion here. Am I? Are you thinking of charging me, detective? Really?"

"No, John, not at all," Lucy assured him. "We just need the full picture so we can catch the bastards that

22

did this. All three bodies in the morgue we can put down as self-defence; the same goes for the guy in intensive care."

"Thanks, Lucy."

"We want what you want, John: to find out what happened to your son. But we need to understand the circumstances of this case to build a proper picture of the sort of people we're dealing with here."

"I'm sorry. Of course, you're right. This is just… it's a really stressful time for me. I'm sorry if I'm coming across a little off. It's not easy to process all this. Is… is there any chance I can take a break, please? To clear my head?"

"Of course, John. Go get some air. We'll pause the interview for a minute. Just remember, the faster you tell us everything, the faster we can find the people who did this."

"Give me ten minutes, detective. I'll be back." John stood up urgently, pushing his seat backwards and scraping the floor with its legs, before promptly slamming the door behind him.

Relieved to be out of the firing line, at least for a couple of minutes, he took a huge gasp of air. The waves of panic kept washing over him, and he was struggling to hold it together. For the first time in years, he could feel his past coming back to haunt him. He knew, at some point, they were going to start asking the right questions, and he needed to figure out how he was going to answer them. Lying to the police, and hindering the investigation into his son's attack, was not something he wanted to do. But he could not tell them the truth either.

There was no way those robbers had been acting alone; they must have been hired to get the real attackers

23

into the house. The fake paramedics had been the real pros, that he was certain of. He needed to focus on them; leave the Russian red herrings to Mork and Mindy over there. Maybe the Russians had been in on it too, or maybe they had been set up. Either way, the paramedics were where he need to start.

He thought about calling his old handler for some advice, but decided there was no need at this point. If he knew Byrne, he would already be all over this by now. For the moment, he needed to keep calm, answer the cops' questions, and wait for the call.

Drifting out of his trance like state, John found himself back at hospital room one hundred and ninety two, looking at his son and his wife through the windowpane. He desperately wanted to go in and re-assure them again; to hold Wendy and tell her why this was happening to them. But something still compelled him to stop. Maybe the guilt; maybe the fear of Wendy's response; maybe the fear of giving up his long hidden secrets.

Instead, he blew them both a silent kiss through the window and headed back to the cops, ready for round two.

****

"Thanks for coming back, John." Lucy smiled warmly.

"No problem."

"So, to recap, we know two Russian citizens entered your house at approximately six thirty-two p.m. last night, on Monday 17th February 2020. They held you and your family at gun point, and demanded that you give over a diamond—"

"That doesn't exist," John interrupted.

"That we now know doesn't exist. You managed to disarm the first guy with a kitchen knife, stabbing him in the stomach and kicking him to the floor, before you switched to guy number two, shooting him, also in the stomach, with assailant number one's own gun."

"It was a Makarov, Russian standard edition,." John added.

"Let's hold there, Lucy. How do you know what type of gun it was, John?"

"From the military, I guess," John replied instantly, annoyed with himself for making such a schoolboy error.

"Okay, we'll move past that for now then. What I really want to know is how the hell you managed to disarm two hitmen, on your own, in the middle of your kitchen?"

"I don't know, detective. Just got lucky, I guess."

"Lucky? John, both men were apprehended within seconds. A professional would be proud of your work, and I don't mean a professional chef. Give us a break, John. You expect us to believe that it was all luck? Even if we did swallow that, you then repeated the same trick ten minutes later with the two 'paramedics'. It's obvious you've gone through some elite level training. Talk to us, we are on your side, remember?"

John said nothing.

Lucy went in again. "Who's coming for you, John? Let us help you."

"No comment."

"Oh, it's no comment now is it, John?"

An awkward silence ensued, until Lucy's phone began to vibrate, breaking the tension. All eyes were

25

fixed on her as Lucy answered.

"Yes, guv? Okay. Yes, I'm with him now. Okay, I'll tell him. Thanks, sir. Yes. Bye." Lucy turned to the detective and whispered in his ear, "James, we need to get back to the station, now. Orders from up top. We have to end this conversation, immediately apparently."

"What the fuck, why?"

"Orders from top brass. Guv didn't elaborate."

John overheard the news, despite Lucy's best attempts to conceal the information, and his whole body instantly relaxed. He had passed the first test, but it had only just started. 'The firm' were involved now!

CHAPTER FIVE

It was a little after eleven, on a rather drab and wet Tuesday morning in Central London.

Colin Byrne was sat at his desk, as he always seemed to be these days, counting down the hours before he could head out to lunch. His job had changed dramatically over the years, and his once exciting, action-filled days had been reduced to endless hours spent staring at a screen. As he was contemplating this monotonous existence, the office phone rang,

"Byrne," he answered, in a less than enthusiastic manner.

"John is back on the radar. Make contact with him; find out what he knows, and report back to me ASAP."

"Okay, boss. But what d'you mean he's back on the rad—" he began to ask, before a loud 'bleep' cut the line dead.

Colin pulled the screeching phone away from his ear and placed it back on the handset in front of him. If John was back in the field…what did that mean for them? He took a moment to process this unexpected Tuesday morning revelation, whilst simultaneously searching his PC and checking the wires on his phone for any connections.

Terrorist attack in Lebanon kills 35.

That didn't sound right.

Plot foiled to blow up Notre Dame.

Definitely not.

Suburban terror: intruders hold family at gunpoint.

"Shit, that's it!"

Colin instinctively knew this was John, but clicked on the wire anyway to confirm his assertions.

Boy in intensive care after father takes down two intruders in their own home... Mr Cooper of Kenilworth Warwickshire, hailed a hero as he disarms two armed intruders... Eleven year old son shot in the crossfire, currently fighting for his life in intensive care.

"Shit..." he muttered out loud, as he immediately called back his boss. "John is in the Midlands, sir. Phone the police up there and tell them to back off. I'm on my way up."

Colin picked up his phone and wallet, flung on his parka, and made for the exit.

****

Wendy was still sitting on the old leather chair beside her son's hospital bed, waiting... waiting for something, anything, to happen. For his eyelids to flicker, or his hand to twitch... but there was nothing. At least he looked at peace, she thought, which was more than could be said of her.

She glanced at her watch. One fifteen p.m. She had barely touched the pastries, or the coffee John had brought for her. She could not face it; her stomach was churning in a thousand different directions. Her eyes desperately needed to close, but they refused, stubbornly remaining open as the fatigue spread into each and every muscle in her body.

At least John was back now, sitting beside her, taking up residence on a blue plastic chair that he had brought in from the nurse's office.

"Do you want a sandwich, sweetheart? You need to eat."

"No, thanks," Wendy replied.

"Ok, Is there anything I can get you? Anything I can do?"

"No, I'm alright. Holding his hand is enough." She paused for a moment. "Actually, there is something, John."

"What is it?"

"I'm sorry to ask but, it keeps going around in my head; I just can't understand it. How did you do that, John, fight them all off, I mean?"

John was silent for a moment, trying to get his story straight in his mind. He turned to look at his wife, his expression serious. "There's something I need to tell you."

"What? John, you're scaring me now."

"I'm sorry, Wendy. I never imagined anything like this would happen."

"Like what? John, seriously—"

"It's okay. It's nothing bad, honey, I promise. I just... I need to tell you something about my past, that will help you process all of this."

"What is it? Just tell me, will you?"

"It's nothing bad, really, I promise." John stood up. "Just something about my days in the army. You see, the thing is... I did receive some combat training over in Afghanistan. That's why I was able to disarm the intruders." He so wanted to tell her everything, but he could not bring himself to reveal the whole truth, not yet anyway. "We all did. Things got pretty hairy over there for a while, all hands on deck, so to speak. I never told you because I didn't want you to worry." He would tell her his secret soon, though, when she was a bit stronger, he promised himself.

"Is that all you wanted to tell me? I was expecting something much worse; I assumed that you had all received some kind of training. Why didn't you mention it before? It's not a big deal."

"Never thought I would have to use it again, so what was the point?"

"Again? Did you face real combat over there, John?"

John paused again. He was getting tired and giving too much away. "No, I meant after the training. Anyway, that's all it was, promise. Just thought you ought to know; I thought it would stop your mind running away with you. I had combat training, which it turns out came in handy. Now we can focus on Ethan, and let the police do their job, okay?"

Wendy was not convinced, but she decided to let it pass, for now. John was clearly on edge, and she could see the beads of sweat forming on his neck, so it came as no surprise when he made an excuse to get out of the situation.

"I'm going for some air; feeling a bit claustrophobic. I'll be back soon."

She watched her husband leave the room, feeling no less confused. John's explanation had done little to calm her fears, in fact, it had made her even more suspicious. John was clearly hiding something, but what? As her exhaustion finally caught up with her, Wendy's mind began to drift, wandering back to her memories of her husband's army days. His chef story had never really sat right with her, but equally, she had never had cause to question it, until now.

John had been away for two full tours, both lasting four long years, and besides the odd phone call or text, she had barely heard from him during that time, and he had not visited home once. John had told her that he was stationed at Camp Bastion, and had little access to comms, but that excuse had never really rung true with her. It had been tough, not hearing from him for months on end, and it had inevitably caused her a great deal of anxiety and frustration. She had started to question everything: what was her husband doing over there that was so important that it meant he couldn't speak to his family? Something more important than cooking the troops dinner, that was for sure. She had always suspected that he was more involved in the war than he had let on, but now, given what had happened, she needed to find out the truth. Whatever it was, she was certain that she could handle it.

CHAPTER SIX

"John? John?" whispered a voice from the shadows.

Instinctively, John rushed out of the deserted corridor he was walking through and into the crowded hospital reception area, just in case he needed the cover. Old habits, he thought to himself, as he scanned the room. Confident that he was now safely hidden within this pack of people, he had time to process the voice that had caught him so off guard.

It soon hit him. "Byrne," he muttered, looking around the room for a tall, thin figure. It did not take long; his eyes quickly spotted a Byrne-shaped silhouette in the corner of the reception. Byrne was waiting for confirmation that John had seen him, and once the two former colleagues had made eye contact, Byrne opened a door marked 'exit', and signed for John to follow.

The pursuit continued through the hospital, with John carefully maintaining a safe distance to ensure that they were not spotted on CCTV together, until Byrne finally made it out of the hospital and into the car park. John waited by the exit, and watched as Byrne climbed into an old, battered, silver Rover and drove slowly out of the hospital car park.

John followed him with his eyes as Byrne indicated

right, then right again, drove round the hospital entrance roundabout and pulled over into a small layby, shielded to the south by a country park. The car hazard lights flashed briefly. John knew that was his cue to take a walk.

****

Wendy's phone rang, snapping her out of her semi-comatose state. She had forgotten to put it on silent. She looked at the number; it was her father-in-law, calling to check in again.

"Hi, Steve."

"Hi, Wendy, sorry to bother you. I can't get hold of John, is he with you?"

"He's just popped outside for some air, not sure why he's not picking up. I'll let him know you called and ask him to call you back, okay?"

"No need, I was just checking in. No change I take it?"

"No change," Wendy repeated.

"He's a tough kid, Wendy, he'll be okay. We're all praying for him."

"Thanks, Steve."

"We've been talking with Amy and she's decided she wants to stay with us for a few days, while you're at the hospital. Is that okay with you?"

"Yeah, of course. Thanks, Steve, and send my thanks to Emily too."

"Will do"

"How's Amy?"

"She's okay, you know. A bit quieter than usual but she understands what happened to you all, if that's possible. At least she's managed to eat something now; Em's cooking seemed to cheer her up a bit."

"That's a relief. Thanks again, Steve. Send her my love, will you? Tell her I'll call her later."

****

The passenger door of the silver Rover opened, and a tall, muscular man climbed in. He must have been at least six foot two, with short dark hair and brown eyes.

"Good to see you're staying in shape, John."

"Byrne, how you doing? It's been a long time."

"Eleven long years, my old friend. I'm so sorry about what's happened."

"What do you know?" John asked abruptly. He was in no mood for small talk.

"The first two are low level Russian mafia, well, they were. The second two, well... we don't have much at the minute, but we are working on it. One thing's for sure they were definitely not paramedics."

"They had English accents..."

"And passports, old boy. But they were not Mr and Mrs Stevenson, that much we do know. The ambulance is phony as well; an old NHS model. You can easily pick them up for less than a grand on the internet."

"Were they Russian as well, then?"

"It's looking that way, John. We've got them entering the country three days ago, on a flight from Dusseldorf. The guys are working hard on this for you. Top priority."

"Damn right! They got my son, Byrne."

"I know, mate, I know. Like I said, top priority. Can't have the FSB coming over here and attacking British citizens. Now, what I want to know is, what can you tell me, John?"

"Think you have it all, Byrne. My guess is they are all Russian: first two were sent in as cannon fodder, so they could get the other two into my house; the plan was to catch me off guard."

"Sounds viable."

"What I can't tell you is why; why they attacked me in my home, and why now, after so long. I've been out for years."

"We're trying to figure that out ourselves. We've been running any connections the first two had with any of your old foes but so far we've got nothing. If we could work out who the medics were, that would give us more to go on, I'm sure."

"Agreed."

"We're also running a trace on the flight from Dusseldorf, to try and connect some dots, but it's not easy. They feel like pros, John, so give us some time."

"Okay, I just hope we have the time." John's mind flashed back to the moment he had turned around to see Ethan on the floor, covered in blood.

"Here, John, take this." Byrne passed him an old Samsung phone. "This is clean; if you think of anything, call me."

"Will do, the same goes for you. I want you to keep me in the loop on this, please."

"Of course, old boy. Will check in again soon, I promise."

"Thanks, my old friend." John opened the door of the car and stepped out. "It sure is good to see you."

CHAPTER SEVEN

After watching Colin Byrne drive away, John walked towards the park. He knew he ought to be getting back to Ethan and Wendy, but his desire to avoid answering yet more questions compelled him to walk in the opposite direction. He had no desire to face Wendy's interrogation again, and besides, he needed some time alone to think.

He walked past the duck pond to his left, then up a steep incline, towards an empty playground at the top of the park. As he made his way to nowhere in particular, his thoughts once again turned to the paramedics. They were the key; if he could work out what their role was in this mess, he was sure the mastermind behind it all would become clear.

He opened the playground gate, sat on one end of the seesaw, and took an object out of his left hand pocket: the Samsung Colin had given him. He stared at the old phone for a moment, rocking gently up and down, desperate for some kind of inspiration to strike. Then, quite suddenly, the light bulb moment arrived. He quickly reached inside his jacket pocket and grabbed his brown leather wallet, pulling at the stitching that was keeping the back of the wallet together. Eventually, he managed to prize it open just enough to reveal a folded piece of paper, hiding in the lining of the wallet. He then took out his bunch of keys, found the thinnest one on the ring and gently dragged the paper up and out of its confinement.

Making sure no one was around to witness, he then carefully opened the paper, which was already half-disintegrated, having been trapped inside the wallet lining for over a decade. Written on the paper, in very faint pencil, were four names and phone numbers.

Steve Watson +1 773 456 5152
Sunif Shavigal +91 281 555 788
Hapnan Mustafi + 964 790 189 6277
Dimitri Gregorev +810 495 499 321

The four numbers belonged to four people John had almost completely forgotten about, and had hoped to never speak to again: Steve Watson, in Chicago; Sunif Shavigal, in Mumbai; Hapnan Mustafi, in Baghdad and Dimitri Gregorev, in Moscow. Looking at the phone on the floor in front of him. John glanced around the playground. It was still just him. Taking a deep breath, he dialled Dimitri's number, and pressed the green button.

His heart was really pumping now; the adrenaline coursing through every vein in his body as he contemplated the enormous risk he was taking. Then again, he reasoned, if they were still out there, and they still wanted him dead, then he needed to find them before they came back for another try. What did he have to lose?

The phone rang out and went through to a female

voice, speaking German. A generic answer phone message.

"Damn!" John shouted out loud, just as a young mother was walking up the hill with her toddler. "Sorry," he called over to her, embarrassed by his outburst. The playground was no place for spy games. Picking up his phone and wallet, he made for the exit, apologising once again as he opened the playground gate, before heading back to the hospital.

He walked briskly, his frustration tangible; every muscle was so taut that John looked ready to snap. His massive risk had not paid off. He wondered if Dimitri was still in the game… alive, even? How could he make contact now? That was the only number he had for him, and it had been scribbled down a lifetime ago. The number was probably not even in use anymore. He would have to find another way.

****

John and Dimitri had ended their 'relationship' on good terms, with their respect for one another's professional work still intact, though things had certainly not started out that way. Back in 2003, before they knew each other, Dimitri had been one of the FSB's top men in the Middle East, and John had been stationed in both Kabul and Basra, regularly travelling between the two. John had been made aware of a potential arms deal going on in Gilgit, a small town in the north of Pakistan, just beyond the border. The Russians were due to supply the Taliban with a ton of AK47's and rocket launchers, and John had been tasked with finding out the drop-off time and location.

John had made contact with his regular CI in Kabul, a man named Abdul Aleem, and had arranged a 'meet' to find out the details. What he had not known at the time was that Gregorev had recently recruited Abdul as well, and that Abdul had since been feeding John misinformation. The following Monday morning, at eight a.m., John went in via the back door of Abdul's grocery shop, as he had done every Monday for the last three months. He had been expecting to pick up the rendezvous point and time from Abdul, however, things had not quite panned out like that.

When he had entered the shop, John had immediately sensed that something was wrong, but before he could fully assess the situation, Gregorev had jumped out of the shadows and pressed his gun, a Makarov pistol, against John's right temple.

"Don't move, and don't even think about following me. This is not your business," Dimitri had snarled.

John had waited a few seconds, buying himself time. The silence had been odd; he had expected Dimitri to either kill him immediately or at least subject him to some kind of threat, but nothing had happened. A few seconds later, the gun had been removed from John's temple, and he had swiftly turned around to confront his attacker, but to no avail. Dimitri had vanished into the wind, along with Abdul. Little had John and Dimitri known that their professional worlds would be inextricably entwined for the next half decade, as they pit their wits against each other to try and stay one step ahead of the enemy.

"That's it," John exclaimed. He had worked out a way of connecting to Gregorev, if indeed Gregorev was still out there. John pulled out the Samsung again and typed a three word text message:

Abdul Aleem's Groceries.

****

By the time John arrived back at the hospital, it was almost dark. He glanced up at the clock in reception on his way through. 5.37 p.m. Shit... Wendy was going to be furious.

He picked up the pace of his walk a little, half-jogging through the hospital, into the lift, onto the first floor and down the corridor, towards his family. When he reached room one hundred and ninety-two, he found Wendy sitting with the two detectives from before.

"What's going on here?" John asked gruffly, as he crashed through the door.

"Thank you for your time, Mrs Cooper. We hope your son recovers soon," said the inspector.

"I told you not to trouble my wife today, detective. What the hell do you think you're doing? My son is supposed to be resting, get out, go on. Get out! My solicitor will be hearing about this."

"Don't worry, Mr Cooper, we're leaving," the inspector smirked. "We'll be back tomorrow though, to speak with you again. Please don't go anywhere."

"Good night, Mr and Mrs Cooper, I hope you get some sleep. We will keep our fingers crossed for better news tomorrow," Lucy added, trying to defuse some of the animosity her boss had created.

"Good night, detectives," Wendy called after them, as the door closed shut.

John went over to the window and watched the two detectives disappear down the corridor. "What did they

40

ask you, Wendy? I don't trust that detective; I reckon he doesn't like me…"

"Calm down, John. They just asked me a few questions about last night; said the faster they could gather all the evidence, the quicker they could find the attackers."

"What did they ask about me, Wendy? Please tell me you didn't talk about my time in the army?"

"They asked about that, yes; wanted to know how you managed to defend us against four intruders."

"And…" John interrupted.

"And I told them what you told me, that you had some training in Afghanistan. Why? What was I supposed to tell them, or not tell them? That's the truth, isn't it? Isn't it, John?"

"Yes… yes, of course it is, honey. I'm sorry for worrying you. He just makes me nervous, that's all. How's Ethan?"

"The doctors have been in a couple of times; his vitals are good, apparently. They are hopeful, but said he's not out of the woods yet."

John sighed with relief. "That's such great news, love."

For the next few hours, the Coopers' barely spoke to each other. Wendy managed to eat a sandwich, and John sat in brooding silence, drinking a coke and watching his son. He must have checked his text messages a hundred times, but there had been no reply from Gregorev. By about ten p.m., Wendy had finally fallen asleep, holding Ethan's hand. John tenderly placed a blanket over her, then settled back into his chair for the long night ahead.

CHAPTER EIGHT

John practically jumped up out of his chair, the vibration in his pocket startling him out of his semi-conscious state. Immediately, he flipped open the Samsung. It was 5.43 a.m. So almost eight a.m. Moscow time. His body was engulfed with anticipation as he clicked on the 'one new message' icon. *Gilgit*, it read. Just one solitary word, looking almost apologetic on the screen.

The initial thrill of receiving the message quickly changed to complete confusion, as John looked blankly at the word. What did it mean? What was Dimitri trying to say? John racked his brain, trying to find a connection, but nothing came to mind. Exasperated, he looked over to Wendy, to make sure she was still asleep, and instinctively checked on Ethan as well. As he leant over to touch the back of his son's hand, it suddenly came to him.

"Jesus," he murmured aloud.

Wendy stirred, but to his relief, she quickly settled back into a deep sleep again. John stared back at the text message again. Of course. Gilgit was the town in Pakistan; the one where the weapons deal had gone down, back in 2003; the one Abdul Aleem had been giving him intel on. It had to be Dimitri. Indeed, the more he thought about it, the more it made sense. Dimitri had always been cryptic; he never let himself become too exposed.

John pondered his old adversary's message for a while longer. Clearly Dimitri was intrigued enough to respond, which was good news, but that was about all he could conclude from the message. Or was it? Thinking about it, they were the only two people in the world, apart from Abdul Aleem himself, that could connect that ill-fated meeting inside the grocery store to Gilgit and since Abdul had died back in 2005, it had to be Dimitri, didn't it? He must be checking that it was indeed John on the other end.

John's mind raced in response to this dramatic development. He had finally made contact with Dimitri. But what now? There was no guarantee that Dimitri would help, even if he did know something. Or worse still, Dimitri might be involved in the plot. Despite having grown to respect and maybe even like one another during the Afghan war, John was still damn sure that Dimitri could not be completely trusted. He did not even know whether Dimitri was still FSB; he could be retired, or working for someone else by now. What if this was a trap? What if they were trying to find out what John had on them?

John sat there for a while, with Wendy and Ethan both sleeping peacefully beside him, as he tried to work it all out. Inevitably, his mind wandered back to his previous dealings with the man who he was risking everything by contacting, and one encounter in particular drifted to the forefront of his mind. Iraq 2008. The first time they had both been on the same side... well, sort of.

Dimitri had been made aware of a black op's FSB operation, on the outskirts of Basra. The operation clearly contravened the then UN peace agreement, which at the time was already hanging by a thread, not to mention threatened to kill and injure many innocent Iraqis. Dimitri, having grown increasingly disillusioned in the FSB leadership during the preceding months, had decided that this op was a step too far, and had reached out to the other side, making contact with MI6 agent, John Steele, which had been John's cover name at the time.

John remembered receiving a call out of the blue from an FSB agent, whom he had already run into, quite literally, numerous times while stationed in Afghanistan. He had accepted the opportunity to meet him, and had received intel on the op directly from Dimitri himself. Later that evening, a special-forces unit, organised by John, had managed to stop the operation before it endangered the local villagers, wiping out the entire elite Russian unit in the process.

John sat back in his chair in the hospital room, recalling the successful op with some pride. In that moment, he realised that, despite his dubious past, Dimitri could be trusted. His moral code would hold true, regardless of his current circumstances, John was sure of it. All he needed now was the opportunity to explain the situation to his man, face to face.

****

Wendy began to stir, stretching her arms and legs as if beginning a morning yoga session.

"Morning, love. How did you sleep?" John asked her

44

softly, instantly putting aside the turmoil swirling around in his head.

"Morning. Anything happened?" Wendy murmured, still half asleep.

"No change, hun, but that's a good thing. Remember what the doctor said? After the first forty-eight hours, his chances will be much, much better."

John waited for his wife to fully come around before standing up and announcing that he was popping out for breakfast again. To be fair, he was in need of some food, but he was even more eager to check his phone for another message from his one and only contact. He doubted it would come, but the possibility still excited him.

"I won't be long," John said, lightly kissing his wife on the forehead. "Half an hour, tops."

As John made the now familiar walk out of the hospital, deep in thought, considering what his next move would be, Byrne was just getting out of a briefing with his boss in London. Having updated his boss on the operation, Byrne had been given his orders; he was to contact John immediately. As he dialled the burner phone he had supplied to John, he could not help but wonder whose number John had phoned the previous day. The trace had placed the number in Zurich… who did John know in Switzerland? Obviously, John was conducting his own investigation, but what had he discovered?

John answered after only a couple of rings.

"Morning, John."

"Morning, Byrne."

"How's things your end? How's Ethan?"

"Still stable, thanks. Doctors say he's doing okay

45

considering. What you got, Byrne?"

"You can't let anyone know this has come from me, it's got to stay off the record, okay? We've placed the second two now, got them entering Dusseldorf three days ago."

"Where from?" John interrupted impatiently.

"Moscow. Looks like your hunch was right, old boy. They're ex-FSB, now working as hitmen for a Russian mobster."

"Who?"

Byrne paused. "Alek Malakov."

"Malakov…" John's heart sank to the bottom of his stomach. All of a sudden, everything made sense.

"You okay, John?" came Byrne's voice from the other end of the line.

John quickly collected himself. "Yeah, it's all becoming clear. I thought he was in Belmarsh, though?"

"He is, but that doesn't mean he's not involved. The working theory here is that he, or his son, Andrei, are the orchestrators. Sorry, old boy."

"No, no, thanks for the info. At least I know what I'm up against now."

"What do you mean 'what you're up against', John? You can't do anything. I mean it, John. You've got to sit tight; leave it to us."

"Yeah, yeah, of course." John replied, both men ignoring the obvious lie.

"We're working on the theory that this is a revenge attack… you know… for that incident in Basra? When you—"

"When I murdered his son, you mean? For God's sake, Byrne, you think I could forget about that? Those kinds of memories don't just leave you. But I thought

46

Malakov was supposed to be out of the picture? He's been inside since 2010. How come this has happened now?"

"He is out of the picture, to a degree. He's still serving at Her Majesty's pleasure; it's Andrei who is pulling the strings, maybe with a little encouragement. Trying to avenge his brother and please his father at the same time. Andrei is now a general in the FSB himself, so has both the means and the motive."

"Okay, thanks for filling me in, Byrne. Anything else?"

"Not yet, no, but I'll check in as and when anything else comes to light. Sit tight, John, and look after your family."

"Will do. Thanks again."

This was bad news. If Alek and Andrei were involved, there was no chance of MI6 doing anything about it, especially if the Malakov junior was still living in Mother Russia. John re-opened his phone and typed another message to Dimitri.

Alek Malakov.

At least he finally knew what to say.

CHAPTER NINE

Dimitri was finishing up his breakfast, reviewing the unexpected events of yesterday. John Steele. The legendary John Steele had contacted him. It had been years since anything this exciting had happened, and Dimitri was intrigued. Ever since he had moved to Zurich to escape the clutches of the FSB, his life had become monotonous and predictable, so this unforeseen drama was welcome, albeit worthy of suspicion. He had responded to John's opening gambit, in code of course, and was now eagerly anticipating John's next move.

Dimitri had lived like a recluse for ten years, in a quiet town just outside of Zurich; a far cry from the jet set lifestyle he had once been accustomed to back in Moscow. A quiet, unassuming man, now very much past his prime and fast approaching his fiftieth birthday, Dimitri had eastern European features, slightly balding grey hair and wore rimless glasses. He filled his days walking his two beloved Alsatians, Bonnie and Clyde, and playing poker online, which was more than sufficient to fund his less than lavish lifestyle.

Women came and went, but none of them stuck. It came with the territory. When you lived you whole life never trusting anyone, romantic relationships were difficult to sustain. But despite some moments of loneliness, for the most part, Dimitri was happy as he was: no stress; no pressure; a world apart from his previous life in the FSB.

He had decided to move to Zurich in 2009, following a major disagreement with the then head of the FSB, Alek Malakov, though truth be told, it had not been so much a decision as a necessity. Malakov suspected him of collusion with the enemy, so his choice had been either forge a new life for himself, far away from the spy world, or have his head removed from his body. Dimitri had chosen the former. The 'hit' was still out on him, even now, but things had cooled down significantly since the early days, and ten years on, Dimitri was confident that he was safe in the life he had created for himself in Switzerland. Still, that security was fragile, and though he doubted John was involved in any of FSB's attempts to track him down, he could not afford to take any chances.

He continued to sit at his pine breakfast table, his coffee and toast consumed long ago, pondering what was so important that it would force an ex-British spy back out of retirement a decade on. The very fact that the old phone – the one Dimitri had set up many moons ago for 'emergencies only' – still worked was a miracle in itself, but being contacted by John had blown his mind. Whatever situation had drawn John back into the game, his need was dire.

Ping.

Another message on his phone. He opened the text, and his heart skipped a beat.

Alek Malakov.

All bets were now off.

****

"Mr Cooper?" called one of the nurses from across the corridor.

"Yes?" John replied.

"These came for your son," she said, pointing to a large bunch of flowers on her desk. "I'm afraid we can't allow them in the ICU, but I've given the card to your wife. Just thought you would like to know."

"Okay, thank you. We will have a look later."

"Here you go, honey," he said, as he re-entered the room, carrying two breakfast pastries. "Make sure you eat them this time."

"Thanks, love. Do you know anyone called Alek?"

"Alek?" John's voice was calm, but his blood boiled with rage. "Don't think so, why?"

"We just had some flowers delivered, for Ethan. They're not allowed in here, but look, here's the card that came with them."

John slowly walked over to her, trying his best to remain expressionless and not let the fear and anger that were bubbling up inside him break through his façade. He took the card off the table and read the note.

Thinking of you and our sons.
Best wishes,
Alek.

John froze for a moment, his rage now replaced by genuine horror. "Probably one of the guys from the restaurant, I reckon."

"Strange message, though. Why have they written 'our sons'?" Wendy persisted.

John shrugged. "Probably a typo or something,

they're not the brightest bunch. Listen, love, I've got to make a few calls. You eat your breakfast; I'll be back in no time."

"Who to, John? Can't you stay with us today?"

"Just the police and a few other people, just to see what's going on. Sorry, honey, it's driving me mad just sitting here waiting for something to happen. I can't do it, I'm sorry. I need to be doing something, you know me."

Wendy sighed. "Fine, if you must. But please don't be too long. I need you here with me, John. I'm frightened, you know."

"I know you are, love. I won't be long, promise."

****

The instant John stepped outside, he was on the phone to Byrne.

"Hello?" Byrne answered after a few rings.

"It's Malakov. That bastard sent us flowers; he's taunting me, Byrne. I'm going after him. I'm not waiting around here for him to come back."

"What do you mean you're going after him? Stop and think, old boy. Where would you go? What could you possibly do?"

"I've got a lead, Byrne. I'll catch you up in due course. For now, get me an armed guard on Ethan and Wendy. I'm worried he might try again at the hospital. Do that for me, and I'll keep you in the loop."

"Of course, John, consider it done. What lead? Where are you going? Let me help you; if you won't listen to reason and stay with your family, then at least let me help you."

John's phoned pinged again. A message from Dimitri. "Listen, Byrne, I've got to go. Got another call. Set up the guard for me today and I'll be in touch."

"Okay, good luck—" Byrne just about managed to fit in before the line went dead.

John clicked on the text.

Elena Meier, Luzern.

"For Christ's sake, Dimitri. Can you not just speak normally for once?" His exclamation was a little too loud for one of the nurses, and she gave him a dirty look.

****

When John opened the message, Dimitri immediately received a read receipt. Closing his MacBook, he shouted 'gassi gehen' to his dogs: 'walkies' in German. He had offered the olive branch; it was now up to John to decide whether or not he wanted to take it.

CHAPTER TEN

John's mind was working overtime. He had never heard of this 'Elena' woman, and he had sure as hell never been to Luzern. What did a little town in Switzerland have to do with all this? What was Dimitri trying to tell him?

Soon enough, he found himself outside the hospital coffee shop, on the ground floor, and decided that a coffee might be exactly what he needed to get his brain in gear. As he waited for the waitress to deliver his flat white, an idea popped into his head. He unlocked his main phone, not the Samsung burner he had been obsessing over for the last twelve hours, but his regular iPhone X, and swiftly opened up Safari.

Typing in Dimitri's clue, 'Elena Meier', he pressed search. Over ten different Elena Meier's popped up, including a link to a math's professor working at the University of Pittsburgh; three LinkedIn pages, and about five different Facebook profiles. This was crazy; he had no chance of working this out. Dimitri must just be fucking with him.

John's frustration quickly turned to despair when he looked up from his internet search to see a grief stricken family walking past him, the father consoling his wife and daughter. That short sharp dose of reality was all he needed, and he immediately felt compelled to continue his seemingly hopeless search. He had to do this, for Ethan's sake.

The waitress called out his coffee order, and as he took it, a flash of inspiration hit him. Placing his coffee on a nearby table, he added two words to his original search term.

Elena Meier Funeral Luzern.

When he pressed the search button, all the results came back in German, so he switched on Safari translate button. 'The cremation of Elena Meier. All family and friends welcome', read the heading on the Facebook event page. John clicked on the link and scrolled straight to the 'about' section.

Cremation and Remembrance,
11am, Thursday 20th February 2020,
Stiftung Luzerner Feurbestattung Krematorium,
All family and friends welcome.

John looked at the date on his watch. Shit, the funeral was tomorrow morning. How was he going to get a flight to Switzerland at such short notice? More to the point, how the hell was he going to tell Wendy? She would never understand him leaving her while their son was in such a critical condition.

He thought on it for a while as he finished up his coffee hit, and came to the conclusion that he had no choice. His family's safety was at stake, and this was the only lead he had. He could not pass it up now. Besides, Wendy was stronger that she realised; she could easily handle things at the hospital. There would be plenty of time to explain when they were safe again. He had to do this.

John checked the time again. Ten forty-five a.m. There was no time to debate the pros and cons; the talking could wait. Now was the time for action. Throwing his empty coffee cup in the bin, he walked over to the reception desk and politely asked for a pen and paper.

My dearest Wendy,

I know this will come as a big shock, but there is something I need to do. I'm sure you believe the best place for me is here with you and Ethan, but our future safety is at stake, and I can do something about it. I need you to trust me, like you always have, perhaps now more than ever. I know you have turned a blind eye in the past when needed, and I beg you to trust me once again. I love you more than anything in the world, and know you will look after Ethan while I'm gone. I will only be gone a day or so, and promise I will have the answers you need when I return. Stay strong.

All my love, John.

John folded up the note and handed the pen back to the receptionist, suddenly overwhelmed by a feeling of trepidation and desertion, as he stood torn between family and duty. It was a feeling he had not encountered since his days in MI6; feeling he had hoped he would never have to encounter again.

****

Byrne was busy typing up his report, in preparation for the afternoon's briefing with his boss and a few other senior MI6 top brass. Everything was on track, and he was confident they would be pleased with his progress. He knew John had made contact with the number in Switzerland again, and appeared to be engaged in some sort of coded conversation with the mystery CI.

Byrne had cracked the second message in no time at all, though the first, '*Gilgit*', still eluded him. That minor frustration aside, he could confidently report that John would shortly be departing the UK to rendezvous with an old CI in Switzerland, who was almost certainly Russian, and most probably Dimitri Gregorev.

This turn of events, although unexpected, would not affect the plan his boss had informed him about the previous night. In fact, it made the whole thing more plausible. Byrne was well aware of Gregorev and Malakovs previous relationship, as was all of MI6, and he also knew that Gregorev, if indeed it was him sending the texts, would be a valuable ally for John in his attempts to track down Malakov.

****

Dimitri had set the wheels in motion at his end, and had done what was needed to cover himself, should things go south. Despite his own need to keep a low profile, he was happy to come out of the shadows for this meet; he had no reason to suspect John wanted to do him any harm, and the fact that Malakov was somehow involved made it too intriguing to resist. Either John had something interesting on Malakov for him, or he wanted info himself; either scenario was quite amenable to Dimitri, and did not pose any immediate danger that he could envisage.

In order to cover all bases, though, a bit of due

diligence would be required. He would have to make a few phone calls; see what he could dig up on the Malakovs, just as soon as he got back from his dog walk.

****

Wendy was still by her son's side. There had been no change in his condition, but she kept trying to convince herself that no news was good news. She was concerned about her husband too; he was not coping with the situation well at all, so she knew she needed to stay strong for them all; hold everything together, as usual.

She felt surprisingly calm considering the situation she had been plunged into, and had even managed to eat the pastries John had purchased earlier and clean herself up a little, steadfast in her determination to be by Ethan's side when he woke up.

****

Having given his letter to the hospital receptionist, with strict instructions to give the note to Wendy after, not before, twelve p.m., John headed straight for the train station. He needed to swing by his house to pick up a passport and a couple of essentials, before catching the Cambridge train at 12.52 a.m. The plan was then to catch another train to Stansted Airport, which should get him there for four p.m.

It was a bit of a ball ache, but as Stansted was the only airport with direct flights to Zurich, he had no choice. His flight did not leave until 8.08 p.m., so he would have plenty of time to get his things in order when he reached the airport; he was more concerned about getting past the police who were stationed outside his home. In theory, they should have no problem with him picking up a few things, but he did not want to raise any alarm bells that might ring in a certain DCI Littlehart's ears.

CHAPTER ELEVEN

The taxi driver pulled up just around the corner from the crime scene, as requested. John had deliberately wanted to stay out of sight, to avoid attracting any undue attention. Observing the hive of activity surrounding his former home, he felt an ache in his chest. Despite still being his home, the house already felt different; soulless somehow. He doubted they would ever be truly happy there again.

"I'll only be a few minutes" he said to the taxi driver. "Keep the metre running."

John could not shake the feeling of loss as he made his way up the road. His family home looked like a scene from CSI; there was tape everywhere; police cars all the way down the street and two large cops guarding the entrance, well, what was left of it anyway. The front door was damaged beyond repair, and the blood stains could be seen all the way from the top of the driveway.

All of a sudden, what he and his family had experienced hit him like a tonne of bricks; the flashbacks nearly knocked him off his feet; the feelings of guilt slapped him around the face again and again; the despair and helplessness overwhelmed him when he relived the moment Ethan had been shot. John stopped dead in his tracks and hastily changed direction, staggering across the road as he made his way back to the cab. His legs felt like jelly; a sense of dizziness consumed him.

"Change of plan," he said to the driver. "Straight to the train station, please."

He took a few moments to calm his breathing and gather his thoughts. There was no way he could go back in there, not now, not ever. He needed to come up with a different plan, and fast. He pulled out his phones, hoping for some inspiration, but instead saw three messages and a missed call, all from Wendy.

Wendy's confusion, her rage, and worst of all, her disappointment, were all present in those messages, and it cut John deeply to read them. No words could soothe her pain now, he realised, and close to tears himself, quickly turned off the handset, removing the only channel of communication between himself and his family. He knew he had to focus on the present if he were to save them, and after a few minutes of deep breathing, John mustered the strength to carry on.

He looked down at the burner phone, clean and untraceable – his only source of communication for the next few days – and dialled Byrne's number again.

"Byrne? Listen, I haven't got much time."

"What do you need?" Byrne asked, immediately focused on the task at hand.

"Meet me tonight at Stansted airport. Six p.m. at our usual place. And bring me a clean passport and some cash."

"Any particular currency?"

"Sterling is fine; I'll change it as needed. Not sure where I'm heading yet anyway," he added, trying to cover his tracks a little.

"Okay, stay safe, John. I'll see you soon." Byrne knew there was no point in trying to talk him out of it; once John was set on a path, it was pointless to try and change his mind. Besides, John had already hung up his end, no doubt to prepare himself mentally for the next few hours and days that lay ahead.

John flopped his head backwards onto the headrest. He desperately needed sleep; he had barely slept since the attack, and he knew he functioned better fully charged. Perhaps he could use the train journey to catch up on some sleep, he thought to himself, more hopeful than expectant. In reality, he knew he would spend the journey torturing himself; going over each and every detail from the last forty-eight hours, trying to remember something, anything, that might help him to track down Malakov.

****

As John was changing trains in Cambridge, DCI Littlehart and Sergeant Muloy were answering an emergency call to the Nightingale hospital, the very same hospital they had visited twenty-four hours previously whilst investigating the Cooper case.

When they arrived, they were greeted at the entrance by the CEO of the hospital trust, and ushered into her office.

"Thanks for coming so quickly," she began. "I called you because I have some disturbing news. Michial Rebrov passed away some two hours ago."

"I see. That is unfortunate," Sergeant Muloy responded. "But why have you called us in?"

"Because, Sergeant, we have concluded that his death was not caused by the wounds he sustained. Somebody assisted his death."

"So he was murdered, then?" DCI Littlehart clarified, already losing patience with the woman in front of him. "Why do you suspect foul play?"

"Because, detective, he was in a stable condition, and recovering from his wounds well. We were even considering taking him off his ventilator today, as he appeared to be able to breathe unassisted. But something changed in the night, and when we came to check on him this morning, one of the machines monitoring his vitals had been disconnected. We suspect he was suffocated."

"Thank you for informing us of this, we will take it from here."

The CEO showed the detectives out of her office. "I trust you will keep me informed of any progress. Our staff have already been briefed, and are expecting to speak to you both. Thank you again for your time, detectives, now if you will excuse me, I must get on."

****

Byrne was sitting in his favourite seat, at his favourite bar in Stansted airport. It was just a few minutes before six p.m., and he had treated himself to a gin and tonic; he deserved it after the wholly unsatisfactory rush hour trip he had just endured. He was positioned strategically in a corner booth, with the whole airport visible from his spot. It was the same place he always sat when these sorts of occasions came about.

Just as he was beginning to ponder John's true

intentions, fearing the worst, he suddenly felt a firm hand pressing on his shoulder.

"Hi John," he said, without turning around. "How do you do that?"

"Do what?"

"Creep up on me every time?"

"Ha, you're easy, Byrne, that's why you work behind a desk at HQ, not out in the real world like me."

"Touché. How are you, old boy?"

John sat down opposite him. "I'm here, that's all that matters. Did you bring everything?"

"Yes, old boy. Would you like a G&T?"

"No, thanks. I need to get my ticket and go through shortly anyway."

"Stay for a while, John. Let's work this out together. Let me help you, old chap."

"No need, Byrne. I'm really only going on a fishing trip, but if anything comes from it, you will be the first to know."

"At least tell me who you're meeting, and where you're heading," Byrne pleaded.

"You will know where I'm heading soon enough, Byrne. You only need to look at the passenger list five minutes after I'm gone. I assume you've used my old alias?"

"Yes. Thought it best since you had very little time."

"Good. Hand it over then. I need to get my ticket."

"John, please, before you fly off, tell me who you're meeting. We can arrange surveillance or cover or something for you."

John once again ignored Byrne's pleas. "Thanks for doing this, Byrne. I'll be in touch". Taking the passport and cash, he headed swiftly towards the ticket kiosk: a man on a mission.

Byrne sat there for a moment longer, sipping his gin and tonic as he watched his old friend disappear into the crowded airport. Eventually, when John was long gone and his heart rate had settled back to manageable levels, Byrne got up and left the bar. This had better go to plan, otherwise it would be his neck on the chopping block, as well as John's.

CHAPTER TWELVE

John had finally arrived in Zurich, exhausted from his long trip. As predicted, he had been unable to sleep during the flight over; even the three Jameson's he had knocked back on the plane had done nothing to calm his racing mind.

The plane had been delayed leaving Stansted, and had not made the time back up, so it was well past midnight by the time he arrived at the little B&B he had booked online. Checking in with the night porter, John made his way up to his first floor room, opened the door and flopped onto the bed. The whiskey was finally starting to do its job.

As he lay there, fully clothed, with the lights off, he began to recall his previous encounters with Dimitri Gregorev. One occasion in particular came to mind: the special op's mission John had organised in Basra, back in 2008. The Russian operation had been sanctioned by Alek Malakov, that much he had known; as the then head of the FSB, it had made sense for Malakov to be the one pulling the strings. What John had not known, and had only discovered years later, was that Malakovs own son had been part of the elite Russian unit that had been wiped out during the fire fight.

That operation was the only reason John could think of for Malakov wanting him dead. He could only imagine that the death of Malakovs son must torment him daily, especially since Malakov was now locked inside for twenty-three hours a day. John wondered what Dimitri might be able tell him in the morning, at the old lady's funeral.

His phone buzzed. "Byrne?"

"Correct, old boy."

"Good. As you've probably worked out by now, I'm in Zurich. I'm meeting an old contact of mine, Dimitri Gregorev. What can you tell me about him, Byrne?"

"Blimey, John, impressive work. How d'you track him down?"

"My methods are irrelevant. What can you tell me about him, and more importantly, his relationship with Malakov?"

"From what I remember about that whole incident they are unlikely to be on speaking terms anymore. Gregorev had to leave Russia sharpish after Malakovs son was killed. It was widely suspected that Gregorev was your informant for that operation, is that right, John?"

"Come on, Byrne, you know me better than that."

"It was worth a try. More significantly, Malakov was of that opinion, and Gregorev didn't hang around to persuade him otherwise."

"Yes, I gathered as much. But surely if Gregorev was in the frame, then my name would have also been on the hit list, and I wasn't in hiding. Why didn't Malakov come after me straight away, rather than ten years later?"

"It is odd, I agree. Maybe he came into new

intelligence about your whereabouts, or maybe they found Gregorev, and he gave you up? Be careful, John. I know you think you can trust him but if his neck is on the line, he won't think twice about sacrificing you."

John knew Byrne was right, but had to take the risk. "I'll be careful, but if Gregorev does know the whereabouts of Alek's other son, Andrei, maybe I can go and reason with him."

"Reason with him? You realise that if you go to Russia and take out an FSB general, MI6 can't be involved in any way whatsoever? It could start World War Three, my friend."

"Who said anything about taking him out? One step at a time. Let's see what Gregorev has to say tomorrow and go from there. I'll call you then, Byrne. Night."

"Goodnight, John." Byrne ended the call and sat bolt upright in bed, processing the new information he had just received. John had confirmed the meet was with Gregorev, which was good, but the situation was escalating way too quickly already. His boss would not be pleased when he told him tomorrow. In fact, perhaps it would be wise to hold off briefing him tomorrow, at least until after John had met with Gregorev. With any luck, Dimitri would be able to shed a little more light on the situation, and hopefully offer something a bit more positive that he could use in his report.

****

John was awoken the next morning just after eight a.m. by the smell of bacon. By some miracle, he had slept the whole night. That whiskey must have done the trick after all. Grateful for the rest, he dragged himself out of bed. He was not looking forward to the day ahead at all; he hated funerals.

As he readied himself to go down to breakfast, he replayed the previous night's conversation with Byrne. Could Dimitri really be trusted? It certainly concerned him that Malakov may have already found Dimitri, and might be using him to get another shot at John. Something had triggered Malakovs attack on his family, and it was not out of the question that Dimitri was the catalyst, ten years on. But no, that was just wild speculation. His gut was telling him that Malakov was on the level. John had made contact with Dimitri, not the other way round, and besides, Malakovs son did not have the intelligence to find Dimitri. If Dimitri did not want to be found, he was damn sure no one would be able to track him down, least of all Malakov junior.

By ten-thirty a.m., John had destroyed a full English breakfast, having already dressed himself for the funeral in a sharp black suit, white shirt, black tie and shiny black shoes. He also wore his Ray-Bans, to protect his eyes from the sunlight that was already streaming over the mountainous landscape. The taxi arrived shortly after he had finished eating, and he quickly settled up the B&B bill; he had decided that he would not be staying another night.

"Can you take me to this crematorium?" he asked the taxi driver, pointing to the address on his phone.

"Certainly, sir. It's about fifteen minutes from here," the driver responded, in very good English.

Fifteen minutes Swiss time turned out to be twenty-five minutes real time, and when the driver pulled up, John could see he was one of the last to arrive. He quickly paid the driver and joined the back of the queue.

A surprising number of people had come to pay their respects, especially given that the deceased was an eighty-six year old widow. Then again, a large crowd would allow himself and Dimitri to remain hidden, so it was not something to complain about.

As the mourners began to make their way inside the crematorium, John looked around for Dimitri, but he could not see him. Wondering whether he might be inside already, John decided to follow the crowd, seating himself at the very back of the crematorium, in the last pew available.

As the ceremony began, John took the opportunity to look around the room. For a moment, he thought he could see the back of Dimitri's head in one of the front aisles, but he could not be sure if it was him. It had been years since John had last laid eyes on him, and this particular man that had attracted his attention could, in all honesty, be anyone.

Forty minutes later and it was all over. The eulogies had come and gone, and the old lady was now off to meet her maker. John stayed throughout, and when the curtain closed on the old lady for the last time, John took his turn to stand up and pay his respects, before walking out of the room.

The very moment his lungs hit the fresh air, John felt a light tap on his shoulder, and turned instinctively to greet Dimitri.

"Thank you for coming," Dimitri said, as he stretched his arms around John. "It's a long way for you. Elena would have appreciated you being here."

"No problem," John replied in character.

"Come on, John, let's take a walk and catch up," Dimitri continued, walking away from the crematorium, towards the forested wood next to the graveyard.

They walked for about half a mile, neither man saying a word, until they reached an old railway bridge.

Dimitri stopped walking and turned to his comrade. "John Steele. You look well, my friend. I'm so sorry to hear about your son. I hope he pulls through."

"How do you know about Ethan?"

"Really, John? When an old MI6 agent makes contact with you out of the blue, after being out of the game for ten years, you feel inclined to do a bit of homework before you meet him."

John instinctively knew that Dimitri was telling the truth. He would have sensed by now if Dimitri were involved in Malakovs plot.

"Fair enough," John replied calmly, instantly reducing the tension. "What can you tell me, Dimitri? My sources suggest the Malakovs are involved."

"Yes, I gathered that from your message."

"When did you last come into contact with them, Dimitri?"

"When I left Russia ten years ago. I swear to you, John, I'm telling the truth. As you will remember, I wasn't exactly at the top of Alek's party list after it all went down in Iraq. I left shortly afterward, and have been living here ever since."

"So, why did you agree to meet?"

"To be honest, I was intrigued. Thought you might have something on them for me."

"Sadly not. That's the reason I'm here. I need you to tell me what you know; anything you have, even if it seems like nothing, it could really help me now, Dimitri."

"I see. And what is my incentive to help you, John?

Now, after all this time? Speaking to you could put me in considerable danger, you realise that, don't you?"

John paused a moment, like a lawyer does before delivering his closing pitch. "Dimitri, if you do know something that can help me, and I am successful, the Malakovs will be out of the picture forever. You can go back to living your old life again, rather than hiding out here in the back of beyond."

"What makes you think I want to go back to all that? I've carved a good life out here for myself, John. Its tranquil, and safe."

"Even so, if the Malakovs are no longer around then you are no longer in danger, right? Surely removing them from the picture would lift a huge weight off your shoulders? Telling me what you know is in your own best interests, Dimitri, and you know it. That's why you set up the meet with me in the first place, not because you needed to scratch an itch."

"I'll give you that, John. You're as sharp as ever, I see. It's good to know that civilian life hasn't softened you too much. I do like the idea of you dealing with the Malakovs once and for all, which is why I have already done some digging for you. Sadly, I didn't find much, only that both Alek and Andrei are back in Russia, living together again. They are back running the organised crime scene in Moscow, and are being protected by the Russian mafia."

"But that's not true," John interrupted. "Alek is still in England, under lock and key."

"You're wrong, John."

"What do you mean I'm wrong? I know this to be true. It came from my man inside MI6. Listen, I don't know what you're playing—"

"I'm not playing, John. I'm telling you the truth." Dimitri insisted. "Alek has been out of prison and back in Russia for over three months now."

"I don't understand…"

"Late last year, the British government agreed to release Alek Malakov in exchange for some classified documents, which his son, Andrei, had somehow acquired. It was all very secretive, apparently. Andrei received some intelligence that would have been potentially embarrassing for the British government had it got out, and Andrei used this intel to negotiate his father's release. After a few months of discussions, it was agreed, and Alek was smuggled out of the UK in exchange for the documents."

"Shit… I guess that explains why he is coming for me now, after all this time. But surely my man in MI6 would have known about Alek's release? What was in these documents, Dimitri?"

"I don't know, John. Honestly, I don't. But it must be something big. It's not every day that the British government agree to release a known terrorist."

"Quite… but why wasn't I informed of this? My informant told me he was still inside?"

"You need to take that up with them, John. Maybe they weren't told either. It was all very secretive; on a need to know basis only. Maybe that information is above your guy's pay grade?"

"You would think the guys at MI6 might have given me a heads up though. They must have known I would be at risk as soon as he was released?"

"John, if he is going after you, I'm sure as hell on his hit list too. Alek will definitely come after me as well, so we need to work together here. What are you planning? I can't just sit here twiddling my fingers now that I know what I know."

"Okay, but first I need to make a couple of calls; find out what the hell is going on. I'll be in touch again very soon."

"Fair enough. I'll sit tight until you call."

"Thanks, Dimitri. I appreciate you putting your life on the line for me."

"No problem, John."

"Just one more thing before you go. It's been bugging me… who was the old lady?"

"No idea." Dimitri smiled. "I read about her in the local paper yesterday. She was a very popular lady around here by all accounts; thought her funeral would make for good cover, in case you weren't feeling too friendly."

John grinned. "I figured as much. Always better to be prepared."

CHAPTER THIRTEEN

John's brain was spinning as he walked away from the railway bridge. Was Alek really out of prison? And, if so, why had Byrne failed to mention it to him? Was Dimitri even telling the truth? Surely MI6 would have informed him? John sighed. That particular fight would have to wait; there were too many other things to sort out now. Priority number one was his family. If Malakov was out of prison, he had the means to hurt his family again, and John could not let that happen. He decided he would have to speak to Wendy, and explain the danger they were in. She deserved to know the truth.

Second on his list was Byrne. John needed to know why the hell he had not been told about Malakovs release, but first, he needed to find out whether Byrne was in the loop or not. If he was, then omitting this huge detail from their conversations was unforgivable, but if he wasn't, which was more probable, John wanted to find out what was so important that it needed to be kept secret from everyone but the top brass of MI6. John had just about had enough of MI6 and their 'need to know' attitude; it had nearly got him killed in the past, and he refused to let their desire for secrecy threaten his life again.

His mind wandered back to his time in MI6, as he considered all the sensitive operations that could be serious enough to embarrass the British government. He could only think of one that would force them to make this kind of deal. If the Russians had intel on that particular secret, MI6 would do everything in their power to make sure that information never came to light. It was a terrifying thought.

Setting aside his fears, John took out his phone and dialled Wendy's number. He might as well get this over with.

Wendy answered after a few rings. "Hello, who is this?" she enquired, not recognising the number.

"Hi, honey, it's me. Are you okay?"

"John? Is that you? What the fuck, John?"

"I know, I know. Listen to me, honey."

"Why should I, John? You left us when we needed you most, and what's that letter all about? Trust me? Trust me? Jesus, John, how did you expect me to react to that? Where the hell are you?"

"That doesn't matter right now. Wendy, I need you to listen to me." John's voice was calm but authoritative. "We are in danger, Wendy. I'll explain everything, I promise, but right now, you have to stop and listen to me."

"Danger, what sort of danger? How could we possibly be in any more danger than we already are? We've just been attacked by a bunch of strangers for no reason whatsoever and Ethan's in here fighting for his life—"

"Honey, stop. Listen, I know you're angry, but I'm trying to explain. I'm trying to work out who those people who attacked us were, and who they were working for, and from what I have learned so far, you and the kids could still be at risk."

"What?" she breathed, her voice thick with terror. "How am I supposed to react to that? I don't... I don't think I can cope with this on my own. Are you coming back now, John?"

"Soon, I promise. In the meantime, I've organised some protection for you."

"Is that why there are two guards standing outside my door?"

"Oh good, they're still there."

"John, they've been here since you left. But why? What's going on?"

John took a deep intake of breath. He had resigned himself to telling her the full story. "I'll tell you everything, but you need to sit down first. This is going to come as a bit of a shock."

****

Half an hour later, John was on another call. He had already tried Sergeant Muloy, but had been forced to settle for her voicemail. He had left a rather cryptic message, asking her, and her alone, to phone him back, stressing the importance of their conversation being in confidence. He trusted that she would at least offer him that initially.

Next it was time to check in on Byrne, and find out what the hell was going on inside MI6. As he re-dialled the number, he could feel the anger building up inside Why had Byrne kept this information from him? Byrne answered swiftly, and John went straight for the jugular.

"Malakov is out of prison, Byrne. Why the fuck did

you not tell me this? I'm out on a limb here, not to mention my family is in danger. This isn't some spy game, you prick, this is my life you are playing with here!"

"Jesus, John, good morning to you too. What do you mean Malakov is out?"

"He was released from prison last year and is back in Moscow. Don't play me on this, I mean it, Byrne."

"Christ, calm down, old boy. I have no idea what you're talking about. Listen, I will make some enquiries and come straight back to you. Calm down, I'm on your side."

"You better be, Byrne. I'm running out of time and I have no idea what the hell is happening here."

"Leave it with me, John. How did you come by this information, may I ask?" Byrne enquired, attempting to decrease the explosive nature of the conversation.

"Dimitri, obviously. He did some digging his end after I sent him that text; found out Malakov was released months ago."

"Be careful, John. You seem to be placing an awful lot of trust in this ex-Russian spy. Stop to consider his motives for a second, will you?"

"I have, Byrne. I have no reason not to believe him at this point; he is in the same situation as me, so we are sort of bound together on this one. If Malakov is really out, he will come after both of us. That's why I need you to verify the intel as soon as possible. How long will it take?"

"I will speak to the boss straight away; tell him the severity of the situation and let you know. Hold tight, John."

"Thanks, Byrne. I need you to have my back here. I

don't know who to trust anymore."

"You can rely on me, old friend, don't you worry. What will you do now?"

"If this rumour turns out to be true, I will find that bastard and figure out a way to stop him."

"Did Dimitri tell you where he was? Malakov, I mean?" Byrne probed.

"In some safe house in Moscow, apparently, protected by the Russian mafia."

"Jesus, John. That's us out, you know that don't you? There's no way MI6 would sanction a black op's mission inside Russian territory, especially one involving an FSB general and Russian mobsters."

"I know, Byrne. I'm on my own again; nothing changes. Just get me the verification, will you? I'll take it from there."

CHAPTER FOURTEEN

John put down the phone – it was feeling dangerously hot from overuse – and thought back to his previous call with Wendy. He could not help but worry that he had not explained clearly enough.

He had begun his confession by asking about Ethan.

"He's the same, John. You would know that if you were here with him, wouldn't you? He's the same, just lying there. The doctors seem happy with his progress though... but we can talk about Ethan in a minute. Tell me why you left, John? I mean it. If you truly want to save our marriage, if we still have one to save, that is, then you need to think very carefully about what you tell me in the next few minutes."

"I'd really prefer not to do this over the phone but I know you won't listen to lies anymore. I asked the police to put the guards on your door because I believe the person that attacked us may try again. I have been speaking to my old army pals and they have been working with the government to find out who did this. It looks like it is someone from my past, seeking revenge. I need to find him and stop him."

Wendy had paused for a moment, taking it all in. "Why do you need to find him though, John? It makes no sense. You should be here, with us, not running around playing cop."

"It's complicated, love. He is someone I had direct contact with in Iraq, and I know how he works. You are safe there because the police are watching the hospital. I would only be putting you in more danger if I came back. I'm the only one who can find this guy, and the only one who can reason with him. I would rather be with you, of course I would, but while I'm far away from you, you and Ethan you are in less danger. It's me he is after, I'm convinced of it. As soon as I find him and sort this out, I will come straight home and we can move on with our lives again. I promise."

"Can we? Can we though?" Wendy had interrupted, sobbing at the other end of the line.

"Yes, of course we can. That's why I need to deal with this now, myself. I need this problem to go away for good, so that we can move on, stronger than ever."

"I still don't understand, John. Why does it have to be you?"

John had paused. "This is the bit that might come as a bit of a surprise to you."

"Tell me, John. If you respect me, you'll tell me the truth."

"Well, the thing is… I wasn't just a chef in the army, love. I did… other stuff, too."

"What other stuff, John?"

"Important stuff, Wendy. Intelligence stuff. That's why it has to be me, you see. I can't really say any more on the phone, but it was through that side of my job that I came into contact with this guy, and it's me he wants to take revenge on."

Wendy had not responded. She had been too

80

preoccupied with processing the news; not the revelation that he had been a special agent – she had always suspected as much – but the fact that he had finally chosen her over his work.

"I'm so sorry about all this, Wendy. It's my worst nightmare; I left all that behind, years ago, so that it wouldn't affect you and the kids. But it seems this guy wants his revenge now, so I've got to deal with him. But I promise, after that, it will all be finished for good, okay?"

"Okay, John," Wendy had finally responded, "My head's spinning; I still don't understand, but I guess I'm going to have to trust you for now. Please come home as soon as you can, we need you here."

"I will, love, I promise. There is one thing I need you to do for me. It will help me find him. Will you do it for me?"

"What is it, John?"

"That sergeant woman, did she give you a card?"

"Yes, I think so... yes, here, Sergeant Muloy." Wendy had replied.

"Can I have her number? I want to speak to her about your security, it has to be her, not the detective guy."

"Shall I text it to this number?"

"Please. Hold tight now, love. Everything's going to be okay. I love you."

"Be careful, John. We need you back with us in one piece."

"Send me her number, hers not his, remember? I don't trust him."

"Okay, John, I've got it. Sergeant Muloy, not the detective. Sending it now."

"Thanks—"

"Before you go, there is something you should know about the two detectives."

"What is it, Wendy?"

"They both came round here again today, asking for you. They were saying that the other attacker, the one in the hospital—"

"Has he woken up?" John had interrupted, a glimmer of hope in his voice.

"No, John. He's dead, and they think somebody killed him deliberately. They think it's you, John, I'm sure of it."

"It was me, Wendy. I shot him, remember?"

"No, John, not that. They think someone went into his hospital room and finished him off, and that detective obviously suspects you. He was saying somebody tampered with the man's vitals machine, and then when he found out you'd done a runner… you have to admit, John it doesn't look good, does it?"

"Fuck's sake," John had sighed down the phone. "Even more reason to speak to the sergeant, then. You know it wasn't me, don't you, Wendy?"

"I don't know what to think to be honest…"

"Trust me, Wendy. I love you, and I will always tell you the truth, from here on in, I promise."

"That's all I can do, isn't it, John? I have to trust you. I don't have any other options."

****

Wendy had collapsed back into her chair, exhausted, as she had tried to digest what her husband had just told her. She had not known where to begin. Her husband was off somewhere, trying to track down a known murderer, who was seeking revenge for something that happened when her husband had been British spy. Not to mention the small fact that this known murderer was still coming after them. It had been a lot to process.

If she were honest with herself, she had always suspected John had been doing more than cooking during his long spells away from home, and though she had been mad at him for not telling her the truth, she had understood that he was trying to protect her and the kids. She had known he was involved in something high-level, and that he had received some sort of elite level training. Every time he had come back home from a tour he had looked like a professional athlete, chiselled and muscular, not your average chef's physique.

He had also always been on duty, not active duty, but when he had supposedly been 'on leave' at home, he had still been on the phone five or six times a day at least. When he had finally 'quit' the army, she had felt an enormous sense of relief, irrational, really, because he had supposedly never been in any real danger. But she had felt it none the less, an instinct that he had been in real danger, and had grown tired of all the lies and deceit in his life.

Despite her suspicions, she had never given those thoughts credence, most probably an act of self-preservation, she had later realised. But now it was different. He had been out of all that for over a decade and their relationship was a new one, based on honesty, trust and friendship. What would become of them now? Was it really John's fault? Another wave of panic had encapsulated her.

No, she could not let those thoughts muddy her mind; she needed to believe in him, now more than ever. After all, he had changed for her; quit that life. He had certainly not asked for his past to catch up with them. Even so, she was not ready to forgive him for deserting them while his son was in intensive care. Not yet. Her emotions were still too raw.

Closing her eyes, she had settled back into her chair. Perhaps, when Ethan woke up, this would all just go away. Like a nightmare, dissipated by the morning sunlight. Clinging to that hope, and holding tight to her son's hand, Wendy had fallen into a restless sleep.

CHAPTER FIFTEEN

As Byrne put down the phone receiver, he glanced at the clock in his office. Four forty-five p.m. With any luck, *he* would still be in the building, he thought. Byrne immediately got up from his desk, left his glass-fronted office and headed down the corridor.

He got in the lift with a couple of colleagues from surveillance and pressed level five. His mind raced with excitement and fear. If Malakov had indeed been released, what could possibly have persuaded the powers-that-be to trade him in?

By the time the lift arrived at level five, Byrne was in all alone. As the doors opened, he stepped out, walked a little way down the corridor, and knocked on the large, tainted glass door. He heard the boss sanction his entrance.

"Yes, Byrne? What have you got?"

"Just spoken again with John, sir. He is in Zurich, with Dimitri Gregorev."

"Interesting," came the reply.

"Yes, um… apparently John would like us to verify some intel," Byrne whispered, almost reluctant to ask the question.

"Carry on, Byrne."

"Well, regarding Malakov, sir, Gregorev has evidence that suggests he is, um… no longer in the UK, sir. Gregorev reports that he is back in Moscow…"

"Really," his boss replied, pausing and lifting his right hand in the air to gesture for Byrne to remain silent.

A few seconds elapsed.

Byrne squirmed and adjusted his necktie awkwardly. Eventually, he could hold it in no longer. "What should I inform him, sir?"

"Wait," came the terse reply. A few more tortuous seconds went by before, finally, an answer came. "Well, this is most unfortunate, and I might add, very close to the bone now. Tell John that yes, Alek Malakov was released in November of last year."

"Jesus," Byrne breathed, forgetting his manners for a second. "May I tell him why, sir? He is not going to be happy; he will want to know why we didn't tell him at the time."

"Thank you for stating the bloody obvious, Byrne. 'Why' is quite another matter entirely. That information is classified, you hear, Byrne? Classified. Neither you nor Cooper can say a word about this, especially not to an ex-Russian spy of all people."

"What should I tell him then, sir?"

"Tell him… tell him that we didn't advise him of this particular decision because we didn't feel it posed any immediate threat to him or his family, and it was on a 'need to know' basis only. John did not need to know," Byrne's boss stated, trying to end the conversation with a decisive lashing of his tongue.

But Byrne felt compelled to push a little harder for his old pal, and tried again. "Will do, sir, but he will want to understand a little more."

"I'm sure he will, Byrne, but that is classified information. Are you familiar with that concept? Tell him we are sorry for his trouble, but he must come home immediately. He is not an active member of the intelligence services anymore, and should not be running around pretending to be so. Tell him," he continued, now in full flow. "We are carrying out our own extensive operation, and if Malakov is indeed proven to be involved, we will make every effort, through the correct channels of course, to bring him to justice. Now, unless you have anything else, will you excuse me, Byrne. I have plenty of work to attend to."

"Of course, sir," Byrne replied, edging towards the door. "Thank you, sir."

****

John was sitting in a small coffee shop, in Luzern town centre, having walked the two and a half miles from the crematorium. He had spoken to Wendy for most of the journey, and had spent the remaining half hour or so reflecting on the events of the day. He was still seething with anger that MI6 had taken a decision of this magnitude without warning him first. He could appreciate that something like this would be highly classified, but still, he felt they owed him some form of warning, especially taking into account the many national secrets he had loyally kept undisclosed thus far. But then, what did he expect from his old bosses? It was things like this that had made him quit in the first place. As he sat in a cramped corner of the coffee shop, positioned so he could see both exits and the cobbled lane outside, John again turned to his trusty friend, the old Samsung Byrne had given him; his only source of communication with the outside world. No new messages. He sighed. If Mohammed would not come to the mountain, then the mountain would have to go to Mohammed. He typed a new message.

Can we meet tonight at your place? I have some news. Text me your address.

****

Dimitri had made it back to his gite, and was contemplating the significance of his meeting with John Steele. It had certainly not gone as well as it could have done. Steele had provided no information with regards to helping him track down the Malakovs, and Dimitri felt that he had definitely been the more useful player in that particular rendezvous.

His overall feeling was that of unease; he was certainly more exposed now than he had been in years. The fact Malakov had gone after John Steele now, so soon after his release from prison, could only mean one thing: he still wanted revenge, and that would inevitably place him in the firing line at some stage in the not too distant future.

What to do? Should he try to help John track Malakov down? Or should he run and hide again? After all, that would be the most sensible move, and it had served him well first time around. Dimitri decided he needed some sort of leverage over John, if he was going to work with him, but in all honesty, apart from knowing that Malakov was out of prison and roughly where he was in Russia, he had nothing.

Attempting to penetrate the Malakovs safe house

would be suicide. They probably would not even be able to get into the country without being exposed and captured. The contacts who had given him the 'tip' on Malakov were helpful, but Dimitri felt sure they had exhausted their usefulness; they were only low level informants and going back to them would most likely be fruitless, not to mention risky. His contact with them had probably already reverberated around the corridors of power in Moscow.

Dimitri pondered for a while, imagining what John might be doing at his end. He felt sure he would be verifying his information and asking some tough questions of his contacts in MI6. But, as had always been the case, John was difficult to read, and Dimitri could not tell what his next move would be.

He did not have to wait long for an answer. His phone pinged again.

Can we meet tonight at your place? I have some news. Text me your address.

Really? John wanted to meet him here? That did not seem wise; surely it was too dangerous? John must still have concerns about his loyalties. Maybe John was trying to test him? Or maybe he genuinely had no alternative but to trust him? Perhaps John thought his house would be a safe place to take refuge for a while? Maybe he did trust him? Yes, the text must mean that John had chosen to believe him; if John thought he was double crossing him, there was no way he would expose himself this much.

Dimitri's mind continued to race; there were a million possible permutations to consider. Twenty-four hours ago, his life had been very simple; just his little gite and his dogs to worry about. But now, thanks to

John Steele, he was right back in the middle of a shit storm, that could have dire consequences for him if John made a wrong move. He walked into the kitchen and filled the kettle with water. This felt like one of his high stakes games of poker: all in, or fold. Except, this time the stakes could not be higher.

"Fuck it," he exclaimed. "In for a penny…"

CHAPTER SIXTEEN

John was losing patience. Why had the sergeant not phoned him back? Surely a call from Inspector Littlehart's 'prime suspect' would immediately jump to the top of his sergeant's to do list? John pressed the re-dial button, and as he listened to the monotonous ringing, he contemplated how he was going to convince the sergeant of his innocence. The idea of him being responsible for the other Russian's subsequent death in hospital was ludicrous to him, but he could, begrudgingly, understand why the police were following that line of enquiry, especially since he had disappeared soon afterwards.

In truth, he did not care all that much. There was not a lot she or her boss could do about it while he was out of the country, but he also knew he needed to have an ally back home, one that he could trust to keep his family safe if things turned ugly again. John knew MI6 would inevitably distance themselves from the whole affair, covering their own backs as usual, and John instinctively felt that, if he had to trust someone, then Sergeant Muloy was that person. In his line of work, instinct was often his most valuable weapon, and it had never let him down before.

John listened as the phone rang out, and was relieved when the sergeant's voice piped up on the other end of the line.

"Hello. Muloy speaking," she answered.

"Sergeant, it's John Cooper. Did you receive my message?"

"John!" She sounded surprised. "Hi. No, sorry, what message was that? I've been in a meeting for the last hour or so. Where are you, John? We need to talk to you."

"I know, Sergeant, that's why I called. My wife told me you went to see her again. You need to listen to me. You are barking up the wrong tree pinning this on me. I'll put you in touch with someone; his name is Colin Byrne. He will explain everything to you."

"If you have nothing to worry about, why not just come into the station and we can sort this all out, face to face."

"I can't do that, Sergeant. Ethan and Wendy are in real danger, and they need your help to keep them safe."

"Why, John? Why are they in danger? And why can't you come in? You must see how this looks."

"I know it looks bad, and I appreciate that I am putting you in a difficult position. But I have no one else to turn to. You need to trust me. Speak to Byrne, and if you still want me to come in, I will do so, but in the meantime, please listen. The people who attacked us targeted us specifically; and my bet is they came back to finish that guy off yesterday, my guess is so that he couldn't talk to you lot. They also sent flowers a few days ago, complete with a threatening note., they want me to know who did this to me and it is far from over. I wasn't even there when that man was killed in the hospital, I was on my way to the airport. Now listen, speak to Byrne, he will explain everything. If you need anything else answering after that, you now have my number. I want to help, Sergeant, but there's something I have to do myself first," John explained.

"What do you mean? You are talking in riddles, John. What are you doing? What airport? And where are you, for that matter? And who is this Byrne guy?"

"Byrne is my friend and was the person who put the guards on Ethan's door, he's one of us, well, sort of. But I'm concerned that he won't be able to keep them there for much longer. I need you to protect them as well."

Sergeant Muloy paused for a moment. She had no idea what was going on, but instinct told her that John was telling the truth. She had to believe him, at least for now. "Okay, John. Text me this Byrne's details and I will contact him. But if I don't find out exactly what's going on here, I won't be able to stop my gaffer coming after you."

"Byrne will fill you in, I promise. I'm not completely sure what's going on myself to be honest; that's what I'm trying to work out now. What I do know is that I need your help to keep my family safe while I work out what needs to be done here. Please, protect my family. I'll be back very soon, and will meet you then, you have my word."

"Twenty-four hours is all I can give you, John. I will do as you say, for now, but you need to help us too, John. It's a two-way street, you know."

"I understand. Thank you, Sergeant. I really appreciate this."

Sergeant Muloy ended the call and placed her phone onto the desk in front of her, a range of emotions engulfing her body. She glanced over at DCI Littlehart, who was sitting at the desk opposite. She knew the right thing to do would be to walk over there straight away and tell him about the call, but there was something about this case, and John in particular, that intrigued her.

She was already starting to suspect that John had some sort of connection with the secret service; the fact that they had been told to end their interview with him on day one, the morning straight after the attack, had been an immediate red flag to her. As a rule of thumb, the less information you received from your bosses when you were pulled from a case, the more interesting the case was.

The style of the attack had also not sat right with her. It was very rare indeed for assailants to enter a house in the early evening, while the owners were at home, let alone to claim that they had been paid to steal a diamond. It was certainly not your typical suburban Warwickshire burglary; it was like something straight out of a spy novel. That, combined with the complete lack of evidence that the aforementioned diamond even existed, made her suspect that the 'diamond' had been nothing more than a decoy.

To top it all off, the victim had gone missing, just hours before the only remaining suspect, and the only person who might have been able to shed any light on the case, had been murdered in his hospital bed. It was all very alarming indeed, and Muloy was convinced that all these factors were not a coincidence. MI6 had to be involved somehow. Was John MI6? Was this Byrne chap? Either way, she was starting to believe that John might be telling the truth.

Her DCI, though, had other ideas, and was busy

coming up with all sorts of conspiracy theories, with John Cooper guilty as charged in all of them. He had even floated the idea that John had organised the attack himself, as part of a plan to kill his family, a notion that Sergeant Muloy had immediately dismissed as outrageous. DCI Littlehart might be her superior, but that did not mean he had all the answers, and Sergeant Muloy was determined to give John the benefit of the doubt, especially now that he had called her personally and told her about this Byrne person, and the two agents at the hospital.

Eventually she decided the best thing to do was to keep her word, and give John his twenty-four hours. Besides, withholding this particular piece of information for a short while, at least until after she had spoken to Byrne, made sense. There was no point going to the boss until she had all the facts. The problem was, she had just promised John that she would place a police guard on his son's ward… how the hell was she going to organise that without her DCI finding out?

She sat back at her desk, contemplating her options, all the while staring at her boss opposite, but he was too absorbed in his own theories to notice what she was doing. Suddenly, it dawned on her. The flowers. The note that had come with them was a credible threat, that was the answer! And if anyone questioned her, she could argue that although she had read the note on the flowers when they had been to see Wendy earlier that morning. She had decided that rather than causing her any unnecessary alarm, she elected to set up a police guard, just to be on the safe side. That line of reasoning sounded convincing enough to her; besides, she had always worked on the premise that it was easier to say sorry than please in these situations.

When John arrived at their chosen meeting place, Dimitri was already waiting in the shadows for him, slightly to the left of the main entrance, as agreed. He gestured for John to go inside and followed a few yards behind, joining the queue after a few unsuspecting locals, to ensure that himself and John were not seen entering together. John accepted his invitation with a brief nod, entering the casino and heading straight for the poker tables to register for the night's main event, as instructed.

The trip into Zurich had been an unnecessary distraction in John's opinion, but Dimitri had insisted, clearly not feeling comfortable meeting John at his own home just yet. This had, in turn, unsettled John, such that when Dimitri took his seat next to John at the bar, ten minutes later, there was an almost tangible friction between them, neither as certain of the other as they had been the previous day.

****

Muloy was already off the phone, having received a warning from Byrne to stay away from 'his man', John Cooper.

"This is a sensitive situation, Sergeant. I assure you that John Cooper is not a suspect in your case, and can be vouched for by us at the SIS," had been Byrne's unchanging response to her questions, before he had finally cut her off at the legs completely, stating, "That's

96

all I'm at liberty to say at this point. Thank you in advance for your cooperation."

Following their brief, entirely unhelpful conversation, Byrne had seen fit to call to Muloy's station chief, and as if by magic, five minutes later, she had received the call to 'get her arse in here' from the chief himself. Like Byrne, he had also made it crystal clear that John Cooper was now off limits.

Despite placing a massive roadblock in front of her case, at least her superiors' reluctance to disclose any further information tallied with John's version of events. She was now more convinced than ever that John was the good guy in all of this; that he was telling her the truth, and that he was inevitably wrapped up in some secret espionage mission that she did not, and probably never would, understand.

CHAPTER SEVENTEEN

"Why here?" John asked, sipping on his Jack Daniels and coke.

"It's nice and safe for both of us, don't you think? It's still early days, John. I'm sure you appreciate that."

"Of course I do, Dimitri, but unfortunately, I don't have the time to build a relationship with you. My son is still on an ICU bed, and I'm concerned that Malakov may try again."

"I understand that, John. Here, we can talk in plain sight. No danger of either of us getting unsettled, if you know what I mean?"

"Okay then, Dimitri. Talk," John replied, gesturing for Dimitri to take the lead.

"Very well. Did your guys confirm my intel?"

"Yes, they did, but they also warned me off trying anything stupid."

"I would be inclined to agree with them, John. I understand your frustrations, but entering Russia is a suicide mission, and I'm certainly not prepared to get involved in anything along those lines. I couldn't anyway, I don't have the access these days."

"What will you do then, Dimitri? Hide again?"

Dimitri shrugged. "That's the plan."

"Hence why you don't want me to know where you live?"

"Correct again. It's not that I don't trust you, John, I'm just protecting myself. I'm sure you can appreciate that."

John sighed. "I suppose so. Unfortunately, I don't have that same luxury. Malakov is on my tail, and I need to stop him, one way or another."

"Look, John, I sympathise, I really do. But if I were you, I would get myself back home and start organising witness protection, or whatever it is you Brits do. This is part of the job, John, you must have considered that this day might come."

"I can't do that, Dimitri. I left this life a decade ago, to keep my family safe, and I'm just not prepared to let my family live in fear for the rest of their lives."

"John, I've been hiding in the back end of nowhere for twelve years. These things happen. It's not that bad, you know, stepping away."

"I can't, Dimitri. I'm going to find him, with or without your help. He attacked my family home; he's not getting away with that."

"Well, all I can say is good luck to you, John. I'm afraid I cannot get involved any further, no matter how much I would like him dead myself."

A long silence descended over them. John withdrew into himself, suddenly feeling completely alone again, and Dimitri anxiously awaited John's reaction to his rather cold brush off. Neither man had the will or inclination to converse with the other. Ultimately, it was Dimitri who finally broke the silence, announcing that he was going to the bathroom, and would be back shortly.

John remained silent as he watched Dimitri get up from the table and walk towards the gents. His newfound sense of hopeless had completely consumed him, and he was unable to think past it. Although he could not blame Dimitri for wanting to avoid getting involved in this fight, he had hoped that this trip would be at least somewhat productive. Instead, he had been left with an overwhelming awareness of the enormity of his task. He could not do this alone, that was for sure. How was he supposed to get anywhere near the Malakovs without Dimitri or MI6 for back up? Dimitri was right; it was a suicide mission.

Downing the rest of his drink, John stood up from their table and left the bar, collecting his coat on the way out. As far as he was concerned, there was no need to waste any more time on this dead end. He felt a tinge of guilt that he had deserted Dimitri so abruptly; he had tried to help after all, and John could not really blame him for wanting to avoid exposing himself further. The problem was, John had nowhere to turn. MI6 were not interested in any clandestine operation on Russian soil, so Dimitri had been his only route to finding the Malakovs, and now, that plan had just gone up in smoke.

As he walked outside and embraced the crisp evening air, a sense of desperation came over him. There was no way he was leaving here with nothing. If Dimitri would not come to him, then he would just have to go to Dimitri.

CHAPTER EIGHTEEN

As John waited for Dimitri to leave the casino, he thought long and hard about the ramifications of his next move. He tried desperately to convince himself that he was only going to confront Dimitri at his home in one final attempt to persuade him to help search for Alek Malakov. But in his heart, John knew that gentle persuasion would not be enough; he was going to have to find out where Dimitri lived and use this intel to blackmail him into coming along for the ride. It was a foul, underhand move to say the least, but he had been backed into a corner; he had no choice but to come out fighting if he wanted to save his family.

John looked around for some props to help him get into character, discovering some old, slightly soggy cardboard at the back of the row shops opposite the casino, and an empty Costa cup in one of the bins. Settling down near the entrance to an ideally placed grocery shop, and using the shadows and cardboard to conceal his appearance, he removed his suit jacket and wrapped himself in the tarpaulin that had come with the cardboard boxes, preparing himself for the long wait.

John had checked every possible exit point whilst inside the casino, as was his normal ritual for every building he entered. Even ten years on from active service, John would still check all the possible exits at restaurants and other social events he attended, just to be safe. It had always driven Wendy mad, but she had eventually put it down to a form of OCD, and had learned to book ahead. John recalled her frustration every time he had demanded the 'premium' table.

"It offers the optimum dining experience," he had always told her, proceeding to happily wait for over an hour for the table he had chosen, or worse still, leave altogether if he did not get his wish. Wendy had always dreaded family holidays, following him around with two ravenous kids, whilst he walked in and out of any number of eateries, trying to find the best restaurant for the evening. He had never been able to tell her the real reason for his bizarre behaviour; perhaps now, he would finally be able to explain.

John contemplated all this while he waited; he was used to surveillance, and managed to relax into it rather than becoming agitated by the whole experience. He was confident that he had not missed Dimitri; his former informant had no reason to feel cornered, so John doubted he would exit the building from the rear door. John might have left their meeting without offering the due courtesy he might have expected, but that was no reason for Dimitri to worry; he would probably have simply put it down to John's eagerness to find an alternative solution to his current predicament.

John had chosen a position that allowed him to see both the casino entrance and the taxi rank at the corner of the street. He had no idea how long he would have to wait, only that he had no other alternative. Dimitri was a keen poker player, so John assumed that this might be a particularly lengthily surveillance. He had seen Dimitri's name on the registration table for the night's 'main event' – not his real name, obviously, but an alias – and John was convinced that Dimitri would not pass up the opportunity to have a gamble in John's absence.

During the long vigil, John's mind once again began to play tricks with him. As soon as he had a moment to think, his brain would replay the attack, focusing almost sadistically on the moment where John had seen his son, lying on their kitchen floor in a pool of blood. He could not shake the image from his mind, and it tortured him constantly.

He tried to occupy himself in different ways, scoping out the casino goers as if on a mission, and thinking back to his encounters with both Alek and Dimitri, but it did not seem to pass the time any quicker. After a couple of hours of boredom, he resigned himself to a long night and began to switch off. Dimitri was clearly taking part in the poker tournament, otherwise he would have been out by now. John just had to hope that his poker game was worse than his spy game.

John ran through the events that had led him here. He was sure that Alek Malakov had sent the people who had attacked them, but he still questioned the need for two different squads. Maybe Malakov had assumed that John was aware of his recent release, and thought he would be well prepared and equipped for anything less complicated? In reality, he could have just sent a lone gunman to do the job. John had not given Malakov a second thought over the last five years, and had become lax in his management of the family's security measures.

The message on the flowers had certainly been from

Malakov, that was clear, and the murder of the hitman in the hospital suggested an organised gang. The injured hitman was the only loose end that could link the attack back to Alek, and it was certainly within Alek's compass to take him out right under the police's nose. John had other enemies from the past, but none that had such a deep vendetta and heartfelt grudge, and certainly none that had recently been released from a UK prison.

The flowers in particular troubled John. They were a personal message from Alek to him, a message telling him that not only would Alek stop at nothing to avenge his son's death, but also that he knew exactly where John's family where. The fact that Alek had not tried to get to John's family at the hospital again gave him a moment of comfort. Hopefully he could keep this fight between the two of them, but he was not naive enough to think that this was over. Alek was a loose cannon, and was definitely not above targeting his family for revenge. An eye for an eye and all that… Alek might even consider it poetic.

John continued to torture himself as he waited for Dimitri to make an appearance. He wanted desperately to be by Ethan's side, but he knew that the only chance of ending this, once and for all, was to take out all the Malakovs himself. It tugged at his heartstrings, but he managed to resist the urge to phone Wendy to check on his family, promising himself that he would call as soon as this whole saga with Dimitri had concluded. His priority at this moment was to convince Dimitri to join him; hopefully he would not have to wait much longer to take his last shot.

****

The casino entrance door swung open, and the bouncer politely nodded to Dimitri as he left. Another early night, Dimitri thought to himself. He really ought to stick to the cash games online, tournaments were not his thing, though if he was honest with himself, his failure today was almost certainly, at least in some part down to his inability to concentrate on anything other than John and the horror that Malakov had inflicted on his family. He felt guilty for refusing to help John in his time of need; he had grown to respect him over the years, and hated the idea of his family being in danger, especially at the hands of Alek Malakov.

Malakov was a thug, too stupid to make it in the FSB and too insane to survive in the Russian underworld. That was, until now, it seemed. Somehow, he had negotiated his own release from the British government, something Dimitri had never expected would happen. Dimitri had realised way back, when he had been working in Afghanistan, that Malakovs time as a general in the FSB would be short-lived. He had always been too reckless, and his decisions had caused embarrassment for the Kremlin one too many times. It had been no secret that Malakov did not fit the new FSB philosophy, and he had been considered a throwback to the old Cold War era.

Dimitri had known that any opportunity to remove Malakov from his post would be greeted with glee amongst his superiors. That was partly why Dimitri had decided to expose him, back in 2008; he had grown sick of seeing so many innocent civilian's die. Though, if he was honest with himself, he had also seen Malakovs exposure as a way to climb the ladder and acquire himself a promotion… unfortunately for Dimitri, things had not turned out like that.

****

John watched closely as Dimitri headed towards the taxi rank, quickly jumping out of his temporary living arrangements and hurrying stealthily after him. It had just gone twelve p.m. and the taxi rank was fairly busy, so John could safely join the queue without being noticed, confident that he would not lose Dimitri while he waited for another cab to arrive.

****

Dimitri was now at the front of the queue.

"Luzern, please."

"No problem. That'll be seventy francs, sir."

"Thank you," Dimitri responded, getting into the back of the rusty old Volkswagen taxi.

****

John was waiting impatiently three rows back. He did not have a moment to lose; Dimitri's taxi was pulling away and the couple in front of him were taking their time, clearly inebriated from their evening out at the casino. John looked on in frustration, until the couple became distracted, looking for something in the lady's pursue. Taking his chance, John jumped to the front of the queue, opened the back door of the cab, an old Citroen estate, and jumped in.

"Swiss Intelligence, follow that car immediately!" he

shouted at the driver, in the absence of anything sensible to say!

The driver did not even pause to think, pressing his left foot down hard on the accelerator. John slammed the door shut, thanking the driver for his quick thinking.

"What's this all about, sir," the driver asked, a little perplexed. "I don't want any trouble."

"No trouble, sir, I promise. I just need you to follow that car in front. When it stops, I will get out and pay you handsomely."

"Hey, you can't be Swiss Intelligence, your accent is English," the driver exclaimed.

"You're right! Yes, sorry of course, no pulling the wool over your eyes I see. Yes, I'm not swiss intelligence but I am here on a mission, working with Swiss Intelligence." John continued with the elaborate charade

"You're a British spy then!" the driver announced, as if he were on some terrible TV show.

'If you like,' John thought to himself in frustration, and yet still indulging the driver's infant imagination. " Yes I'm MI6" he continued "But I'm not here to spy on your country, so you need not be concerned. The guy we are following is a Russian agent, and I'm working with Swiss Intelligence to track him down. You will be doing your country a great service by helping me. Now, make sure you stay well back, and I'll pay you handsomely for your assistance."

"I'm not sure I want to get involved in this… how handsomely, sir?" the driver asked.

The promise of money could almost always convince people do things they would usually think twice about. "Follow that taxi and I will pay you four times the meter rate when we get to where we're going, how's that sound?" John replied, not taking his eyes off the black cab a few hundred metres in front of them.

"Okay… but where are we going?" the driver asked, instinctively taking his foot off the accelerator pedal as he pulled behind a bus.

"I'm not sure, to be honest. My guess would be Luzern, but exactly where, I don't know. That's why I need you to follow him without drawing any attention to us.

"Okay, sir. Leave it to me," replied the driver, beginning to enjoy the excitement of this unexpected turn of events.

****

Dimitri, a few hundred metres in front, and completely unaware that he was being followed, settled back into his seat for the short journey ahead. He was relieved to be heading home and happy to have put the whole unsatisfactory, if short-lived, episode behind him. The experience had made him realise that he was happy to be out of the game, and he urged himself to remember this feeling the next time he felt a little bored walking his dogs in his quiet little town.

Occasionally, he caught himself reminiscing about his previous life, but time had clouded his memory, choosing to recall only the more glamorous moments of the job and conveniently omitting all the horrifying, dangerous ones. The constant uncertainty; always looking over his shoulder; the very real fear of getting caught in some forbidden territory. Yes, he would make sure to remind himself of the perils of his previous vocation the next time he got itchy feet.

****

John was gripping the edge of his seat, all the muscles in his body taut with anticipation and adrenaline. Maybe he did miss his former life, just a little bit. Back home, working in the kitchen, he had always convinced himself that he was better off out of the game, and was always telling himself that it was not worth the constant danger and long spells away from the people he loved. But the surge of excitement he felt right now – the thrill of this particular chase – reminded him of the reason he had joined in the first place, and he could not help but feel a tinge of regret that he no longer served for Her Majesty's Secret Service.

"Get a little closer. If they turn off this highway at any point, you will need to be able to get off quickly."

"Okay, but I don't want them to make us."

"Make us," John repeated, a smidgen of sarcasm in his voice. "Pleased to see you are getting into character, my friend."

They continued to follow Dimitri for another ten minutes, turning off the highway at the Luzern junction, as John had suspected, and into the Swiss countryside. The side roads were almost completely unlit and there were very few cars on the roads, all of which helped John's plan. Houses were few and far between, and on either side of the pot-holed roads, miles and miles of undisturbed forestry surrounded them. It was the perfect location to keep a low profile.

The taxi driver had managed to keep a safe distance back whilst still comfortably tailing the leading taxi.

"You're doing well, driver," John announced. "I suspect we are close now, so stay well back and be prepared to slow down. I want to park well back from them when we do finally stop, so that we don't draw attention to ourselves."

The taxi meter said 72.38 francs in great big blue numbers, so John took out the three hundred Swiss francs that he had withdrawn earlier at the casino and placed the wodge of money on the passenger seat next to the driver. "Here you go. Thank you for your help, I trust this will cover your inconvenience?"

"Yes indeed, sir, thank you," the driver replied. "There isn't much around here as far as I know, sir, just a few private gite's and a farmyard or two."

"It looks perfect. Keep your wits about you now," John urged.

****

"Not far now," Dimitri advised his driver. "If you take the next left, I'm just up there on the right, about six hundred metres or so."

"Okay, sir, no problem."

"That's it, left here. I'm the first cottage on the right. That's it," Dimitri continued, as he signalled for the driver to pull over. "Anywhere here, please," he added, not wanting to disclose his exact address.

****

John had seen Dimitri's car turn left and gambled that this was his end destination, or at least very close. "Okay, if you just pull over here, driver. I will travel the rest on foot."

The driver did as instructed, and John got out of the cab.

"Please turn around and go back the way you came; don't go any further down this road."

"Okay, sir. Thank you," the driver whispered as he did a three-point turn and slowly accelerated away into the distance, trying not to make a sound.

John was on his own again, but this time, without a weapon or a plan. It was not an ideal scenario, he thought to himself, as he began a slow walk towards what he assumed was Dimitri's home.

After a couple of minutes, John had almost reached the turning. He stopped and looked for a gap in the bushes that separated the road from the forest; finding a small opening, he climbed through the gap as silently as could. Once on the other side of the bush, he was confronted by a thick, woody maze, and he was forced to duck down to avoid the low branches. After carefully making his way through the densest part of the forest, he cut the corner and travelled silently onwards in the direction of the gite's opposite.

He could just about make out three of them in the distance, across the small adjoining road. The one nearest to John was in complete darkness, only visible because of the light from next-door shining on it. Next door was certainly occupied, with lights on in every possible room. The third, which was by far the smallest of the three, was barely noticeable but for a couple of lights glinting in the distance.

John reached the road and leaned forwards out of the bushes, trying to get a slightly better view. Suddenly, to his left, the cocking of a shotgun sounded in the silence.

He paused for a split second before whispering, "Dimitri?"

"Unfortunately for you, John, no," came the response.

John's whole life flashed through his mind in the few additional seconds it took for him to process what was happening. As he began to conjure the few words that might just save his life, his ears were exposed to a deafening sonic boom, followed by a loud snapping sound. He hit the floor with a thud, and with that, the sleepy little Swiss village once again returned to its previous tranquil silence.

CHAPTER NINETEEN

John lay motionless, his face planted in the mud. After a few seconds of silence, he realised that he could still hear his own breathing. He was still alive.

Lifting his head a few centimetres off the ground, he plucked up the courage to turn in the direction of the gunman. No one was there. Slowly and carefully, so as to make as little sound as possible, John pulled himself to his feet. He could smell the smoke of the gunshot, and could feel the residue on his face and in his hair.

He checked his body for damage. Nothing. Then he saw him, lying face down on a coffin of branches, his body suspended an inch from the ground. John lifted his mud laden black shoe out of the undergrowth and kicked the man off his balcony of branches, onto his front.

He did not recognise the man, though this was hardly surprising: the right side of the man's face was no longer there. Horrified, it suddenly dawned on John that the residue dripping down his face and entangled in his hair was not gunpowder at all, but in fact pieces of the recently deceased man's brain.

"Jesus," John whispered to himself. "He must have been right behind me."

"He was, John," came a voice from the darkness.

John jumped backwards in shock.

"Stay there, John. Don't move. It's me, Dimitri. Are you armed?"

"Dimitri, thank Christ! No, I'm unarmed" John replied, raising his hands instinctively into the air.

"At ease, soldier," Dimitri quipped, "What the hell are you doing here, John? And who the fuck is that?"

"Erm," John paused, trying to compose himself. "No idea. Looks like you saved my bacon though."

"Bacon… what are you talking about, John?"

"Sorry, it's an old English saying. Is there somewhere we can talk?"

"Yes, John, there is. But this time, you can do the talking, and I will keep holding this gun if you don't mind."

"Of course," John conceded. "I guess we need to deal with this guy first?" he continued, trying to avoid the inevitable cross-examination for as long as possible.

"You can deal with him, John. I will sit here and watch, if that's okay with you. Here, I brought you a shovel."

"Thanks…" John replied, resigned to his immediate fate.

CHAPTER TWENTY

John ruffled through the deceased's pockets, desperate to find some clues about the man's identity. Inevitably, he had very little on his person, apart from a well-hidden flick knife, some cash of varying currencies and an old burner phone, not dissimilar to John's old Samsung. John took the phone out of his inside jacket pocket and called over to Dimitri.

"Got a phone here, might help us to identify him?" he said, as he tossed the burner into Dimitri's awaiting palms.

John continued his search of the body, finishing his check of the inside pockets of the man's black leather jacket before moving on to the outside zipper, situated slightly above his heart, now stained red from all the blood. Finally, John checked his jean pockets. Finding nothing else of interest, he completed a final scan of the body, piled up the few artifacts he had found – the only remaining evidence that the attacker had ever existed – and began to dig.

Dimitri watched on, one eye on John's progress and the other on the phone that he was trying to gain access to. The gun pointed in John's direction was more of a token gesture than anything else; he wanted John to understand that their relationship had significantly deteriorated following John's recent betrayal of his trust.

"So, why did you follow me, John?" Dimitri asked, gesturing for John to keep digging.

"Straight to the point as always, Dimitri," John joked. "You know, you could really do with working on the subtlety of your interrogation technique—"

"Cut the crap, John. You owe me an explanation."

"Look, I'm sorry, Dimitri. I appreciate how you must feel about me invading your personal domain and putting you in potential danger."

"Potential danger?" Dimitri laughed. "I've just killed a man not fifty metres from my front door because he was coming to kill me, or you, or potentially both of us. I'm not interested in your apologies, John. My cover is blown; I'm going to have to move now, thanks to you. So do me a favour and tell me why you followed me."

"I wanted to try again," John responded, without looking up from the hole he was digging.

"What do you mean, try again?" Dimitri demanded.

"I wanted to see if I could persuade you to help me. You are my only hope, Dimitri."

"Bullshit," Dimitri exclaimed. "You followed me so that you could blackmail me, didn't you? Well, that plan is fucked now, isn't it? Not only do you now know where I live, but so does our friend here, and most probably the people that sent him. My home for the last ten years is no longer; all because of you."

"I suppose you could look at it like that."

"Yes, I do look at it like that, John. How else am I supposed to fucking look at it?"

John paused and gathered his wits. This was his

chance to turn the tide in his direction. "Well, maybe, just maybe, me following you here actually saved your life—"

"Hah!" Dimitri exclaimed, outraged. "It was me who saved your life, John, not the other way around."

"Yes, yes, I know, and I will forever be in your debt, Dimitri. But consider, for a moment, that this guy came here to kill you, not me. In that case, me getting in the way inadvertently saved you, didn't it?"

Dimitri paused for a moment, considering this elaborate take on the evening's events. He could not help but appreciate John's creativity, and the longer he thought on it, the more he felt it was plausible. "It's an interesting theory," he finally conceded.

"I have four, Dimitri. Four working theories."

"Good. What are they?"

John composed himself once more. He really needed to make this count if he wanted to get out of here alive. "It is possible that, by following you back here, I somehow led our friend over there to this place, via some implausible taxi conga across Zurich and that, by some miracle, he managed to avoid being noticed by two very experienced spies along the way."

"Well, I didn't spot you, did I?" Dimitri said, realising too late that he had just unnecessarily inflated John's ego and revealed his own vulnerability.

John smirked briefly, but chose to ignore this particular victory; considering the current state of play – him holding a shovel and Dimitri holding a gun – it was probably best not to gloat. "If that theory is correct, then it is fair to assume that I was the primary target, and that you were either a secondary target or not on their list. Agreed?"

117

Dimitri nodded. "I think he followed you to the casino, and then followed you here. You did his job for him. I bet the guy couldn't believe his luck, two birds with one stone, as you British say."

"I accept that it is a possibility," John said coolly. "But my other two working hypotheses are also credible."

"Go on," Dimitri gestured again.

"Theory two is that the gunman was already here in the woods, waiting for you to return from your evening out, and could not believe his luck when I started thumbing through the forest over the road."

"It's possible, but it doesn't explain how he found me, does it? I've successfully managed to stay hidden here for ten years," Dimitri responded, unimpressed with this particular theory. "It all sounds a bit too convenient for my liking, that you just happen to show up on the same day that they finally track me down."

"I appreciate that, but it's not that incredible, is it?" John retaliated. "Alek is out of prison; maybe he has been tracking you down too. Surely it would be just a matter of time if he wanted you enough."

Dimitri grunted, well aware of how ludicrous this argument was becoming considering the situation they had found themselves in.

"If you think that's implausible," John tried again, "Then I accept that maybe I inadvertently led him here."

"Inadvertently, my ass," Dimitri dismissed.

"No listen, hear me out. Maybe he has been tracking me ever since they attacked my house. The moment I contacted you and arranged to meet, Malakov could have been on your tail, he would have known I was in Switzerland, and if this guy was tailing me, then he could have easily picked you up at the crematorium."

"That's possible, I admit. It's still your fault either way," Dimitri shrugged.

"I did not intentionally do anything to harm you, Dimitri, you must see that." John was starting to feel rather unsafe.

"Calm down, John, it's okay. I'm not going to shoot you and bury you out here in the woods," Dimitri said calmly, lowering his gun to the ground for the first time. "Go on, what's your final theory?"

"Simply that all this was inevitable the moment Alek got out of prison. He was always going to come after both of us; the fact that we got to each other first is probably the only reason we're both still alive."

Dimitri remained silent; his expression thoughtful.

John continued, "You see, if they had managed to kill me the first time around, you would have been none-the-wiser about all this; a sitting duck waiting for them to track you down and finish you off as well. It might not have been tonight, but they would have got here eventually. The fact that we are together and alive gives us an advantage of sorts, don't you think?"

Dimitri slowly got to his feet. "Interesting theories, John," he said whilst simultaneously kicking some dirt over his victim's face. "Come on. Let's finish this job and get out of here before the sun comes up."

CHAPTER TWENTY ONE

John felt a slight breeze wafting over his forehead and slowly opened his left eye, his right still concealed by a cushion that had left a small imprint on his cheek. Lifting his torso upright, he spun his legs around, flicking off the old musty blanket as he moved. Two large Alsatians immediately confronted him. He paused for a moment to assess the threat, but quickly realised that he was only in danger of being licked to death. As he rubbed his face and sat up on the sofa bed, he began to recall the events of the previous night.

He could just about make out Dimitri, sitting at the breakfast table in the room opposite, smoking a cigarette and sipping from a large mug.

"Got one of them for me?" John called over.

"A cigarette?" came the reply.

"No, a coffee."

"In the pot on the side. Did you sleep well?" Dimitri enquired politely.

"Yes, thank you. I thought we were supposed to be taking shifts?"

"Yeah, but I couldn't sleep. Besides, you needed it more than me."

"Thanks, I really did," John replied, as he took his

seat at the breakfast table, having already acquired a mug of lukewarm espresso. "What now then, Dimitri?"

"Good question, my friend," Dimitri murmured philosophically, without looking up. "I have been sitting here considering that one all night."

"Have you found the answer yet?"

"Not sure there is one, to be honest. It's all such a mess, isn't it?" Dimitri sighed, staring at his empty mug. "The first thing we need to do is get out of here. I've packed my case and arranged for us to meet some people in Kyiv tomorrow night."

"Us? Are you in then?" John asked, having already read the answer across Dimitri's face.

"The way I see it, I can either run or fight. I'm too tired to keeping running, John."

John nodded in appreciation. "Thank you. I will be forever in your debt, my friend."

"Hah, I've heard that before," Dimitri chuckled.

"Why Kyiv though, Dimitri? And what people?"

"It's nearer Russia than Zurich, isn't it? Plus there's an old contact of mine there who might be able to help us. Now, drink up. We need to be gone."

John sipped from his coffee as he watched Dimitri approach the two dogs, both still sitting and looking up at their master from the corner of the room.

"Goodbye, my friends. It's been wonderful knowing you," Dimitri said as he knelt down to their level, trying to conceal the visible tears in his eyes.

"What will happen to them now?" John asked, touched by Dimitri's tangible emotion.

"I've arranged for a friend to collect them later this morning. I've told her I need to go away for a few weeks, they will be fine. I just hope it's not the last I see of them. They've been my best friends ever since I went into exile."

"I am sorry, Dimitri. Really, I am."

"Always with the apologies," Dimitri muttered as he brushed off the emotion. "Now, come on, let's go. We have a long journey ahead of us."

CHAPTER TWENTY TWO

Byrne had arrived at work for the final time this week, or so he hoped. As usual, he loaded up his computer and briefly checked his emails, but he could not escape the nagging concern in his stomach. He had not been able to contact John since early yesterday morning, and he knew in his gut that something was wrong. He must have called John's burner phone at least ten times yesterday, without receiving any response. He just knew that John was in the middle of something extremely dangerous.

His morning calm was soon destroyed completely by a loud crashing sound from the corridor outside his office. He looked up, first hearing, then seeing his boss come bashing through his office door.

"Hello, sir. To what do I owe this pleasure?" Byrne enquired, surprised by this most unexpected visit. Byrne knew that visits from the boss were never trivial affairs, and he feared the worst. "What is it, sir," he asked instinctively, his heart sinking and his thoughts quickly moving to John. "Is John okay?"

"That's what you should be telling me, isn't it, Byrne?" his boss, Sir Steven Redcalf, interjected. "I've had no updates from you about this blasted Steele charade since Wednesday, despite specifically asking for daily briefings. We can't afford to take our eye off this one."

"No, sir, of course. Unfortunately, I've had nothing to report, sir," Byrne said apologetically.

"Terrific. Fantastic work, Byrne," Redcalf replied sarcastically.

"I have been trying, sir. He just isn't picking up his phone."

"Try him again now, Byrne."

"Was about to, sir."

"Well, go on then, old chap." Redcalf gestured at Byrne, taking the seat opposite.

"With you in the room, sir?"

"Yes, man. No secrets here. I've already had the chief of police asking for an update on this case this morning, something to do with a Sergeant Muloy?",

"I know of her, sir. No need to worry; I dealt with her yesterday."

"But I do worry, Byrne. We can't have the press finding out about this. I can imagine the headlines now: 'house burglary reveals secret spy in suburbia'. It's not good, Byrne, not good at all. Now, make the call. Let's see what Steele's been up to."

Byrne began to dial the number again, but this time, on his office phone, buying himself a few seconds to think. As he copied the number into the phone keypad and gestured to Redcalf that he would put the call on speaker, he was frantically trying to work out why his boss had ventured all the way down to level two for an update. It was most unusual, and Byrne was beginning to sense that he was not being given the whole story.

The phone began to ring and both men held their

breath, eager to hear a response on the other end of the line.

After what seemed like an eternity, John answered.

"Hello."

"Hi, John, its Byrne. Thank god you're okay, where have you been?"

"Byrne? Jesus, have I got a story for you."

Byrne quickly interrupted his flow and announced "Redcalf is here with me, John. What have you got?"

"Wow, I'm honoured," John replied, as he glanced over to Dimitri in the driver's seat and raised an eyebrow. "I don't think I spoke to you more than twice, sir, when I was in MI6."

Redcalf glanced over at Byrne and gave him a glare that made it clear he would have preferred to remain anonymous.

"Hi, John. Everyone here at MI6 was so sad to hear about this whole affair. I can assure you that we're working day and night to find the perpetrators."

"Me too, sir," John quipped,

"But you see, that's just it. We can't have you running around, renegade. What if something were to go wrong? We can't be responsible for your actions, John. Please try to see it from our side."

"Sir, with the greatest respect, something has already gone wrong. My son is in Intensive Care, and I've been shot at twice in the last five days."

"Twice?" Byrne exclaimed.

"Yes, Byrne. Twice. Last night someone came for us at Dimitri's home. Luckily, Dimitri saw him before he saw Dimitri, otherwise I would be a dead man."

"Jesus, John, you need to come home, now. We can work out what's going on together; we are stronger together, John."

"Yes, exactly, Byrne," Redcalf added. "You must come home immediately. It is not safe for you out there without our back up. You must come home immediately and let us deal with this sorry mess."

"No can do, sir. We both know it's Malakov, and we also both know that you won't go after him in Russia. But I will. Just help me find out where he is, that's all I'm asking."

"Come home, Steele, and we can discuss it."

"I'm sorry, sir, but I can't do that. If I come home now, I will spend all my waking hours waiting for him to try again. I need to tackle the problem head on. Besides, Dimitri is also involved now; they are after him too. Dimitri can help me track him down."

"Are you sure they tried to kill you, John, not Dimitri?" Byrne added, somewhat naively.

"Pretty sure! I mean, he had a shotgun pressed against the back of my neck, Byrne, before Dimitri blew his head off. Besides, what does it matter?"

"Sorry, John. Just trying to put the pieces together. Do you think they were after you or Dimitri, seeing as it was his house they went to?"

"Both, I suspect, but it really doesn't matter. We are connected by the events that took place all those years ago, and we are connected again now."

"Do you know who it was?"

"No, do you?" John fired back, becoming increasingly irritated by the direction of the Byrne's questioning.

To Byrne's relief, Redcalf summoned the energy to speak again. "Come home, John, that's an order. We can work this out together. If not, I will have no choice but to have you arrested. We can't have you travelling around with an ex-Russian spy executing people."

"Will you help me enter Russia, Redcalf?" John asked, getting to the heart of the matter. The pause on the other end of the line was all John really needed to hear. "You forget, Redcalf, that I don't work for you anymore. If you won't help me find Malakov, then I have no choice but to do it myself." With that, John flipped the phone shut and threw it out of the window into the lush Swiss countryside. "Looks like it's just us two now, my friend"

Dimitri glanced over at him, momentarily taking his eyes off the road. "It appears so, John. It appears so."

CHAPTER TWENTY THREE

John waited in the petrol station while his newfound partner filled up with diesel. Dimitri's vehicle of choice was an old but sturdy black Hyundai Tucson, ideal for the tough terrain ahead.

Dimitri opened the driver's door and threw a couple of bags of food and a couple of drinks at John. "Supplies for the road trip," he shouted across, as he started up the four by four.

They headed back onto the A96, and drove for a good twenty minutes before either of them spoke again.

"So, how long is this going to take then, Dimitri?" John eventually asked.

"We'll drive through Munich on the A9, pass the toll, then stay over in Prague for the night. At least, that's the plan."

"How long until we hit Prague?"

"About ten hours, give or take. It's a straight road from Prague to Kyiv, via Poland, so should be fairly straightforward. The whole trip will take about twenty hours, so take the opportunity to get some rest. You're going to need it."

"Let me do some of the driving, Dimitri. It will help me pass the time. In fact, why don't you pull over now.

128

I'll drive for a bit; you can catch up on some sleep."

Dimitri paused for a moment, struggling to set aside his scepticism. He could not help but second-guess his old enemy, despite knowing that John was only trying to help. Pushing his doubt from his mind, he conceded.

"Okay, John. I'll let you know when I've hit the wall. I will try and get you to the A9; it's straight to Prague from there. Even you won't be able to get us lost!"

"Hey, my geography isn't that bad!" John protested, a small grin invading his face.

"We might have a bit of trouble getting into Ukraine tomorrow though," Dimitri continued. "The border is still active. I'll speak to my friends from Kyiv tonight; see what they can do."

John sat back and closed his eyes, waiting for his turn to drive, but almost immediately, Ethan and Wendy popped into his mind again. "Shit," he said out loud.

"What's up, John?"

"I've just realised, I've thrown away my only way of contacting Wendy…"

"Do you know the number?"

"Maybe… I think I remember it. She's had the same number for years; I really ought to have memorised it by now."

"Okay, look in my rucksack, in the front zipper. There are three or four clean phones in there. Take one for yourself."

"Really?"

"Of course. Can't imagine I will need them all before we get to Prague. I can always pick a couple more up there if we need to."

"Thanks," John mumbled, as he stretched behind the driver's seat and scrabbled around in the bag. Once he had grabbed one, he sat back in his seat and switched the device on.

****

Wendy had finally moved from her hospital chair, and was now standing at the end of Ethan's bed, talking to the doctors. There had been a development in the night, so when her phone rang, it came as an unwanted distraction. She quickly checked the number. Withheld. It was probably some PPI scam or something, she thought, not registering that it might actually be her husband trying to make contact.

She rejected the call and continued her conversation with the specialist. "Sorry about that, doctor. You were saying?"

"Yes, Mrs Cooper. I'm afraid Ethan picked up an infection during the night; he has a high fever, but we are treating it with antibiotics and monitoring him very carefully. I'm afraid the next few hours will be vital, once again."

"Thank you for informing me, doctor," Wendy managed to spit out, her head feeling like it was about to explode off her shoulders from all the pressure she was under.

"I will be back around again later this morning to check on him. Is there anyone we can call, your husband?" the doctor offered.

"No, thank you, doctor. He isn't reachable at the minute," Wendy replied, angry that he was not with her and embarrassed to have to explain that to the doctor.

"Stay strong, Mrs Cooper. We will see you soon."

"Jesus," John shouted, frustrated that Wendy had not answered his call. "You'd think she would pick up, wouldn't you? What could be more important than this?" he vented, folding his arms like a petulant schoolboy.

John and Dimitri exchanged very few words for the next couple of hours, and John drifted in and out of consciousness, unable to resist the drowsiness induced by the bumpy roads. When he did finally wake fully, he quickly realised that he had slept for at least a couple of hours, and could see from their new surroundings that they were in Germany already. It had always amazed him how different Germany was to Switzerland, despite being just over the border.

"I thought you were going to wake me, Dimitri," John protested. "You're not very good at taking shifts, are you?"

"I guess not," Dimitri smiled. "Can't seem to switch off. I keep trying to work out what would convince the British government to let Alek out. It just seems insane to me."

"I know. I keep wrestling with that one myself," John replied. "For the British government to even consider an exchange, the intel Andrei acquired must have been extremely embarrassing indeed. I don't think they have ever agreed to anything this high level before."

"What did he have on them, John? You must have some idea?" Dimitri probed.

"Trust me, there are a number of things that would cause my government a lot of problems if they came to light; things are no different on your side, I'm sure.

What I want to know is how did Andrei manage to get his hands on it in the first place?"

Dimitri paused on that thought, and continued to drive a while. Eventually, his eyes could no longer take the monotony, and he decided to throw the towel in. "Okay, John, your turn. We are about three hours outside of Prague now."

"No problem," John replied.

As the two men walked around the car to take up their new positions, Dimitri pressed his left palm into John's chest, in a motion that suggested John needed to stop walking.

"Hey, what you doing, Dimitri?"

"John, if there is anything you are not telling me, now's the time," Dimitri whispered into John's ear. "We are in this together now, so no more secrets, okay? I'm prepared to risk my life to help you, but I need to know everything you do, otherwise this won't work."

John thought for a moment, then nodded at Dimitri, confirming his understanding of Dimitri's new terms of engagement.

Neither man spoke for a long time after that, but both were now fully aware of the contract they had just made with each other. John watched the road and listened to a German radio station, while Dimitri sat and stared out of the passenger window, still unable to sleep. Eventually, as dusk was falling, they made it to the outskirts of Prague.

"Thirty kilometres out, Dimitri," John informed his passenger. "Have we got a room organised?"

"No, not yet. Drive into the city centre and park in one of the multistorey car parks. There will be loads of B&B's around there; it'll be easier if we pay by cash."

CHAPTER TWENTY FOUR

"Good news, Mrs Cooper," Dr Rubani began, as he walked into the room. "Ethan's fever has already come down significantly; it looks like the antibiotics are taking effect. He is a fighter, your boy, must take after his mum, eh?"

Wendy lifted her head up wearily, just about registering what the doctor was saying to her. "Oh, thank god. He doesn't look any different…"

"No, he won't, Mrs Cooper. He is still in a coma, and not yet out of the woods by a long stretch, but the fever is reducing, so his body can start to recover from the trauma again now."

"Thank you, doctor," Wendy mumbled.

"Mrs Cooper, if you don't mind me saying, we are all worried about you too. You can't take all this strain on your own; no one should be expected to. Is there anyone we can ask to come and be with you?"

Wendy looked at the doctor, and his kind, concerned eyes finally broke her. All at once, the emotion flooded out, and she dropped to her knees, falling out of her chair and onto the floor, weeping uncontrollably.

"Nurse, nurse," the doctor shouted, as he realised what was happening,

A nurse quickly rushed into the room and tried to hold her up, but it was no good, Wendy could not catch her breath, and was starting to turn an alarming, pale blue colour.

"Quick, bring a ventilator," Dr Rubani said softly but firmly, taking control of the situation and gently lowering Wendy to the floor. He began to perform CPR, pressing increasing firmly on her chest as he failed to get the response he wanted. For some reason, whether because of her son's dire situation or because he felt sorry that she was having to deal with this situation alone, he felt an usually strong responsibility towards the welfare of this woman.

"Where's that ventilator? I'm losing her," he yelled down the corridor as the panic began to set in.

Finally, his prayers were answered, as a nurse appeared alongside him and quickly attached Wendy to the ventilator she so badly needed. It took a minute or two, but slowly her heart rate and oxygen levels started to improve. She was breathing okay now, albeit with the aid of the ventilator, but she remained unconscious.

"Nurse, organise a bed for her in here, so that she can be close to her son when she wakes up."

"Yes, doctor," replied the nurse, deciding that this was not the time to complain about the bed shortages in the ICU. "I'm sure we can find space for her around the corner."

"And keep me aware of their progress throughout the night, both of them. If anything changes, let me know immediately, and I'll come in."

"Yes, doctor, of course," she replied, as she helped the male nurse to carry Wendy onto the temporary bed they had just wheeled in.

"Give her forty milligrams of bromide for now, and codeine to help calm her down at little. Hopefully it will make her sleep, she looks exhausted. Take the usual bloods so we can rule out anything sinister, but I strongly suspect it's just a panic attack. Okay?"

"Of course, doctor, I'll keep you updated," the staff nurse assured him, as she wheeled Wendy away.

As the disturbance calmed and Ethan's room returned to its eerie silence, Dr Rubani glanced over at the boy, lying there in the ICU bed, oblivious to the drama that had just unfolded in front of him. In that moment, he realised why he felt so attached to them both, and why he felt such anger toward the father. Surely nothing could be more important than being by your son's side while he is fighting for his own very existence in this harsh world you had brought him into?

CHAPTER TWENTY FIVE

John was settling in to their room for the night, a shitty little twin room in a backstreet B&B in the centre of Prague, where no doubt countless filthy lads on stag dos had stayed before. John did not really care; he just wanted to phone Wendy and make sure all was well. Dimitri had offered to pop out and get them some food, so John took the opportunity to call his wife again. Hopefully she would pick up this time.

He listened as the phone rang out, becoming increasing angry at the prospect of her missing him once again.

"Hi, this is Wendy, I'm not around at the moment..." the voicemail began.

"For Christ sake," John shouted, smashing the phone lid shut, just as Dimitri came back through the bedsit door.

"What's up now, John?" Dimitri asked.

"Oh nothing, Dimitri, just my wife. She's still not answering my calls. I really would feel better if I could check in on them. I guess she's still angry with me; can't blame her really, she doesn't know anything about all this."

"What does she think you are doing then?" Dimitri

asked, slightly surprised to hear about Wendy's ignorance.

"She doesn't know anything about my previous life, so I guess she can't understand why I'm not with her and Ethan when they need me most."

"Understandable, then, her reaction I mean. That must be difficult for her, John, not knowing anything. Here, hopefully these will help take your mind off it for a bit: pizza and a few tins."

"Cheers, Dimitri," John replied, as he gratefully accepted a beer. "I'll try her again in the morning, hopefully she will have calmed down a bit by then."

John moved over to the makeshift dinner table that Dimitri had put together with sofas and a drinks table from the corner of the room, and took his seat for dinner. They both executed their much needed re-fuelling mission in silence, hungry and exhausted after their long trip across central Europe.

John paused for a moment, out of breath after demolishing his twelve inch pizza, and noticed that Dimitri was staring off into space, seemingly in his own world. Something must be on his mind. John waited for them both to finish their pizza, then passed his comrade another can of beer. "Are you okay, Dimitri? I really am in your debt. After this, if there is anything, anything at all that you need, I owe you one, okay?"

Dimitri nodded, pulling the ring pull on his second Pravha. "Good these, aren't they? Brewed in Prague, apparently."

"Yes, they really hit the spot," John answered, taking a giant gulp.

Both men returned to their own quiet contemplation, and stayed that way for a good while, exchanging more beers and acknowledgments but no conversation to speak of.

Gradually, as the alcohol began to take effect, John started to lower his guard, and once again asked what was on Dimitri's mind.

"Do you really want to know, John?" came the response.

"Yes. I wouldn't have asked if I didn't, would I?"

Dimitri took a deep breath. "The truth is, I feel like I'm flying in the dark here, not with the Malakov problem, but with our own relationship, or partnership, or whatever you want to call it. You seem to be ahead of the game, and I'm following along for the ride, and I'm not sure I like it. I said it in the truck, and I will say it again, John. We can have no secrets now; we need to be on the same page if we are going to get this done."

"I completely agree, Dimitri, but I'm not sure I follow. What do you think I'm hiding from you?"

"Not hiding exactly, John, more like withholding some key information, information that might help me put all this together."

"Like what?" John questioned.

"Just a couple of things, like what you have been telling your wife for the last twenty years… it seems a little weird to me, John."

"Well, as implausible as it may seem to you, Dimitri, my wife has never had any knowledge of my work with MI6. She thought I was a cook in the army, and never had any need to question it, until now, I guess. If I think about it, which believe me, I have been doing a lot of this last week, then I think she turned a blind eye to it all, trusting in the fact that it wouldn't affect her and the kids. It's ironic really, given the events of the last few weeks."

"And after you left MI6?"

"Never thought it important; that life was finished, and we built a new one together. I didn't see the need to throw a spanner in the works."

"I guess I can understand that," Dimitri responded apologetically, after a few seconds reflection. "Never been married myself, so no idea how all that stuff works between a man and his wife."

John looked over and could see that Dimitri was still not satisfied. "Go on, what else? Spit it out, man."

"I guess what troubles me most is how this all came to pass in the first place. What was it that persuaded them to make the swap? I struggle to understand how any government could conclude that releasing Malakov was a reasonable solution."

John paused for a moment, as was his way before any important speech. He was conscious that he wanted to be honest with the man in front of him, but was also aware that he needed to be careful about how much he revealed. He did not want to say anything that would implicate his own government in something underhand. "Well, your guy told us Malakov was exchanged for some sensitive information, classified files, right?"

"Yes, I know that bit, John, but what files? And how did Andrei come by them?"

"I haven't got the answers to either of those questions, and I'm quite sure MI6 haven't either. They will be frantically trying to find that out for themselves right about now."

"But what's your take, John? You must have an idea?"

"In terms of who, I've got no clue, honestly. From

140

the service's point of view, this will be their priority. That's probably why they are so reluctant to help us out; if there's a mole giving the Malakovs intel then everything will stop until they find out who it is."

"Especially if they are leaking intel important enough to get Alek released," Dimitri chipped in.

"Exactly, but I've been out for ten years, haven't I? Same as you. Do you know who's running the FSB and GRU offices now, Dimitri? We're as clueless as each other."

Dimitri sighed. "I guess you're right.," he conceded. "Let's focus on the 'what' for now then. Like you say, I'm sure there are plenty of people working on the 'who', from both sides."

CHAPTER TWENTY SIX

Byrne was sitting in his flat, doing exactly the same thing trying to work out who the mole in MI6 was.

He had been re-assigned since his asset, John, had gone dark, and he desperately needed a result to make up for the scolding he had just received from Redcalf. Losing contact with John had not gone down well, hence why he was putting in some hours now, sitting on his sofa with a glass of red wine in hand.

It had been a tough day, and although Byrne was still licking his own wounds, he could not help but worry about John's predicament. He was angry at the way the agency had treated John, and he had grave concerns about the magnitude of threat the Malakovs might pose in the future if the intel they had on the government was as damning as he suspected. It was a labyrinth of conspiracy, of which he had yet to find the entrance.

****

Both John and Dimitri were now laying on their allocated beds, still fully clothed, of course, and still with their beers in hand. It reminded John of his early army training days; he only wished he felt as carefree now as he had felt back then.

Dimitri was seemingly pre-occupied watching some old spaghetti western on the telly, so John spent the time developing his story for when Dimitri inevitably quizzed him again. He wanted to be transparent with Dimitri, but was not prepared to divulge any national secrets just yet. There was no point in taking out the Malakovs only to be rewarded with a trial for espionage when he got home.

His mind inevitably wandered back to his time in Iraq, and although he tried, he could not help but fear that all this was connected to those days somehow. He could not overlook the dark secrets he had learned on that particular tour; it was the real reason he had left MI6, and it terrified him to consider what Alek could do with those sorts of state secrets.

****

Back in 2008, shortly after Dimitri had passed on the info about the weapons exchange, John had been putting a report together, detailing the current position of weapons of mass destruction in Iraq. To John's surprise, Dimitri had made contact, for the second time in as many months, requesting some information about a rumour going around. Usually, such rumours were quickly dismissed, but this particular rumour had grabbed Dimitri's interest, for it alluded to the existence of an 'off the grid' British government facility in the Iraqi desert.

As John had been in charge of reporting on these matters, and knew the location of all the British government facilities, both 'on' and 'off' grid, he had confidently rejected all talk of such a facility. Dimitri had refused to tell John how he had come by the information, so both men had decided to leave that particular conversation where it was, lost in the sand dunes of time.

However, Dimitri's questioning had, inadvertently, triggered a switch in John's brain. He had struggled with the seed that Dimitri had planted, and though he had tried to ignore it, something in his gut had refused to let it go. Perhaps upset that he had not been involved in such an important operation, or maybe concerned that the rumour might indeed be true, John had eventually decided to investigate further.

At the time, his position had been such that he had the clearance to start digging, but that was what had concerned him most. If this rumour were true, he should have been informed, so there must be a reason why he had been kept out of the loop, if this off-grid facility did indeed exist.

A few days later, during a briefing with his boss, the newly appointed Sir Steven Redcalf, John had taken the opportunity to add an extra operation to their agenda, to see whether Redcalf would inadvertently let something slip, if indeed there was anything to let slip, which he still believed was highly unlikely. As they discussed all the active operations in John's remit, including Basra, Baghdad, Najaf and Erbil, John casually mentioned an operation in Rawa, a small town in the Syrian desert. It was a fictitious operation, but one that would allow plausible deniability if Redcalf spotted his deliberate mistake; Rawa, had been one of the first places the British had checked for weapons of mass destruction, at the start of the war in 2003, so if questioned, John could put it down to a typo from an old agenda.

"Rawa?" Redcalf had queried, when John had asked him whether he was up to speed on that particular operation.

"Yes, sir."

After a long pause, Redcalf had continued. "I don't have anything in Rawa, John. Is that an old op? Or maybe you mean Haditha?"

"Oh, apologies, sir. I think you're right, that must be from an old agenda. One, two, three, four…" he had counted. "Yep, that's all of them. Thank you, sir."

"Keep up the good work, John," Redcalf had replied in his usual matter-of-fact way, with no degree of suspicion in his voice.

"Thank you, sir. Goodbye."

John had put the phone down and inhaled a huge breath of relief. He had just about got away with it, and he now had a clue. He had never heard of Haditha, let alone run an op there. What was going on? He needed to find out, and fast.

CHAPTER TWENTY SEVEN

Wendy was awake, sitting up in bed and drinking a cup of tea. The nurse had left her with a plate of chocolate bourbons, insisting that she needed to eat to build up her strength again.

At least the drama was over now, she thought to herself. Her vital signs were all back to normal, according to the nurse, and she had been left with nothing more than a slight migraine and an aching in her heart, pulling her back to her son.

She had already negotiated with the staff nurse, who had advised her several times that she would be best staying where she was for a while, insisting that she needed rest and that Ethan was still sleeping peacefully, so there was no need to worry. But Wendy had been adamant, and after a great deal of pleading, the nurse had finally relented, agreeing that she could see her son just as soon as she had been checked over by the doctor.

It was just after eight a.m. now; Dr Rubani was due round anytime, and Wendy was trying desperately to gather all her things together so that the moment he had checked her over she could get back to Ethan.

"Nurse? Nurse?" she called over to one of the ward sisters. "I can't seem to find my bag. Did you bring it through with me last night?"

"Let me just check for you, Mrs Cooper. Don't worry, I'm sure it's not gone far."

Wendy sat herself back on her hospital bed and caught a glimpse of Dr Rubani at the other end of the unit, near Ethan. "Sorry, nurse? Nurse, can I have a quick word?" Wendy asked politely, from a few metres away.

The young nurse walked swiftly across to Wendy's bed.

"I don't know if they have told you, but that's my son down there," Wendy informed her.

"Yes, I know, Mrs Cooper."

"Well, I had a funny turn myself last night, so the doctor put me here for the night, but you see, Dr Rubani is over there, look," Wendy said, waving to the other end of the corridor. "He's about to check on Ethan and I really need to be there to discuss his progress with him."

"I appreciate that, Mrs Cooper, but the nurse who was on shift before me left strict instructions not to let you go until you've seen the doctor."

"Exactly! Could you please pop over to him and remind him that I'm here? See if he will give me the once over before he goes in to see Ethan? It would save him time, and will get me out of your hair," Wendy pleaded.

The nurse looked at her with sympathy and pity, the same pity that almost everyone had been looking at her with this past week. It was a look that was starting to grate on her ever so slightly.

"Let me see what I can do, Mrs Cooper. Oh, and apparently your things have been left in Ethan's room,

147

the nurses thought they would be safer there than on the floor out here. I hope that's okay?"

"Yes, that's fine. Thank you."

****

John and Dimitri had risen early, and were already on the road, heading out of Prague city centre and towards the A1.

"Once we hit the A1 it's a straight road through Poland and into Ukraine; another ten hours or so and we'll be there," Dimitri confidently announced.

"What's the plan when we get there? Did you speak to your guys in Kyiv?"

"Yes, I called them last night. They've organised for us to get through at Yahodyn; they are expecting us tonight at ten p.m. exactly, that's why we had to leave so early. We don't want to miss our window, we might not get another one."

"Have they got men there, then?" John asked.

"No idea, to be honest. He just said go through at ten p.m. and asked for my registration. It's a slight detour, but they said we must avoid Ustiluh at all costs. Can't be going through there with your British passport. I'm assuming you have a British one with you, right?"

John nodded.

"Good. That won't get us into Russia, but it's okay for Ukraine apparently."

As both men settled down for a second day on the road, John decided to take the opportunity to once again try and call his wife.

Yet again, the phone rang out and went through to voicemail. "Hi, this is Wendy, I'm not around…"

Dimitri waited for John to respond in his usual manner.

"For Christ's sake!" John shouted, throwing the phone onto the back seat.

Dimitri allowed himself a brief smirk, making sure he concealed it from John. "Why don't you leave her a damn message next time, man?" Dimitri offered, in an attempt to calm things down a little.

"No, I need to speak to her so that I can explain what's going on. What can I possibly say on a voicemail that would help make sense of all this? I get it, she's pissed with me, but it's not just about us, is it? I need to know what's going on with Ethan."

Dimitri glanced over apologetically and shrugged his shoulders. "Maybe send her a text with your number?" He said, trying to offer some comfort to his partner.

"I guess that's not a bad idea. I'll try her again in a couple of hours; if she doesn't pick up, I'll send her my number, and just hope that she phones me back."

****

The young, pretty nurse had quickly caught Dr Rubani's eye, a little too quickly in Wendy's opinion, and the doctor was now making his way over to her hospital bed.

"Good morning, Mrs Cooper," Dr Rubani smiled.

"Good morning, doctor," she replied.

"Glad to see you are feeling better now, Mrs Cooper. You gave us all a scare last night."

"Yes, sorry about that," Wendy replied, not sure why she was apologising.

"I've taken the liberty of phoning your father, Mrs

149

Cooper, to let him know what is going on here. I did try your husband first, but no luck. I hope you don't mind, they were on Ethan's registration."

"No, not at all," Wendy answered, acknowledging that she needed all the help she could get.

"He's coming in later this morning to look after you. Meanwhile, I'm happy to discharge you based on these results," he continued, looking at Wendy's notes. "I'm confident that it was simply a panic attack, so I will give you some tablets for the anxiety. Take two a day, with food, please. The nurse will bring them down to you later."

"Yes, doctor, thank you."

"No problem. Besides, I strongly suspect that you won't be going far, will you, Mrs Cooper? So we can still keep an eye on you, can't we? Now, when you are ready, you can head down to your son's room. I will be in shortly to give him a once over, but I've already been told that he had a good night, so it seems its good news all round this morning."

CHAPTER TWENTY EIGHT

Byrne was making his way up the M1 for the second time this week, on a Saturday, his day off. He wasn't exactly sure why, but knew he could not just sit around while his old friend was missing in action. There was no chance of him getting any more information out of Redcalf back at GCHQ, so he had decided to try a different tactic.

Byrne was used to being left out of classified meetings, being fed half-truths, and just generally being ignored these days. He was eighteen months from retirement, and always looked for the path of least resistance; the easy life. In fact, he spent most of his days trying to stay out of the firing line, and avoided getting embroiled in troublesome cases where possible.

His had been a potentially glorious career; as a young recruit to MI6 in the 1980s, spotted in the halls of Oxford University and groomed for front line action, one would have assumed that he had an exciting life ahead of him. But it had never quite materialised like that. Poor health, and a few badly advised misdemeanour's, had held him back, and by the early 2000s he had been pigeonholed into the vetting and handling departments, very much stuck behind a desk.

Ironically, those first few years of desk duty had been the most stimulating of his career, as he had spent the time working remotely with John and a few others on operations based in Afghanistan, Iraq, and briefly Eastern Europe. He had gained the trust of a small circle of operatives, and John in particular had always insisted that Byrne was involved in any operations that came his way.

If he was honest with himself, the spark of excitement that had once fuelled his spy career had long since burnt out, and though he had always offered his 'guys in the field' every assistance, and made sure they were as safe and informed as possible, his work at MI6 had become just a job to him. Looking back on his time as a spy, his finest work had definitely been during the years he had spent with John Steele. For some reason, John had brought out the best in him, and had found a way to re-ignite his passion for this work.

Maybe that was why he was on his way up the motorway again? Or maybe it was the particular injustice of this case that had motivated him to step in. Either way, he needed to find out where John was. He could not let him do this alone.

****

Wendy, having retrieved her bag from the floor of Ethan's room, rummaged around for her phone. There was a message from her dad, saying that he would be at the hospital after the traffic had died down, and two missed calls, both from an unknown number. She resolved to answer the mystery number next time it called her, and took her phone off vibrate.

As she sat, patiently waiting for Dr Rubani's latest prognosis, she began to reacquaint herself with her son. He was still lying there peacefully; the tubes and machines attached to his body were the only indication of the horror that he had been through less than a week ago.

"Mrs Cooper?" Dr Rubani said, interrupting Wendy's momentary reflection.

"Yes, sorry, doctor."

Dr Rubani smiled sympathetically. "I'm afraid it's another case of no news being good news."

"Oh, okay. Do you know when he will wake up, doctor?"

"When he's ready, Mrs Cooper. He's beaten off the fever and all his vitals are positive. I'm sure he will make an appearance again soon. Just keep praying for him, Wendy. Is your father still coming today?"

"Yes, yes. He'll be in once the traffic has died down, probably sometime around eleven a.m. I expect."

"Good, you need someone to look after you as well."

"Thank you, doctor, but I'm alright, honestly."

"We can arrange for someone to sit with you if you like?" the doctor offered.

"No, thank you. My father will be here soon enough."

"Well, if you change your mind, just let the nurse know, okay? I will be back again this afternoon. Stay strong, Mrs Cooper. You are doing great."

Wendy nodded her appreciation and sat back down in her chair. The doctor had left, and it was just her and her baby boy again. Reaching out for Ethan's hand she closed her eyes, and tried to rest, but her mind was cluttered with visions and flashbacks, and all she could feel was fear and panic. The thought of losing Ethan was too much to bear, and she tried to block it out of her consciousness, but in quiet moments like this, it crept up on her, consuming her.

In addition to her fears about Ethan, she was scared for John. Not knowing where he was right now terrified her, and she longed to know that he was safe. Her instincts told her that John had to be trying to find out about their attackers, and she was becoming more and more convinced that the withheld calls were him trying to make contact. Wendy once again glanced at her phone, berating herself for missing him. No new messages.

Just as another wave of hopelessness began to engulf her body, something pulled her back into the real world. A voice. A male voice. Wendy looked up, expecting to see her father in front of her, but instead was confronted by a strange looking man, offering out his hand.

"Hi, Wendy. You don't know me, I am a friend of John's. How do you do."

"A friend of John's?" she said, as she accepted his hand. "Do you know where he is?"

"No, sorry, Wendy. I was rather hoping you could tell me that."

"Who are you?" Wendy asked, growing concerned.

"Apologies, how rude of me. My name is Colin Byrne, I'm a friend of John's from his army days."

Wendy's heart sank as she realised this conversation would inevitably be concealed with half-truths and mystery.

"You see, I'm concerned about John, as I am sure you are. I was in contact with him earlier this week, just after the attack happened, but have unfortunately lost contact with him now. I really need to find him again, so that I can help bring him home. Is there anything you can tell me, to help track him down? Has he been in contact with you?"

Wendy paused a moment, digesting this new information. She looked at the man in front of her and, strangely, did not feel any fear.

"How do I know you are who you say you are, Mr…?"

"Byrne," he reminded her. "I appreciate your predicament, Wendy, honestly I do. But if I had wanted you dead, surely you must realise that you would already be so? Apologies for speaking so bluntly, but it's true. Not to mention that those cops out front would not have let me in. I had to show them my credentials to even get on the ward. Look, I respect that you don't know who to trust right now, Wendy, but you need to listen to me. I will tell you the truth."

Wendy sat down, and made a gesture for Byrne to do the same. Suddenly, her numbness had been replaced by excitement. Could this man tell her what was really going on? "Okay then, Mr Byrne. Tell me the truth, and I'll consider trusting you."

CHAPTER TWENTY NINE

Redcalf had been summoned to Chequers, for an unscheduled and hastily arranged meeting with the Prime Minister, ahead of the monthly COBRA meeting in Downing Street.

It was now a few minutes after two p.m. Redcalf had hoped to be back in London in time for some much-needed down time with his family, but as the meeting had been scheduled for one p.m., and he had still not laid eyes on the PM, he was beginning to lose hope of that particular dream becoming a reality.

He had already planned what he was going to say, pre-empting what the PM would want to talk about. To be fair, it wasn't difficult; the PM's office had been on the phone to him every day this week, wanting an update on John Cooper's current whereabouts.

"Sir Steven, my apologies for keeping you waiting. Please, do come in." The Prime Minister, Alistair Cowan, summoned him personally from the door, gesturing for him to enter the adjacent room.

"Thank you, sir," Redcalf replied, walking carefully past him and into what was clearly the study. The Prime Minister followed, shutting the door behind them both.

Hundreds of books surrounded the men, adorning

156

every wall on tightly packed shelves, and a mahogany desk stood resplendent in the centre of the room, dimly lit by the antique lamps placed sporadically but strategically around the room.

"Take a seat," Cowan said, as he took his place behind the desk. "Your presence is much appreciated. I'm sure you realise why I have asked you to come down here today."

"Of course, sir. I assume you wish to discuss the John Cooper case?"

"Indeed, Steven, indeed. It is a fairly troubling predicament we find ourselves in, isn't it?"

"Yes, sir. I appreciate that losing contact with John is not ideal, but the last contact we had with him was only yesterday. He was still in Switzerland, but we now strongly suspect that he is currently moving towards Russia. I heard him myself, during the last call with his handler, threatening to team up with Dimitri Gregorev, a Russian ex-spy friend of his."

"A Russian spy friend?" Cowan pondered. "Is that not an oxymoron, Steven?

"Yes, quite, Prime Minister. But we have reason to believe that Dimitri Gregorev may be useful to us, and may well assist us in meeting our objectives. He has his own reasons to want Malakov dead, sir. Malakov is the reason Gregorev had to flee the FSB and Russia back in the late 2000s."

"Interesting. Well, as long as you don't foresee any further problems, then I'm happy for you to continue as discussed," Cowan stated, eager to remind Redcalf that he alone would be responsible for the outcome. "What I want to know is, what do you intend to tell the chaps in our COBRA meeting on Monday morning? I suggest we keep the circle of knowledge extremely small on this one."

"I agree, sir. I will give them an official update on John's whereabouts. We still have forty-eight hours until the meeting, so who knows what intel we will have acquired by then. Rest assured, sir, I am convinced that John will continue to seek out the Malakovs and ultimately solve our situation for us, one way or another."

"Excellent. Well, in that case, I won't waste any more of your time. You seem to have it all in order, Steven."

"Thank you, sir," Redcalf replied, realising that this whole meeting was purely a charade, conducted purely so that the PM could delegate responsibility, and any potential consequences, away from his desk.

As Redcalf walked out of the study, towards his driver in the courtyard, he could not help but worry that perhaps he was losing his grasp of all this, just a little. He would certainly feel a whole lot better about things if he still had eyes on John.

CHAPTER THIRTY

Wendy sat forwards in her chair, ready to begin the interrogation. A million questions were running through her mind, and she was eager not to waste the opportunity.

"So, Mr Byrne..."

"Colin, please, Wendy," came Byrne's instinctive response.

"Colin, then. The only way this will work is if you let me ask the questions, and you give me the answers, okay?" Wendy informed him, keen to take control of the conversation early.

"Yes, Wendy, that's fine. I appreciate that your mind must be racing. I will tell you what you want to know, and then we can work out how to get John back, together. How does that sound?"

"Good, I think," Wendy replied. "So, remind me, who are you again? How do you know John? And why are you helping him now?"

Colin chuckled. "Straight to the point, ey?"

"Well, where else is there to start, Colin?"

"Quite." Colin took a deep breath. "The thing is, Wendy, John has lived a complicated life. You see, he wasn't always able to tell you the whole story. He's a

159

national hero, Wendy, really, he is."

"What do you mean, a national hero?" Wendy sniggered, finding that difficult to imagine, especially at the moment.

"Well, you must have suspected that he wasn't just a chef in the army, Wendy? All those long periods without contacting you while he was away on tour… you must have thought that odd, for a chef?"

"Go on," Wendy replied, gesturing for him to continue.

Colin paused, then sighed. He might as well be honest; Wendy was John's wife, after all. "John worked for the secret services, Wendy. He gave many years of service to our country, he just wasn't allowed to tell you." There was silence for a few minutes, before Colin added, "But he decided a few years back that he wanted a normal life with his family. You, Wendy. He left all that behind because he loved you, and I promise you, he never looked back, even though some very important people tried to change his mind."

Wendy's body visibly sank as she expelled all the air inside her, more from relief than anything else. Finally, after all this time, someone had told her the truth.

"Surely you must have suspected that something wasn't quite right?"

Wendy looked at the man sitting opposite her. She had only known him for ten minutes, but he had already shown her more respect, more courtesy, than anyone else had ever done before, including her husband. She knew, deep down, that John had almost certainly wanted to tell her, but had decided not to in order to protect her. She also appreciated that he must have already been a spy when they had first met. To hear that he had chosen her and the kids over his job was comforting, and incredible, but she still could not help but feel a little betrayed.

"You're right, Colin. Maybe I did suspect something; believe me, I've have had plenty of time to think about it these past couple of days. At the start of our relationship, I turned a blind eye to the things that didn't make sense. I was in love; I chose not to focus on the negatives."

Byrne looked at her with a genuine air of sympathy, and Wendy once again noticed that she was not scared of him. He had a way of putting her at ease, even though they had only just met. She felt instinctively safe with him, like she had felt with John in the early days. Her gut was telling her that he was on her side.

"When he first met you, in 2002," Colin explained, buoyed by the progress he had made, "He was already an important person, Wendy, heavily involved in the fight against terror following 9/11 and all of that. He did so many critical things that helped keep our country safe, things that, unfortunately, nobody will ever know."

"So, when I met him, he was already a spy?" Wendy asked.

"MI6, yes. Spy is such an ugly term, don't you think? Anyway, almost immediately after Amy was born, his heart went out of the life. He could juggle a relationship and his job, he used to say, but not a family as well. That was why he quit just after Ethan was born; he couldn't go through that pain again. He told me that personally." Byrne could see that Wendy was obviously comforted by his words, so he went on. "He loved you, Wendy, and still does. He chose you over the life, you must remember that. That's why he is wherever he is now, doing whatever he is doing. It's because he loves you all."

CHAPTER THIRTY ONE

John and Dimitri were now in Poland, and making good time, though the conversation was not exactly flowing. With both men not finding trust easy to come by, theirs was still an uneasy partnership. Dimitri had barely said two words to John since they left Prague, apart from the predictable travel debrief at the start of the journey, and he was still hogging the wheel, leaving John alone with his thoughts and demons in the passenger seat.

Resting his feet on the dashboard and reclining his chair halfway back, John had decided that the only way to cope with the rest of the journey was to attempt to sleep through it. He tipped the front of his new cap, the one he had just purchased from the petrol station, over his eyes slightly, making it clear that he was not open for business. His mind was playing around with the pieces of the puzzle; there were still too many missing parts for comfort, and two giant holes right in the middle of the jigsaw: how had the Malakovs come by this information, and what were the government planning to do about it?

More immediately pressing was the unease between himself and Dimitri. He wanted to build the faith between them, and recognised that he needed to lead the way. Dimitri had already said as much, but what could John divulge that would make Dimitri trust him? Once again, Haditha popped into his mind, like an itch that demanded to be scratched. Haditha had been the main reason John had left MI6, not that Dimitri needed to know that. It was fair to say his new family life had also played a part in that decision, but the information he had discovered in Haditha had definitely been the driving force; after discovering that, he had known there was no future for him in MI6.

****

In the early 2000s, John had been in charge of securing intelligence on various facilities in the Middle East, which the British government suspected might be developing either weapons grade chemicals or military grade weapons. Having been stationed in Basra for nearly four years, his remit was finally coming to an end.

The initial splurge of activity following the invasion had presented few results; certainly no weapons of mass destruction, contrary to what the British media had been telling the public. It had thus been decided that the next phase of the operation needed to be a little more clandestine; out of the public consciousness, which was exactly where John worked, where he excelled, in fact. He was to remain in the shadows, building intel and informants, so that MI6 could slowly form a true picture of what Saddam's Iraq looked like.

This had not been a quick job though, far from it; the first eighteen months had resulted in little, if any, credible intel, but slowly, John had built his network:

Iraqi ex-military; a few of Saddam's key allies, who were not currently listed on the infamous deck of cards; key government and opposition leaders, and fellow spies from other countries.

His reputation in the spy community had proved useful, and had enabled John to yield strong intel from otherwise unobtainable sources; he was a perfect fit for the job, and had no reason to suspect that he was being kept out of the loop regarding what the British were doing in Iraq.

He had been based in Basra's southern palace, the onetime southern residence of Saddam himself, with license to roam Iraq and investigate any leads that might come his or his government's way. Each fortnight, at the COBRA meeting, he would tell his superiors back in London about the intel he had gathered on various targets, and advised them on whether they were credible or not, recommending military interventions when required. Fortunately, taking such drastic action had been a rarity, for the war was ending and credible threats had been few and far between.

During the COBRA meetings, John would have an agenda of places he had updates on, and would receive new targets to feed back on the following meeting. It had been very much a rolling operation, and one that had inevitably brought other nuggets of information his way, which John had always reported these separately to the chief.

After his new boss had hinted at something happening in Haditha, John had carefully considered his next course of action. He had been reluctant to leave any breadcrumbs on the internal servers, so had decided to go up there himself and check it out. After making a few calls to the main players in the area, eager to feel them out first, he had arranged to meet one of them the next morning in Rawa, about one hour from Haditha itself.

At first light, John had made his way to meet his informant, an Iraqi who had once been a captain in Saddam's army, but who was now very much a mercenary, selling himself or any information he had to the highest bidder. He was an expert on the Syrian desert though, so if anybody knew something about this mystery facility then, chances were, it would be him.

John had known it would not be cheap, but had heard enough about Mustafa Yasin to trust his intel would be genuine if he had anything to offer. Guys like Yasin had reputations to uphold; one bad word from John and word would soon spread that Yasin was not to be trusted.

John had arrived for the rendezvous an hour early, and had taken his place in the corner of the small coffee shop in Rawa that he had often frequented when he had first come over to Iraq. He had wanted to scope out the place first, just to make sure he was not being set up, and had ensured that he was seated away from the window, but with a good view of the action out in the street, so that he could see what was going on without making himself an easy target for any snipers out there. This particular coffee shop was ideal because the entrance on either side was relatively open and it only had one way in and one way out. John could control the situation if things went south from the inside, and could also get out in good time should he be concerned about a potential ambush.

Over the years, he had developed a good rapport with the coffee shop owner, so had chatted to him briefly before settling down in his seat. He had been the only person in the shop, and had sat in silence, assessing the situation and sipping on his coffee, completely in his zone, with just him and his instincts for backup.

Just before ten a.m., John had looked out into the desert, and had seen an old range rover heading into the village from the desert beyond. Immediately, he had readied himself for action, knowing by some sixth sense that it was Yasin in the car.

Yasin was a small bull of a man in his late fifties, his shaven head disguising his receding hairline and silver hair. Parking the range rover, he had entered the coffee shop and sat down opposite John, who had offered him a coffee. Yasin had gladly accepted, and John had promptly asked the owner, in his best Kurdish, for another espresso and two bottles of water. The two men had never met before, but they had spoken plenty of times on the telephone, so John had felt comfortable jumping straight to the point.

"Thanks for coming, Mustafa. I'm looking for some information about a facility in Haditha. Can you help me?"

"Haditha… Russian? American?" Yasin asked.

John had gone along with this initial charade, eager not to admit that it might be British and expose his weak hand to the informant. "Not sure, but it's definitely in and around Haditha. I don't know of any facilities, active or otherwise, out there, so if you can find me one that would be sufficient, I'm sure."

Yasin had thought for a moment, thanking the owner for his coffee and water, before asking John the obvious next question. "How much?"

John had already prepared for the question. Unable

to use his usual channels for paying informants, he had been forced to use his own private funds. On the journey up, he had carefully calculated how much he would need to buy him this information, without raising suspicion or pricing himself out of the market.

"Two million dinars," John had answered. It was equivalent to about one thousand fiver hundred US dollars. "Half now, and half on completion."

Again, Yasin had thought for a moment, finishing his coffee before agreeing. "Okay, that works. I know someone who used to work in a facility up there; he might be able help you locate the place. I will call you later after I have spoken to him, but he will also need paying."

John had looked at Yasin, square in the eye, as if to say, 'don't take the piss' before calmly adding, "Another million for your man if the intel is accurate."

"Excellent, I will be in touch." Yasin had said, tucking his chair under the table and offering his hand to John.

John had shaken Mustafa's hand and watched him walk back to the range rover, quickly making a note of the registration number. Now, all he could do was wait.

CHAPTER THIRTY TWO

Wendy continued asking questions about John's mystery life, and Colin continued to oblige her with the answers she craved, albeit moving on swiftly when needed, so as not to disclose any national secrets. He felt increasingly confident that they were building a solid foundation of trust from which to move forward, and was careful not to push his own agenda onto Wendy too quickly.

By now, the conversation had moved to the café, where Colin had ordered a sandwich and drink for them both. Both parties seemed to be feeling comfortable with each other, and Wendy had learned more about her husband in the last hour than in fifteen years of marriage. Though this fact somewhat concerned her, for now, she had decided to focus on the task at hand: getting John back home, safe and sound. Her other concerns would have to wait until he was safe in her arms.

"So, when did he involve you in all of this, Colin?" Wendy asked, moving the conversation forward.

"I involved myself, Wendy, the morning after the attack. I heard about what had happened and came straight up here to see him at the hospital. We met just here, in fact, in the café. As I told you, I was his 'go to' back here in the UK when things got tricky, and I thought he might need my help again now."

"Well, he doesn't seem to need it at the moment," Wendy challenged him, gaining more and more confidence by the second.

"True, that's a fair point, but I think he's just playing it safe for now. He doesn't know who to trust at the minute, and is therefore keeping his circle as small as possible." Colin looked at the sandwich in front of him but chose not to pick it up, keen to keep the conversation flowing. "You see, when our boss told him yesterday that he wouldn't be getting any assistance from us if he ventured onto foreign soil, I think he flipped a little. He is used to working for long periods alone, or at least, he was, so I guess he decided that if we weren't going to help him, there was no point in staying in touch."

Colin looked over to Wendy and glanced down at the untouched chicken and chorizo sandwich on her side of the table. Wendy shook her head, and promoted him to continue talking.

"He is scared, Wendy. He knows what Malakov is capable of, and he doesn't want to just wait around the hospital for the next attack, that's not his style. But he made sure you were all protected first, didn't he, before he left?"

"But why leave us? Why not stay here and protect us himself?"

"I guess he wants to get to Malakov first, before he gets to you again," Colin suggested.

Wendy thought about her husband for a moment. That hypothesis certainly made sense; even if she did not agree with him, she could see his rationale. "So, what's his plan then, Colin? Sounds like you know him best?" she continued, somewhat sharply.

"I'm not sure, Wendy, but I do know that he made contact with an old Russian acquaintance of his and went over to see him in Switzerland."

"Switzerland? Why Switzerland?"

"Oh, long story, not important, except that this Russian also has reason to dislike Malakov, so John thought he might be able to help locate him."

"And?" Wendy asked.

"And yes, he did know something. He knew that Malakov was back in Russia. The timing lines up with him coming after John, after all these years, and the flowers confirmed it."

"Flowers?"

"Yes, remember the flowers you received with the strange message, something about 'our sons'?"

"Yes?"

"Well, that appears to have come from Malakov, a sign that he is not finished yet. You see, John and Malakovs son had a bit of a run in a few years back, so it seems Malakov was sending a message."

"Jesus, Colin, what message? What run in? Do you think they targeted Ethan on purpose? What do you mean back in Russia?" Wendy was speaking too quickly, her brain struggling to keep up with all this new information.

"That's another long story. It's not relevant to all this, Wendy, honestly, except that those words confirmed to John that Malakov was behind the attack. In terms of targeting Ethan, I really don't think that was deliberate. Ethan just got caught up in it all. Malakov has been in prison for years, so his release lines up with

171

the attack."

"Prison, where?"

"In the UK."

"Why on earth would the government let him out then, if this Malakov is as bad as you say?"

"That we don't know; indeed, that missing piece of information is what concerns me most of all. That's why we need to track John down, and quickly. He doesn't know what he is walking into, none of us do."

"What do you mean, Colin?" Wendy asked, becoming increasingly concerned.

"I mean, whatever leverage Malakov had over the British government, it must have been pretty significant for them to let him out. Whatever that information is makes Malakov doubly dangerous in my opinion, and not knowing is my biggest concern."

"What do you think it is, Colin? You must have a theory."

"Honestly, I don't know. Those kinds of secrets are way above my pay grade," Colin answered, before pausing for breath. "I tried to get some answers for John a couple of days ago, but I was told, in no uncertain terms, that the information was classified. John doesn't know either, which I'm sure is another reason for him wanting to be on the front foot. I suspect he is going to try and get into Russia and track Malakov down, find out what information he has, and settle it, one way or another. You must understand though that there is no way the British Government can be seen to be involved in any way at all; John knows that. That's why he's gone dark. It would start World War Three if we were caught trying to assassinate a Russian citizen, an ex-general no less, on Russian soil. I'm sure the PM and the powers that be wouldn't mind Malakov being taken out, but they can't be implicated in any way. If John is successful, it will suit them nicely, but he is on his own, that's just the way it is."

Wendy sighed, acknowledging the rationality of what Colin was saying, but her heart was heavy; full of pain and betrayal. She had neither the knowledge, nor the energy, to help her husband. Her focus needed to remain with her son.

"What do you need from me, Colin? I can't leave here, not with Ethan still in the ICU."

"I know, Wendy, don't worry. You can leave it to me. I will track him down; I just need to know if he has been in contact. If I can speak to him then maybe I can help him in some way."

"But I haven't spoken to him either, not since yesterday morning."

"What number was that on, Wendy?" Colin asked, pleased to finally be on task.

"My mobile."

"Do you mind if I have a look, Wendy."

"Not at all, here you go." she replied, unlocking the phone with her finger.

"Great, thanks. Okay, that's the number I gave him," Colin explained, as he scrolled through her call history. "What are these withheld calls, Wendy? Three since yesterday. Why didn't you answer them, it has to be him, doesn't it?"

Wendy looked at Colin, a little embarrassed. "I had a bit of a funny turn last night, so I missed them, sorry. I'm okay now though, so you don't need to worry about me."

"Are you sure? Though, I guess you are in the right

place if it happens again. The next time he calls, please tell him the following, okay?"

Wendy nodded.

"Tell him, I've been here, and that I want to help you 'off book'. Get him to phone me on this number, I will text you now so you have it, and let me know the moment he makes contact, okay, Wendy?"

"Yes, of course, will do, Colin. Thank you for helping us, really, thank you."

"No problem, Wendy. I'm here for you. I will leave you in peace now, but I'll stay close by, okay? I'll check into a hotel up here and wait for your call; the moment he calls you, let me know, okay?"

"Of course. Thanks again, Colin. Nice to meet you."

"Nice to meet you too, Wendy," Colin smiled, as he began to walk away. "Stay strong, okay?"

"I will. Everyone seems to be telling me to do that at the moment," Wendy sighed.

"Easier said than done, I suppose." Colin turned around and walked straight out the front entrance of the hospital, not wanting to look back at Wendy. Poor woman, he thought, as he pulled out his phone again and made a call.

"Hi, Johnson. Yes, it's Byrne, hi. Sorry to phone you at the weekend. Listen, I need you to run a track on a phone, I will text you the number. Yes, belongs to Mrs Wendy Cooper. Just between us two, okay? Thanks, pal. Call me with any activity."

CHAPTER THIRTY THREE

"John. John, wake up. We're only an hour from the border now," Dimitri informed him.

"I'm not asleep, Dimitri, I'm just resting," John replied in a gruff voice, as he pushed the cap up his forehead to reveal his face. "I've been thinking about what you said, you know, about me holding back on you."

Dimitri glanced over and gave John an approving nod, raising an eyebrow as if to say 'and?'.

John continued. "I know that we need to be in this together fully if we are going to succeed, and I know you are risking everything, coming out here with me. I guess it's just… well, old habits die hard, my friend."

"I get it, John, old habits…"

John sat up sharply in his seat, pulling the recline lever back to its upright position. "No, seriously, I mean it. Over the last few hours I've been going through everything in my head because I want us to be on the same page. I don't want to keep secrets from you, Dimitri."

"So, what have you come up with?"

"Most of it you already know, but… there is one thing you might not. I think I might know why he got out of prison in the first place... I think I know why he was released."

"Go on..."

"Well, it's like you said. It must have been something big to convince my government to trade him. Many years of hard intelligence went in to capturing him, so in my mind, I can think of only one secret that could possibly be damaging enough for them to even consider his release, at least, from my time at MI6 anyway."

"Sounds interesting. What is it, John?"

"Do you remember, towards the end of your time in Iraq, when you came to me with a query about a mystery facility out in the Syrian dessert?"

"Vaguely," Dimitri answered, as he racked his brain. "Didn't you tell me it was all nonsense?"

"Yes, I did; at the time, I believed it to be so. I was in charge of monitoring all facilities in that area, so since I knew nothing about it, I reasoned that it must just be a rumour. But following our conversation, it nagged away at me, and I eventually decided to check it out. In my meeting with the chief a few days later, I dropped an additional operation into the agenda that wasn't in my remit, just to test the water, so to speak. I wanted to see if he might divulge any operations he was aware of that didn't involve me, you know, in the confusion. To be honest, I was concerned that I might be being kept out of the loop in my own country, and wanted to find out what was going on, if anything."

"Yes, I can imagine. It could have been very dangerous for you, not knowing," Dimitri chipped in, eager to keep John talking.

"Exactly! Well, anyway, he did. When I mentioned a phantom op in Rawa, he paused, and asked me if I meant

Haditha. I said I had no knowledge of it and quickly passed the Rawa point off as an error on the agenda. He left the meeting none the wiser, and I hung up the phone with my suspicions confirmed. He was clearly being briefed on operations that I had no knowledge of. It was then that I knew something wasn't right, and I committed myself to finding out exactly what was going on in Iraq under my nose."

"I knew it," Dimitri replied. "Something about that tip off seemed interesting at the time. I wish I had trusted my gut, maybe things would be very different for me now if I hadn't let you fob me off."

"I didn't fob you off, Dimitri, I didn't know! And when I found out, I wasn't exactly going to bring you in on it, not when I was in the dark myself. Anyway, listen, this is the important bit. The following day, I decided to follow the trail, and drove up to Haditha. Do you remember it? Just north of Rawa?"

"Yes, vaguely."

"When I got there, I met an old contact of mine, and he put me in touch with an Iraqi who he said used to work in a facility in Haditha."

"Interesting…"

"I met him that evening, and he told me exactly where to find the facility. He said the US closed it down early on the invasion, back in 2003, and this guy was out of work and bitter about it; he didn't like the Americans. Anyway, he seemed to suggest that it was some sort of chemical lab, so I checked it out, and it turns out that it wasn't the Americans who closed it down. The British got to it first."

"Sounds like your team were not all that good at sharing," Dimitri said, taking the opportunity to score a minor victory. "But how does this relate to Malakov, John?"

"Good question. Look, I have to be a bit careful here, Dimitri. You must understand, given your connections and our past relations. I'm not about to reveal any compromising national secrets to you, but I can say this, and this is the only part that's relevant to us right now, I promise: when I took a look at the facility, it certainly wasn't closed down."

"Shit."

John nodded in agreement. "My thoughts exactly. It was very much active, and almost impossible to find, even with the exact co-ordinates. It was also surrounded by a three mile security perimeter, so I knew something was up even before I made it inside. Let's just say that if Malakov somehow managed to lay his hands on intel about that place, it would certainly be enough to spook my government into releasing him. I'm convinced that he knows something, and that's why they let him out. It was top level, Dimitri, I wasn't even involved, and I was their main man in the Middle East, for Christ's sake."

"But what intel did Malakov receive? And from whom? And how did the Brits make sure he had no way of blackmailing them further after his release? Files are easily copied, as we well know."

"I'm afraid that's where I'm at, Dimitri. I don't have any more answers, so we'll have to work together on those. But we are on the same page now, yes?"

"Yes," Dimitri agreed, reluctantly. He paused, looking down at his watch as he pondered their next move. "It's six thirty p.m. now, so let's head towards Dorohusk, get some food and rest up a bit. We are still three and a half hours from our window at the border, so

178

we have plenty of time. You can fill me in some more about this working theory over dinner."

John smiled, sensing that some of the barriers were finally coming down. "Good idea. We can put a plan together for when we get to Russia, but first, I need to phone Wendy again."

CHAPTER THIRTY FOUR

Half an hour later, John and Dimitri had parked up in the Polish border town of Dorohusk, and John had made his way down a small back alley to try and call his wife. Pressing redial, he looked up to the sky and prayed. If she did not answer this time, he would have to send her a text, despite all of his instincts telling him not to.

To his immediate relief, his wife's voice interrupted the ringing on the other end of the line.

"Hello? Who is this?" she asked.

"Wendy, it's me. Thank Christ, I've been trying to reach you for ages."

"Oh, John, thank god. Are you okay?"

"Yes, yes, I'm safe and well. More importantly, what about you and the kids? I've been losing my mind with worry."

"Ethan's stable, but we've had a rough couple of days. He got an infection yesterday, and his temperature was running high, but it's gone now."

"Shit," John interrupted. "How?"

"It's okay, John, honestly. It's gone now, back to normal, and the doctors are pleased with his progress. They say he could wake up any time. Maybe you could get back in time? Where are you right now?"

"I'm trying, love, honestly I am. I'm in Poland would you believe, but I haven't quite finished the job here yet. As soon as I'm done, I will fly straight back."

"What? Poland? What are you doing there? What job, John? This is getting ridiculous, you should be here with us."

"I know, I just can't be at the minute. Listen," John pleaded. Must be the day of truth, he thought, with a hint of irony. First Dimitri; now his wife. "I'm going to tell you the truth, hun. You deserve to understand why I'm not there. You might want to sit down; this may come as a bit of a shock."

"I'm sitting down, John, go on."

"You see, Wendy, I... I wasn't just a chef in the army—"

"Yeah, I know. You were a big shot spy, John, for MI6. Your friend, Colin, came and told me all about it."

"What the...? Wendy, be careful what you say, for Christ's sake. This line might not be secure. What do you mean Colin came and told you?"

"Colin Byrne. He came to the hospital today. He is worried about you, John, and wants to help you, that's why he told me the truth about your work, so we could work together to make you see sense. He said he wants to help you 'off book'?" she continued, assuming 'off book' was some form of code.

"Really?" John answered, surprised and somewhat outraged by Colin's audacity. "Well, that's good of him to fill you in on all my secrets behind my back."

"It wasn't like that, John. He is genuinely worried about you; he said he thinks something is going on at his work, and he thinks they have treated you badly. He wants to try to help. I believe him, John."

"What exactly did he say, Wendy?"

"He said you are a national hero, and it's not your fault. He said you are in danger, and he is worried you won't be able to find Malakov alone."

"He told you about Malakov? Jesus…"

"Yes, he did. I appreciate you are trying to protect us, but now's the time to let us help you, John. Listen to me."

John paused for a moment, shocked by what he had just heard. He ran through his options in his mind, and decided to continue putting his faith in this new skill he had recently developed, Telling the truth.

"Okay, Wendy, I admit it, it's all true, what Byrne told you. But I left that life years ago, for you and the kids. You have to realise that."

"I know, John, Colin told me. Listen, it's okay. I understand. I know that you were still working for them when we met, but that you left when we had the kids. I can forgive the lies and secrecy, but I need you to be honest from now on, John. Please."

"I promise. No more secrets. As soon as I have finished here, I will come back, and we can start again. But you have to trust that I know what I'm doing. If I come back now, this will never end; we will always be looking over our shoulders. He won't stop until he gets me, and maybe even you three. I need to find out what he knows, and deal with it myself. It's the only way, Wendy. You have to trust me."

Wendy paused, listening to the desperation in her husband's voice as he continued to plead with her.

"I need to stop him myself. The government and my old work colleagues at MI6 won't help me. I have to do this myself."

"Colin will help you, John. If you won't come home, at least speak to him."

John contemplated this option. He really would prefer to keep the number of people involved to an absolute minimum, but he knew that, if Byrne were on board, he could perhaps help them track Malakov down faster.

"Byrne came to the hospital, told you about me, and asked to help?"

"Yes. He said that he wants to at least talk to you; he said he knew you wouldn't come home until it was finished, but he wanted you to know he was willing to help. He asked me to contact him as soon as you made contact. He is staying in a hotel round here, to be close by."

John let out a huge sigh before finally surrendering his position. "Okay, okay. Give him my number; I will text it to you after. Just him, though, and read it to him, don't forward the text, okay?"

"Okay. Thank you, for listening to me. If you have to do this then I want to at least help you. It sounds like you will need all the help you can get."

"I just don't want to put you in harm's way, love."

"If you let me in, then you won't, John. We need to be together on this now. That's the only way."

"You're right, I'm sorry for keeping this from you for so long. I'm gonna have to go now, love. I will call again in the morning. How's Amy doing?"

"Okay, I think, holding up. Dad brought her in today to see us. She's strong; must take after you."

"Sounds like it's you she takes after, love, not me."

CHAPTER THIRTY FIVE

"You're in room one hundred and six, just down the corridor on the left," the receptionist said to Byrne, as she passed him the room key. "Do you require anything else tonight, sir? It's just the one night, is that correct?"

"Yes, one night. No, thank you, that will be all," Byrne replied impatiently, eager to get to his room. As he made the short walk to his hotel room, a budget Premier Inn just off the M6, he could not help thinking to himself how unglamorous his job had become; long gone were the Halcion days of unlimited expense accounts and luxury trips around Europe.

Entering the room, he immediately dropped his bag on the floor, as the door automatically shut behind him. He took out his phone. No missed calls, and nothing from Wendy. Damn it. He had left the hospital feeling confident that he had her on his side now, but he could not be totally certain that she would play ball, and even if she wanted to, if and when John spoke to her, he might put an end to the whole idea there and then. He was on the bubble, as poker players liked to say; on the edge, waiting for the next development in the plot to unfold. It could easily go either way.

Although it had only been a couple of hours, he had

hoped Wendy would have sent him something by now, anything really, just to cement their newly formed partnership. But he had received nothing, and that made him feel uneasy. He did not want to phone her and pester her, after all, such behaviour might pressure her into the wrong course of action, especially given Ethan's fragile condition. But equally, he could not just hang around in this tiny little room, waiting for something to happen.

He thought for a while, flicking between TV channels and trying to figure out what to do. It had been a few hours since he had given Johnson the number; he might have something by now. Conscious that it was a Saturday night, and not wanting to appear impatient, Colin opted for a quick text, just to see if anything had come up yet.

Hi Johnson, sorry to hassle you again. Just wondered whether anything has jumped out at you re: that number? Thanks, Byrne.

That would have to do for now. He just hoped Johnson had found something.

****

Wendy was sitting in her usual position, having just received John's text message, which consisted of just his new number sent with an x. She thought for a while about their conversation and the peril her husband might be in. She so desperately wanted him home, but knew she had exhausted that possibility. Now was not the time to criticise his choices; now was the time to try to help her man.

She picked up her phone and dialled Colin's number, remembering that she needed to tell him the number herself and not just forward the text, she was now completely resigned to her new reality. A gangster's moll of sorts! The response on the other end was immediate, almost like Colin was sitting with his phone in his hand, waiting for it to ring.

"Hello? Byrne."

"Colin, hi. It's Wendy."

"Hi Wendy, good to hear from you. Any news?"

"Yes, John just phoned me; those missed calls were him, as you suspected."

"That's great news, is he okay?"

"Yes, he says he's fine. He's in Poland, and wants to track that Malakov guy down."

"Of course he does. Poland… interesting. Did you tell him about me?"

"Yes, I told him about our conversation. He wasn't very pleased initially, but he softened a little after I told him I thought you had done the right thing, coming to me. He admitted everything to me, Colin. He explained why he couldn't tell me when we first met, and why he needs to do what he's doing now. I'm still not convinced it's sensible, or safe, but I can see why he feels it has to be this way."

"I'm glad you were able to have that chat. Is he prepared to listen, Wendy?"

"I think so, yes. Not about coming back, of course, but he's prepared to speak to you if you still want to help him."

"That's my plan. I know as well as you do that he's not going to stop until it's done, but if I'm helping him in the background that's got to give him an advantage, hasn't it?"

"I agree, and I told him as much. He's given me his

186

number to give to you. Have you got a pen to take it down?"

Colin looked around the room and grabbed the handily stationed Premier Inn complimentary pen and paper sitting next to the rather less useful miniature kettle. "Yep, go ahead."

Wendy sounded out the number as clearly as possible and Colin read it back to her twice to make sure it was correct.

"Okay, great. Thanks again, Wendy. I will give him a call straight away. Speak soon, stay strong," he concluded, remembering what she had told him earlier.

"Thank you, Colin," Wendy replied, with just a hint of a smile in her voice. "Please keep in touch; let me know as soon as you know anything."

"Of course. I'll be in touch." With that, he ended the call, eager to begin the next.

He quickly dialled Johnson's number. The call took rather longer to connect, but after the sixth or seventh ring, Johnson picked up.

"Hello?"

"Hi Johnson, Byrne again. Sorry to pester you, but this case I'm on is developing quickly. I've got a new number for you, forget the old one, unless you found something?"

"No, Byrne, only had a quick look but there's no unusual activity on it. What's this all about, Byrne? Can't it wait until Monday?"

"No, it can't I'm afraid. One of my field guys needs this urgently. I wouldn't ask otherwise."

"Fine, what do you need?"

"Thanks, old boy. I owe you one. I have a new number, will text it through now," Byrne continued, choosing to ignore the sarcastic grunt on the other end of the line. "I strongly suspect it will locate to somewhere in Eastern Europe: Poland or maybe the Ukraine? Can you please confirm for me asap? And get me all the activity from the last forty-eight hours: calls, texts, etc."

"Yes, yes, I know the drill, thank you, Byrne. Leave it with me; I will call you when it's done."

"By tonight, if possible," Byrne added.

"Jesus, Byrne, you don't ask for much, do you?" Johnson sighed. "Lucky for you, it's only my ready meal and Saturday night telly I'm sacrificing."

"Rock n' roll," Byrne commented, immediately regretting his words. "Seriously, thank you, Johnson. It's a massive help. Speak soon."

CHAPTER THIRTY SIX

"Right, it's nearly time, John. Are you ready?" Dimitri asked, as he settled the bill from dinner.

"Ready for what exactly, Dimitri?"

"Honestly, I'm not sure. It's just after nine p.m. now, so I suggest we drive to within half a mile of the border and wait there for our window. It's just a quick drive down the M07 so we can be there within five to ten minutes."

"Whatever you think is best. This is your neck of the woods, Dimitri. I'm in your hands."

Dimitri nodded in acknowledgment. "I suggest we drive through the furthest lane from the border terminal a couple of minutes before ten p.m. It should be fairly quiet at that time; no more than a couple of cars in the queue at most."

"Then what?"

"Then, when it's our turn, we go through slowly and calmly, hand over our passports and they should let us through. It would probably be best if you don't speak. Just let me do the talking, okay?"

"Why? What's with all the spy games?"

"Come on, John, really? You know the score. Your British passport going into Ukraine will raise eyebrows, and would usually prompt a visit to the interview rooms. Worst case, they could send you packing on some technicality or another. They still don't like the West meddling in their affairs, even now, and you can bet your last dinar that the FSB will have intel feeding back to them from the borders, even though it's not their country anymore."

John held up his palms in surrender. "Like I said, I'm in your hands."

"That you are, John. My guys have briefed the guy on that post not to raise any alarm and let us through; he is a Ukrainian nationalist, working with my contacts, so he thinks we are helping the cause in Crimea or something. Either way, he should be friendly."

"I'll just keep my mouth shut then. What happens next, once we're in Ukraine, I mean?"

"I'm not all together sure, John. My guys said they would meet us on the other side, whatever that means. I'm sure they will reveal themselves in due course."

"And what do these guys want from us exactly? What do they get out of helping us?"

"They are old pals, John. They owe me, let's just leave it at that. Those years tucked away in Luzern weren't all wasted; when Putin had a go at Crimea again, I gave them some intel that helped the fight, so they are more than happy to oblige me now."

"Ukrainian freedom fighters as our hosts... not exactly the Ritz then."

"A bed's a bed, John. Besides, this is the easy bit. Without their help, there would be no chance of us getting into Mother Russia! We have that to look forward to next."

John raised an eyebrow at Dimitri, and both men

silently finished up their coffee's.

"Right, let's head back to the jeep, John. I want to make sure we get there in good time."

****

Byrne was still lying on the single bed in his tiny hotel room, somewhere south of Wolverhampton, debating whether to call John now or after he had received more intel from Johnson. In the end, he decided it would be more beneficial to wait, just in case John was not all that amenable to the idea of talking to him.

With a whole lot of time to waste, and nothing particularly productive to do, Byrne's mind began to obsess over the key problem in the centre of all this; the key question that had been troubling him since this whole episode had begun. What was so important to his bosses that they had agreed to let a Russian terrorist mobster out of his life sentence?

He knew some intel critical to the whole framework of the security services was at the root of all this, and equally, he knew that he had no chance of getting himself inside that particular circle of knowledge. For a moment, he wished he had worked a little harder, maybe applied for some of the promotions that he passed up on over the years. Maybe then he would be able to help his friend now.

He again considered a 'leak' in the firm, logically going through any possible candidates, but not able to take any seriously enough to pursue. Malakov acquiring classified files was certainly plausible, but still, there had to be a leak somewhere for Malakov to have laid his hands on them. Also, the chances of the government agreeing to the release without having one hundred percent certainty that it would not come back to bite them again further down the line was zero. Files were easily copied, as was data, so it was difficult for him to see how they could have received those types of assurances.

Colin reached for his inside pocket and pulled out a couple of tablets, swilling them down with a tot of whiskey from his silver engraved hipflask. All this was starting to give him a headache. Laying back, he closed his eyes for a moment's peace. It didn't last long though as his phone almost immediately began to vibrate, and he jumped up off the bed, answering the call eagerly.

"Johnson, that was quick. What you got?"

"The phone is now tracked, and is currently sitting just outside a place called Dorohusk in Poland, right on the Ukrainian border."

"Excellent work, that makes sense. We can follow it from there, yes?"

"Yes, open your app. I have created a new file for you called 'Cooper'. You can track him now yourself."

"Great," Colin replied, already trying to figure out how he might be able to change the title of the file. "How did you know it was John?"

"Come on, Byrne, give me some credit. A 'Mrs Wendy Cooper'? I've been watching the news, you know. If you do want to change the title, you just need to go into settings. I suggest you do so before the morning."

"Thanks, Johnson," Byrne replied, slightly embarrassed by his own stupidity. "Anything else on the phone of interest?"

"Nope, just four calls to Wendy's number and a text,

again to Wendy. No other contact or internet activity."

"Okay, great. I owe you one. If we could perhaps keep this between us for now, at least until Monday morning, that would be much appreciated."

"Okay, Byrne. I can hold it until Monday late afternoon, but then it will need to be logged."

"Perfect, thanks again, old boy."

****

Dimitri had pulled up in a lay-by, half a mile from the border, and looking down at his watch, he confirmed the time to his partner.

"9.42 p.m. Perfect, we have fourteen minutes."

John sank back into his chair, and began to drift off into his own private silence again, as had been the case for much of their journey. He fully expected the silence to last the full fourteen minutes wait time, but to John's surprise, Dimitri continued to talk.

"John, I've been thinking about what you said over dinner, about the mole in MI6, the one you think leaked intel to Andrei."

"And?" John enquired, intrigued by this turn of events.

"Well, I just can't see it, to be honest. It doesn't add up to me, a mole in MI6. It's a bit James Bond, isn't it? How long must this person have had to be entrenched in the system for them not to be noticed? And even if Russia did have someone in that deep, I'm convinced they wouldn't have been reporting to a general in the army, would they? More like the head of the FSB, or even Putin himself."

John nodded, agreeing with his partner's thought

process.

"If whatever went down in Haditha was powerful enough to bring everything down, surely they would have buried it forever, along with anyone that knew about it?"

"I know what you mean. It seems rather far-fetched to me too. But what if the intel Malakov received was limited, and not the main leverage they had? What if the mole was the main trade; the government would know they had a leak, so maybe they agreed to the swap as long as Malakov gave them the mole in exchange? It wouldn't even need to be a mole, would it? What if Andrei got to a secret service employee in the UK; would just need to be a civil servant really, low level. If he found something on them, and used it to blackmail him or her, or threatened their family in some way, then its plausible that the employee would be compelled to give them something, correct?"

Dimitri nodded, a thoughtful expression on his face.

"So, this employee does some digging, and finds something they consider to be old and small, not really knowing its importance. Then, Malakov senior gets hold of it, and sees its value, maybe not the exact content, but the significance of it all. He gets his son to spin a tall tale of a deep cover Russian spy in MI6 leaking top secret files on Haditha. That would be enough to get my bosses to the negotiating table, maybe even scare them enough to do the trade, wouldn't it?"

"Perhaps," Dimitri considered. "It's certainly food for thought, as you Brits say. We can do some more digging once we reach the other side. It's time to go now."

CHAPTER THIRTY SEVEN

Dimitri started up the jeep and slowly pulled out of the layby, filtering back onto the road that led to the border crossing.

"Okay, John, this is it. It's five minutes away now, so we haven't got long. I'm going to drive straight in and wait in the furthest queue as instructed, okay?"

John nodded, entirely focused on the task ahead of them. He was not concerned about the border crossing; it had all been arranged in advance, so there was no need to believe anything would go wrong. Besides, even if it did not go to plan, he was not breaking any laws. No, it was the next bit that concerned John. Ukrainian freedom fighters were not exactly the most stable of partners, and even if they did mean well, the atmosphere could quickly change at any point, for no apparent reason, if they did not like the way things were going. These kinds of militia groups were ruthless; meeting with them was definitely going to be the most dangerous part of the journey so far. He needed to remain alert.

Dimitri drove straight through the empty slip lane and pulled into the fourth and final queue at the border junction. Four vehicles separated them from the moment of truth. It was busier than they had expected, but they had no reason to worry yet. Dimitri was in the queue now; his guy on the kiosk must surely have clocked the number plate by now?

Neither man spoke again for the next few minutes, both quietly contemplating what they were about to embark on. John took out his passport and pushed it over towards Dimitri, who gladly accepted it and placed it underneath his own. One by one, the vehicles in front of them made their way up to the kiosk and through into the Ukraine. John noticed his hands starting to become clammy with sweat, and his heart was racing in anticipation. Game time was upon them.

A couple more minutes of silence followed until it was their turn. Dimitri placed the trusty old jeep in first gear and lightly pressed his foot on the accelerator. He crawled alongside the kiosk and switched his foot onto the brake pedal, deliberately leaving the handbrake off.

"Passports," barked the imposing looking man at the desk, in a strong Russian accent. Dimitri reached up and handed over the two passports, making sure John's was now on top; he figured that if this was their guy, then if he had not already clicked who they were, the British passport would be a sufficient reminder. Equally, if he was not their guy, then maybe this would in some way convince him that they had nothing to hide.

The guard looked at the passports without a flicker of emotion, and after thumbing through the top one, he stared through Dimitri, straight at John. Either he was doing an excellent job of acting out his role in this whole charade, or something was not as it should be.

John looked forwards, making sure he did not make eye contact with the guard for more than a moment, attempting to maintain a composed demeanour without coming across as arrogant.

The guard's eyes returned to the passports, and after a few more moments of unnecessary torture, he finally said something in Russian to Dimitri. John could just about make out the word 'visit', and assumed he was asking Dimitri about the nature of their trip. Dimitri replied with a short sharp Russian sentence that John could not decipher, and once again, the air fell silent.

They waited for what seemed like an eternity, as the temperature in the jeep rose to uncomfortable levels, until the guard eventually switched to the second passport. John immediately felt a sense of relief flow through his body. The guard spared them the drama a second time round as he scanned through Dimitri's Russian passport in no time at all, and waved the men through.

Dimitri said something else in Russian, and John watched Dimitri's hand as it reached for the gear lever. It was then, and only then, that John felt confident that the guard above him was in fact their man after all. Top marks for suspense, he heard his inner voice say. No chance of him being made by the Russians.

The guard lifted the barrier and they drove the jeep through. Dimitri and John dared not look at each other, both of them staring straight ahead until they could no longer feel the guard's eyes in their rear view mirror.

John was the first to speak, breathing an audible sigh of relief. "What now, Dimitri?"

Before his partner had the chance to answer, both men simultaneously saw a white light blinking in the distance, and their eyes were instantly drawn to the set of headlights shining at them through the darkness. The headlights flashed once, then twice as Dimitri slowed down. The lights appeared to move in the night sky, backwards at first, and then out of sight completely, to be replaced by a new set of lights, this time red ones. Brake lights, John realised. He watched on as they slowly disappeared into the darkness,

"I guess we follow those lights. Welcome to the Ukraine, John."

CHAPTER THIRTY EIGHT

It was one fifteen a.m. on a Sunday morning, and Redcalf was still wide awake. He could not sleep; the pressure of the situation was growing heavier on his shoulders, and despite having consumed at least half a bottle of Jack Daniels since dinner, he was existing within a sort of living purgatory; exhausted but unable to rest.

His family had long since retired to bed, and he had been left alone downstairs in his study. The lights were dim; melancholy music was playing softly in the background, and he had only his demons and mistakes of the past for company.

The meet with the PM today had done little to ease his anxiety, and he had not been able to concentrate on anything else since his return home. Sure, he had played with the kids; sat with them for dinner; watched some inane TV with his wife before she had gone up to bed, but all with a vacant look and a distracted demeanour that frustrated his wife at the best of times. They had not argued, but he knew she was disappointed in him, though if he was honest with himself, he was relieved that she had not tried too hard to engage with him. He did not have the energy to deal with that right now; he needed some time alone with his thoughts.

Redcalf pondered what John would do if he found out the whole story, and as he sat in his leather chair, pinned behind his mahogany desk, he wished more than anything that he could turn back the clock. Unfortunately, this was a skill he had yet to master, so instead, he searched for a more realistic solution, none were forthcoming. Finding John was his top priority right now, though part of him also hoped that John would find Malakov and settle their argument once and for all. If John could dispose of Malakov, it would save them a whole lot of trouble down the line.

He lay back in his recliner and began to reflect on the decisions he had made all those years ago, something he often did, without ever reaching a satisfactory conclusion. Haditha would be the stain on his career for the rest of his life, and nothing he did now would change that. All he could do now was make sure nobody ever found out about the whole sorry affair.

He recalled his first mistake, as the new chief, when he had spoken to the famous John Steele, a.k.a. John Cooper, for the first time. The fact that he has allowed himself to walk into that trap so naively, and set this whole chain of events in motion, still haunted him. If only he had known what he knew now; he would never have been so foolish. Then again, he had not known what Haditha had to hide back then. He could not be blamed for that. It was his predecessor's mistake, not his. However, he could certainly be blamed for the many mistakes and cover ups he had been involved in subsequently. Fucking Haditha would be the obituary of his career, and he knew it.

Ironically, it was only a few months after being in the

job that Redcalf had realised the importance of that initial liaison with John Cooper on the phone. He remembered it well, the day Cooper had walked into his office and laid it all out on the table for him to digest. It was difficult not to realise the gravity of a situation when it was spread in front of you like that; the undeniable truth of their actions. That truth had haunted him ever since. Sure, he had managed to placate Cooper at the time, a significant achievement under the circumstances, but it had meant the end of John's fantastic service, a toll that Redcalf only truly came to appreciate in subsequent years.

John had retired with a full pension, and begun a new civilian life far away from the murky realities of the Middle East. He had received no pomp or ceremony; the great sacrifices he had made for the country had remained a secret, not that any of that had meant much to John anyway. It had been the only way for the two men to bury the whole Haditha saga, and one or two other national secrets, without fear of John being tracked down in the future.

This had all come with one condition, of course. John had insisted that what was going on at Haditha stopped immediately, and never started up again, there or elsewhere. This had been the one condition of John's silence, and one that Redcalf had gladly accepted. John had made it abundantly clear that, should he get wind of anything like Haditha happening again, he would go straight to the press, and to the Americans and Russians for good measure. Redcalf had believed him; never before had he seen such rage and disappointment in an operative's eyes, and he had known from that moment that John was not to be messed with.

Redcalf remembered John making a point of picking up a couple of files from the desk in front of them and waving them at him.

"I will take these as insurance," he had said, before leaving the office. "And I'm quite prepared to use them, if necessary. Think of them as a constant reminder of our agreement."

John had gone on to explain that as long as Redcalf kept to his side of the bargain, the files would never see the light of day again. He had also promised to fully immerse himself in his new civilian life, and had informed Redcalf that he would never hear from him again, unless of course the need arose to tell the world the sordid tale of Haditha.

To Redcalf's relief, John had been good to his word; for more than ten years, Redcalf had not heard a word from his former star agent, and after a while, he had forgotten about that day in his office, until the name Malakov had crashed its way back into his world. Redcalf knew the guilt he was feeling was justified, and wished he could find a better, more agreeable plan to resolve the Malakov problem. But he knew there was no other option but to leave John to it, and he had long since resigned himself to that fact.

Alek and Andrei were one thing, but a renegade John Cooper acting against him could be disastrous, for him and the firm. There was no way John could ever find out that he had failed to keep the agreement they had sealed all those years ago in his office. If John discovered that Redcalf had broken the deal, there would be hell to pay, from all sides. It was an eventuality that he could not allow to happen.

CHAPTER THIRTY NINE

"Ok, we are nearly here, get ready for landing," the co-pilot said in a broken English accent, as he leaned backwards from the cockpit. John nodded to the man and glanced down at his torso, pointing out that his seatbelt was already fastened, ready to go.

John was not exactly new to small planes; he had been on a few during his years of active service, and had many stories he could tell of near misses and bumpy landings, but this journey had been particularly uncomfortable. Maybe it was his time out of the game, but this Antonov Ukrainian aircraft was making him feel very uneasy. And the pilot wasn't helping his anxiety either; John suspected neither of the two men up front had the necessary credentials to fly this thing.

They had spent five hours stuck in a space barely wide enough to fit a shopping trolley, but at least the end was in sight. Landing the plane was now the only thing standing between John and solid ground.

"Where are we going?" John whispered, as he glanced over at Dimitri to his left, trying desperately to distract himself from the prospect of two unqualified pilots trying to land this rusty old plane on a tiny piece of landing strip in the middle of nowhere.

"Kyiv, I think," came the hushed reply. "Ukraine is bigger than you think."

"You can say that again. Its daylight out there now."

"It's nearly seven a.m. local time. They are another hour in front of Poland; two's hours plus Greenwich mean time."

"Bloody hell, that's flown by. I must have fallen asleep."

"You've been out for most of the flight. It won't be long now though. The drive to the safe house should only take another hour or so, and then we can freshen up. Have you given any more thought on how we're going to get into Russia?"

"I want to see what your guys have to say first," John replied, not wanting to discuss such sensitive information within their earshot. "Let's arrange a meeting with them for early afternoon, and we can see what options we have. Is it just the two of them?"

"No, I've never spoken to these two. My contact, Vlad, said he will meet us at the safe house."

"Okay, until then, let's keep our own council."

"Stop worrying, John, these guys are on our side."

"I know, but all the same."

"Two minutes to landing," the co-pilot interrupted.

John turned his neck to face forwards again as he braced himself for landing, still a little concerned about the pilots' motives for helping them. Still, they had got them this far, and if they managed to land the plane without killing them, he might be willing to reconsider their trustworthiness. Maybe.

****

Byrne sat up in his hotel bed and stretched his arms up to the ceiling. He had slept well, content in the knowledge that he finally knew where John was and, crucially, that he could track him from here on in, assuming he kept this knew phone with him. Byrne considered that maybe his success, well, Johnson's success really, was the reason he was putting off the call. The last thing he wanted to do was rock the boat and risk losing John all over again.

He briefly rubbed his eyes and took a sip of the stale, lukewarm glass of water on his bedside table, before reaching to the end of the bed where his MacBook lay, precariously balanced half on and half off the bed. As he lay back, MacBook now in hand, he crashed his head onto the painfully thin headboard and cursed the sorry room he was in, for the umpteenth time.

After taking a moment to recover from the indignity of his situation, he carefully opened the lid of his MacBook and clicked on the newly installed tracker app, waiting impatiently for it to update. Eventually, the signal settled on somewhere just outside Kyiv. John had moved into Ukraine, as Byrne had predicated. He thought for a moment about what John's potential plan for entering Russia might look like, and wondered if, and how, he could be of any assistance, stuck here in this dingy hotel room in the arse end of Birmingham.

He quickly pushed aside the negative thoughts, and plucked up the courage to find out the answer first-hand. He had rehearsed this conversation a hundred times in his head; now was the moment of truth. It was just after eight a.m. in the UK so it must be about ten a.m. out there now. John should be awake at least, regardless of what else he was doing. It occurred to Byrne that he spent most of his time on the phone these days; he so wished he could speak to John face to face, it was so much easier to read someone when you could see them.

The phone connected, taking him by surprise for a second.

"Hello?" John's voice piped up on the other end of the line.

"Hello, John? It's Byrne."

"Byrne, good to hear from you. Listen, I can't speak now, just on a bit of a road trip. I will phone you in an hour or so, okay?"

"No problem, John. I'll be here."

"Great," John responded, before hanging up and throwing the phone back into his inside jacket pocket.

"How long now, comrade?" John asked the driver in front. "I've got a call to make soon."

"Twenty minutes, no more,' came the stilted response. "We are nearly in Kyiv."

John looked out of the tinted windows, at the desolate wasteland surrounding the potholed old road they were travelling down, and could not help but wonder how the hell he had ended up here.

CHAPTER FORTY

When they finally arrived at the safe house, it was a lot grander than John had imagined. A long drive and gated entrance welcomed them into the circular courtyard area, which sported a gravel track surrounding an ornate water feature, and many different flowering plants. The beauty of their surroundings felt quite out of place, considering the occupiers of the estate.

"See, John? Nothing but the best for you, my friend," Dimitri said, as he looked over to his partner and winked. On the steps to the main house, the welcome was equally enthusiastic, with at least five or six men waiting patiently to meet their new guests. Only the submachine guns hanging over their shoulders gave any indication of the true nature of their hosts.

Dimitri exited the car first and immediately went to the smallest of the men, who was standing in the middle of the steps. He was the only one without a gun, and obviously the leader.

"Vlad," Dimitri exclaimed, as he embraced his compatriot with a giant bear hug, slapping him somewhat violently on the back.

"This is John, who I mentioned to you. Thank you, once again, for accommodating us, Vlad. This place…"

"A pleasure to meet you, John," Vlad interrupted "It is an honour. Dimitri has told me about your plight. We shall assist you in any way we can."

"Thank you, Vlad. Your help is much appreciated," John replied, noting Dimitri's overzealous greeting and apparent longstanding friendship with the terrorist in front of him.

"No problem at all. Please, don't feel uncomfortable at all during you stay with us. Whatever you need, please ask one of the guys and they will be happy to assist you."

"Thank you, I will," John assured him, choosing to play ball.

"I won't keep you any longer. You must be exhausted from your trip. Vitali here will show you to your rooms," he said, pointing to a tall, menacing-looking man who stood in the shadows. "Perhaps we could begin talking in an hour or so? One of my men will knock on your door and bring you over. Is that okay?"

"Absolutely," Dimitri interjected quickly, as he placed his arm around John's shoulder, as if to tell him to relax and take advantage of the break on offer.

John reluctantly agreed to freshen up before they spoke with Vlad, deciding that it would be a good opportunity to check in on Wendy and Ethan.

The main building was spectacular, and John imagined it had once been a palace of some sort. Quite how this bunch of terrorists had come to acquire it, he had no idea. Surrounding the main house were a number of outbuildings, and John was suddenly struck by the size of the terrorist organisation that had taken him in.

They followed Vitali around the gravel courtyard and

down a side garden, that led to an outhouse about four hundred metres down the track.

"This used to be the servant's quarters, but I'm sure you will find them comfortable," Vitali said, as he led them down the path.

When they entered the building, John could see three doors. The one on the right was open, and led to a separate kitchen area, which clearly belonged to this house. The other two doors were closed.

"This is you, John," Vitali explained, as he pushed open the first door. "And that one over there is yours, Dimitri. I will come back at around one p.m. No problems?"

Both men shook their heads, and Vitali's hand, before nodding to each other and going their separate ways. As John entered his room, he was delighted to see a bed and an en-suite bathroom, complete with a shower and fresh towels. The shower was tempting, but he decided to phone his wife first, and sat down on the bed, opening his burner phone. This action served as a reminder that he needed to call Byrne, though he decided Byrne could wait until after his shower. An update on his son, however, was a priority.

CHAPTER FORTY ONE

A little while later, John was enjoying the full hospitality on offer in his room. He had poured himself a whiskey from the crystal decanter, and was now enjoying a steaming hot shower, feeling fully invigorated by his latest conversation with his wife.

Ethan was hanging in there, and he felt a positivity rushing through his body as he cleaned the mud and dried sweat out of each orifice. This was the finishing straight now, and John could see the end in sight. In a couple more days, and if all went to plan, he would be back alongside his wife and son, where he belonged.

He was still uncomfortable with the idea of sharing all this information with his wife, but equally, he realised that it was probably the only way to save his marriage, if indeed, that was still possible after all they had been through.

Leaving her in the dark any longer would definitely have left irreconcilable wounds, wounds that she would never recover from. At least now she understood why he was doing what he was doing, and why he was the person he was. If he was honest with himself, it felt good to have no more secrets. He was convinced that now, when he finally did get back to them, they would all be able to move forward from this together, as a family.

Byrne, on the other hand, was a completely different matter; a complete pain in the arse, to be honest. What help could an old washed-up pen pusher really offer him? He considered just ignoring him all together, but he had promised his wife that he would speak to him, so he felt obliged to at least call the man, despite his reservations.

Once he was out of the shower, he dried himself with the fluffy warm towels, put some fresh combats on, and phoned Byrne. As predicted, Byrne answered in seconds, now safely out of his own purgatory and on his way back to the hospital, to check in on Wendy. He figured he might as well while he was still up north, and to tell the truth, he genuinely wanted to make sure she was okay. He had become more attached to her than he had initially realised.

"Hi John, how are you doing? I'm on my way over to see Wendy and Ethan," he said, hoping to gain something favour.

"Oh, good man," John replied, put slightly off guard. Immediately, he adopted a more patient approach. If Byrne was willing to make the effort to check on his family, he could at least make an effort to be considerate. "Wendy has filled me in what you told her... I ought to throttle you, man." he joked.

"Oh come now, old chap," Colin replied, recognising the humour in John's voice with relief. "It needed doing. I probably saved your marriage, old boy. You can thank me later."

"Is that so?" John replied flippantly, before getting down to business. "Look, I can't speak long, I'm in the middle of something, would you believe. I will know more later though, maybe something will come up that you might actually be useful for. Can I call you this evening?"

"Yes, of course. I just want to help, John. Are you meeting with the Ukrainian Nationalists?"

"Jesus, Byrne, how did you know that?" John exclaimed.

"Just figured. I can see from the app that you're in Ukraine, who else would be crazy enough to help you into Russia?"

"Are you tracking me, you little…"

"Yes, John, of course I am. It's for your own good. Stop playing vigilante; you need us, my old friend," Colin added in a serious tone. "Besides, someone needs to know where you are, especially if you go missing."

"Great, thanks for the vote of confidence…" John grimaced.

"You know what I mean. Anyway, it's me and only me, I promise. We have until Monday evening before it needs to get logged at HQ, so you're safe for now. We can work out another way to communicate then, if it's still necessary."

"Thanks, Byrne. Look, I've got to go now. I'll call again later."

"Make sure you do, John. Good luck!"

John had hung up the phone before he heard the 'good luck' bit, although it would have been like water off a duck's back anyway. He was far too locked into the task ahead to waste time with small talk. Relaxing into his soft bed, he shut his eyes, and waited for Vitali and his chums to come knocking.

But like an ancient curse, as soon as his eyelids closed, he was transported straight back to Iraq, straight back to that evening in Haditha. He remembered it so vividly, it was like someone had slipped a hallucinogen into his whiskey: the smell of the dusty roads where he had been dropped, a few miles from the target; the taste of the dry air as he had paused to check if he was still following the correct co-ordinates; most of all, the fear in his blood stream, as he stood, scared to death of what he might find underneath the desert below his feet.

He remembered leaning against the wall of the complex, as the sun rose over the horizon, having made it over the perimeter and across the open desert without being seen. He had panicked then, terrified that his position would be exposed by the morning light. But fate had been on his side; the vehicle that had only moments before helped to distract the guards, allowing him to dash over to the complex, had once again come to his aid. From his position at the side of the complex, he had seen a group of people, about thirty or so in total, alighting from the vehicle in single file, aided by an armed guard. At the same time, another group, all wearing white coats and lanyards, had been making their way out of the main entrance, towards the coach. It had to be some sort of swap over, John had thought at the time. A shift change, perhaps.

John had known then that this was his chance. Patiently, he had waited for the new group of workers to form an orderly line, before stealthily sliding himself along the side of the complex and casually joining the back of their queue. Panic had set in again, as he realised that the guards could now see him, but it had been quickly replaced by relief; none of the guards had given him a second glance.

As he waited patiently in line, he had felt his

confidence growing; his whole body humming with anticipation. Having made it this far, he remembered feeling almost certain that he would gain access to the bunker, and finally uncover what was going on in Haditha. The first guard had waved for the front of John's queue to starting entering the building, and John had slowly made his way forward, waiting for his turn to enter. A steel lift was taking groups of three or four employees down into the depths of the bunker, and as he drew closer, John had noticed a scanner just inside the entrance, checking everyone's ID. He recalled the sinking feeling he had felt at that moment, knowing that he had failed.

His military training had kicked in then, and he had immediately started looked for a means of escape. Now that he knew this facility existed, he could start digging in the more conventional way, but for now, he needed to get out. Looking up, he had spotted the coach, still waiting to depart, its engine now running. It was now or never. Quickly and quietly, John had swapped one queue for another, before darting over to the blind side of the coach. Desperately, he had pushed at the luggage compartment, praying for it to open, and sure enough, it had. Relieved, he had dived into the unoccupied storage area and slammed the door shut; lucky for him, the noise of the engine had been enough to mask the sound. Adrenaline surging through his body, he had lain there in silence, waiting, until finally, the coach had pulled away.

THUD.

John opened his eyes, startled. Where was he?

THUD. The door. Someone was knocking on the door.

"John, are you in there? It's time to go."

John immediately shot up, taking a moment to gather his bearings.

"Yes, just coming, sorry. I must have drifted off," he replied, relieved to have escaped his recurring nightmare, for now.

CHAPTER FORTY TWO

John opened the door to find Dimitri and Vitali waiting patiently in the corridor for him.

"Vlad would like to meet with you in the main room. He has a few things to show you that he thinks might be of interest."

"Lead the way, Vitali," Dimitri responded, sensing that John was not in the mood for pleasantries.

Vitali escorted the two men through the estate, with Dimitri following close behind and John tailing them by a few metres. He was still waking up from his impromptu nap, and was struggling to shake Haditha from his mind; by the time they reached the main reception, he had just about managed to re-establish himself in the present. The inside of the building was even more beautiful than the outside; two crystal chandeliers adorned the ceiling, and the marble stairways and giant mirrors created a stunning entrance.

The main sitting room was just off to the right and was opulent in the extreme; huge columns extending from floor to ceiling added a sense of theatre to the room, while the sweeping light fixtures and plush furnishings offered a glimpse into how the nineteenth century Russian nobility had lived.

Vlad was sitting in the centre of the room on a decadent settee, surrounded by lime cushions. A gold leaf coffee table separated his sofa from its sister three-seater.

"Welcome, please sit," Vlad said, as he pointed to the sofa opposite him.

John took up the invitation; the spread of documents covering the coffee table had immediately piqued his interest.

"So, you want to find Malakov?" Vlad continued. "We may be able to help you with that."

"I'm glad to hear it," John replied, as he leaned forwards, his elbows resting on his knees. He still felt somewhat uncomfortable with this potential alliance.

Vlad glanced over at Dimitri, sensing the friction in the air, but choosing to overlook it, and continued regardless. "You see, we are not fans of the Malakovs; if something were to happen to them, none of us here would lose any sleep over it."

"Andrei Malakov was heavily involved in the army invasion of Crimea," Dimitri added. "He was the general that led the operation, so there is no love lost between the Malakovs and the Ukrainian Nationalists."

"Oh, so I'm actually doing you a favour then, by tracking him down," John replied, unable to control the discomfort and dislike in his voice.

"Yes, I suppose you are, John. This is more a mutually beneficial relationship."

"Mutually beneficial… what's your side of the deal then, Vlad?"

"Straight to the point, I like it. We can help you get into Russia, and we can also tell you where Malakov senior is living. After that, it's up to you: we get you in, you finish the job. Is that acceptable to you, John?"

John glanced at the papers on the coffee table, beginning to take the man in front of him a little more seriously. "What have you got on him, Vlad?"

"We know where Alek has been staying since his release, and we have managed to source the schematics of the building. Here, see for yourself."

Vlad passed Dimitri a map from the coffee table, and both he and John scrutinised it carefully. It was a map of a hillside retreat on the outskirts of Moscow, complete with reconnaissance photos. The estate was surrounded by trees and mountains on all sides, and was completely isolated. The only access was by a solitary mountain road leading up to it, which was heavily guarded at the bottom and top.

"So, do you think it's doable, Vlad?" Dimitri asked.

"Not a chance," Vlad laughed. "Like I said, that's up to you. If you are crazy enough to try, that's your business. We will get you into the country, no more."

John pondered their options for a moment, scanning the documents. "Can we take these?"

"Yes, of course, all yours. I really hope you succeed in your mission; it will be in the interests of all of us, yes?"

John nodded reluctantly. "What do you have in mind to get us into the country, Vlad?"

"This I think you will like. Come with me over to the window."

John and Dimitri looked at each other. They knew they were overly indulging their host, but their intrigue eventually triumphed, and they made their way over to the rear window, brushing shoulders with another armed guard on the way.

"What do you see?" Vlad asked. "Over there by the Mercedes in the driveway, what do you see?"

"A van," Dimitri responded, slightly confused.

"Not just any old van, Dimitri. It's a first response vehicle."

"Requiem International Funeral Home," Dimitri read on the side of the van. He squinted to try and make out the smaller text below, but his eyesight failed him.

"It's a funeral van," John interjected, frustrated with this ridiculous charade. "Like a hearse, but designed to take bodies to the funeral home, not from it."

"Exactly, John. And it's not just any old funeral van. It's a Russian funeral van, owned by a firm in Moscow."

"Requiem International," Dimitri repeated.

"Exactly. This is actually a replica, but it's identical to one of theirs; it even has the same number plate. They use it as a first response vehicle to transport their dead soldiers back from inside the Donbas."

"Donbas is a region of eastern Ukraine that Russia are currently invading, John," Dimitri explained.

"Thank you, Dimitri, I am aware."

"Requiem have a contract with the army to bring back any dead soldiers into Moscow; these vehicles are regularly seen crossing back into Russia, and they never get stopped, for obvious reasons."

John nodded, starting to see where this was going.

"Vitali and his cousin here, Maxim, will drive you over the border. All you have to do is stay quiet and relax in the back. No one will check the van."

"Sounds like an excellent plan, Vlad. Thank you," Dimitri interjected, eager to please his host, more through fear than because of any genuine admiration for his comrade's plan.

220

"Hang on, in the back? What do you mean by 'in the back' exactly?"

Vlad chuckled again, delighted that John had been the one to spot this slight twist in the tale. "Obviously, you will be the corpses, John," he said, after pausing briefly for full dramatic effect. "There is no way any border patrol officer would dare to stop a government contracted vehicle, let alone open a leather body bag inside a hearse."

"Is it safe?" Dimitri asked, with a slight hint of concern in his voice.

"It's okay, Dimitri. You will be able to breathe. We will seal the bags when you leave here, just in case they do stop you, but we have specially designed your body bags with small air pockets, so you will have no problems. We have also recreated the drivers' uniforms, complete with IDs for our men, for full authenticity," Vlad continued. "But we don't expect the van to even be stopped, let alone searched. We have gone to a lot of trouble here, John. I hope you approve?"

John looked over at Dimitri, deliberately pausing for a moment, while he thought of a response. He need not have worried; Dimitri quickly answered for him.

"Sounds like an excellent plan, Vlad. Thank you, once again."

John nodded reluctantly, not as comfortable with this plan as Dimitri seemed to be. He still had questions. "Assuming this works, and we get through the border, what happens when we get into Russia?"

"Good question, John. We have organised this for you too. We have sourced the keys to an old, derelict warehouse near the centre of Moscow. We will drop you there, and then, it's over to you. Oh, and we have also organised a car for you, should you need one. It will be parked outside the warehouse; Vitali will give you the details on the way. I trust that this is all you will need from us?"

"It certainly seems like you have thought of everything for us, Vlad. This warehouse, is it definitely empty? No drug addicts or squatters?" Dimitri enquired.

"No, certainly not. It's out of the way, on a rundown industrial estate; it's the perfect place for you to base yourselves until you complete your mission."

John rested his hand on his lower lip; everyone knew he was thinking of a response. After a few moments, it came. "Thank you for your thoroughness, Vlad. It sounds like this plan might well work."

"Excellent, it's settled then. Just let us know when you would like to depart, and I will make the arrangements. A drink, to celebrate?"

"We will go tonight," John informed him. "The faster I get this done, the sooner I can get home."

"You mean you won't be staying the night? Do you not like our hospitality?" Vlad laughed. "It's okay, I'm only joking. I will try not to take any offence."

"No offence is meant, Vlad," Dimitri said. "It's just as John says; there is no point in waiting around. Is it possible to leave tonight?"

"Yes, of course, no problem. I will make the arrangements and Vitali here will come get you when it's time. But before you go, you will at least eat with us? Preparation for the long night ahead, yes?"

"I think we can manage that," John answered, finally setting aside his frosty demeanour. "I have a few calls to make, so if you will excuse me, I will head back to my room now. I look forward to dinner."

222

"No problem, John. It is an honour to be assisting you in your most noble mission."

The men shook each other's hands and sealed their agreement with a shot of Russian vodka.

As they followed Vitali back to their rooms, Dimitri leaned over to John, delighted that the meeting had ended with less animosity than it had started.

"Well done, John. We are getting close, yes?"

"Yes, Dimitri. It might just work. Besides, I can't see anyone else lining up to smuggle us over the border, can you?"

CHAPTER FORTY THREE

John shut the door behind him and collapsed onto the single bed in the corner of the room. He was relieved to be alone again, but somewhat concerned that he had now been reduced to recruiting terrorists as allies. Not to mention that Dimitri had suddenly turned into a 'yes' man. It was very odd that Dimitri seemed so intent on pleasing Vlad; there was certainly something that did not feel right about their relationship. But whatever was going on between them, both Vlad and Dimitri had been useful allies so far. Besides, John had little choice; these temporary alliances were the only assistance he was going to get out here.

Never before had he missed his family as much as he did now, and this last week had certainly reaffirmed his decision to leave the spy world for good. In his desperation to find Malakov, and get back to his family, John realised that he had left himself unnecessarily exposed. He considered for a while how he might be able to build in some sort of contingency into the plan, meticulously going through every detail in his head and working out were the potential for treachery lay.

Although Dimitri was still something of a mystery to him in many ways, John was confident that he would see this through with him, mainly because he had his own stake in this particular battle. To be fair, the same could be said of Vlad; what benefit would there be in organising all this and then killing him now? There would be much more reward in taking out Malakov via John, with relatively little risk on his part. Yes, John was confident they would also deliver on their part of the plan.

Yet, for some reason, something still felt off. Maybe it was an as yet unidentifiable flaw in Vlad's proposal, or more likely it was 'Haditha', still playing tricks with his mind. He stared up at the white ceiling a little longer, searching for answers in the broken old coving, until Byrne flashed through his brain once again. Maybe Byrne could finally be of use to him. He had seemed desperate to help, and apart from Wendy, he was about the only person John completely trusted in this whole sorry mess. Perhaps he could do some homework on the Malakov estate, and who knows, there might be other ways he could help, John thought to himself. After all, Byrne had made a career of fighting the enemy from a safe distance.

Deciding to just bite the bullet and call him, John picked up the phone once again. True to form, Byrne answered the phone immediately, and they talked for a while, with John explaining his need for assistance and Byrne willingly accepting the invitation. Once the formalities were complete, John began to divulge the details of the meeting he had just finished with Vlad, and explained the plan that would get him into Russia, He whispered all the way through, conscious that Dimitri was in the next room; instinct told him he was still best keeping this conversation a secret.

Byrne listened intently, and eventually asked John what his gut was telling him about Vlad and his crew. John admitted that, despite his misgivings about them personally, he did think their plan was sound, and he could not see any reason for them to double cross him at this point. Byrne agreed, and both men started to look through the documents John had received from Vlad. John was taking photos and sending them on WhatsApp for Byrne to look over, and Byrne, in return, was validating what he could on the web.

Byrne searched the co-ordinates of both the estate and the warehouse, and immediately pulled up the warehouse on his screen. It looked deserted enough, and he passed this evidence down the phone. John seemed pleased that they had managed to lay eyes on the area in advance, though Byrne stressed to him that the visuals might not be one hundred percent up to date. Eventually, after some persuasion, John agreed to let Byrne book a B&B in the centre of Moscow just in case a plan B was required.

Byrne was delighted that John had finally let him in, and feeling increasingly important, he began to investigate the Malakovs' estate. Unfortunately, Google Maps only showed a few miles of farmland, and there was nothing else available on Google Images. A local residential guide did make reference to a property in the hills, but that was about it. John, unsurprisingly frustrated, but not surprised by this, asked Byrne what he thought about the idea of him and Dimitri attacking the estate.

"Suicide," Byrne replied.

John could only agree, and both men paused for a

while to digest the magnitude of what they were doing.

Finally, John confessed his concerns. "Even when we get to the warehouse, how the hell am I going to get to Alek?" John sighed.

He was greeted with inevitable silence at the other end of the line.

Of course. If he could not come up with a plan, what chance did Byrne have? "Fat lot of good you are, Byrne," he joked, trying to lighten the mood a little.

Their silence ended, the two men continued to look through the other documents. They were mainly long lens pictures of Alek and Andrei together; some of them featured Alek with his wife, and in a few, Alek was pictured with another, younger looking woman. They had to hand it to Vlad. He had done his homework.

"Does Alek have a daughter, Byrne?" John asked, after another pause in their discussions.

"Not that I know of John, why?"

"It's just this photo. I'm looking at him here, being very friendly with a younger woman, outside a restaurant. Here, look, I'll text you a picture of it now. Do me a favour and get me her name, will you? Even better, get me the name of that restaurant they are in front of."

"Will do, John. What are you thinking?" Byrne asked excitedly.

"Not sure to be honest, Byrne, but if this is a mistress, she could just be the weakness we are looking for."

CHAPTER FORTY FOUR

Dimitri was less concerned by Vlad's plan, in fact, unlike John, he had spent the last few hours catching up on some sleep. Whilst John had been napping at every possible opportunity on the way over here, Dimitri had found it difficult to switch off. Perhaps his subconscious had finally relaxed now that he was in safer surroundings, or maybe he was beginning to feel more comfortable in John's company. Either way, he had crashed out for over three hours, and only just made it in time for dinner.

Vitali had asked them to be ready for six p.m., so that they could leave for the border just after eight, and he was not the sort of man you wanted to be late for. Dragging himself off the bed, Dimitri quickly popped his head into the corridor and knocked on John's door.

"Are you ready, John?" he asked through the door. "Vlad will be here in fifteen minutes."

"Yes, I'll be ready shortly," John replied, momentarily pausing his conversation with Byrne on the phone. He waited for Dimitri's footsteps to grow silent, before continuing. "Listen, Byrne, I haven't got long left before dinner so I need to go now. I will do some digging at my end, see if Vlad knows anything about this mistress, and you see what you can find. I'll try to call you before we leave tonight, but if not, I will call when we arrive in Moscow, okay?"

"No problem, John. Good luck, my old friend."

****

Dimitri, in the next room, was changing his shirt for dinner and getting his bags ready for their departure. He was feeling remarkably calm and refreshed after his sleep, and felt confident that he and John would be successful in their mission. Despite still having no idea how to infiltrate Alek's estate, he had faith in his partner. He knew John would be covering all the angles, and for some reason, he felt strangely safe in the hands of the famous John Steele.

They were putting themselves in immense danger, entering Russia and seeking out Malakov, and there was no guarantee that either of them would make it back alive. But Dimitri was content that the end would definitely justify the means; a world without the Malakovs would be a much safer place, and he for one would rest easier in his bed at night knowing they were dead. Yes, it was time to end the years of hiding, and he was never going to get a better opportunity than this.

****

John packed his rucksack ready for the journey ahead, leaving it by the bed before walking out of the door. He was frustrated that he would need to 'play nice' with Vlad one more time before he could depart, and as he knocked on Dimitri's door, he considered the importance of this other woman, and hoped that this might be the stroke of luck he was looking for. There was no telling whether Alek would be expecting them, so the element of surprise was John's only real weapon and he needed to make it count.

****

When they arrived for dinner, Vlad was still in character, the conscientious host, but his wife and two daughters had now joined him. The dining table had been elaborately laid for twenty-four guests, even though it looked like only six would be dining.

John looked at the lavish setting and could not help but despise his villainous host. But he recognised the need to be civil in this particular scenario, and followed Dimitri's lead, first shaking Vlad's hand and then kissing the ladies outstretched palms. Vlad invited them to take a seat, and John reluctantly accepted, feeling thoroughly out of place in this environment.

Dinner was an opulent affair, as expected: five courses in just over an hour. First the servant brought out some sort of cold soup, followed by white fish of some variety, and then a joint of beef 'for his English guest' Vlad proudly announced, theatrically carving it at the table. Coffee and cheese followed, and all courses were consumed with endless bottles of white and red wine. Dimitri took full advantage of the feast in front of him, but John went steady on the booze, conscious of the job ahead later that night.

Finally, the food trays were exhausted, and as the ladies retired to the sitting room, John took his opportunity.

"Vlad, thank you once again for your help, and for this excellent meal. There is one other thing I would like to ask you before we depart, if I may."

"Certainly, John. Glad to be of assistance," Vlad replied taking his guest to one side.

"It's about the photos you gave me earlier. I had a quick look through them before dinner; great work by the way."

"Thank you. They were not taken by my own hand, I must confess."

"Yes, well, a couple of them appear to feature Alek and a young woman."

"Ah, yes," Vlad chucked. "The mistress."

"I suspected as much. Do you know anything about her, Vlad?"

"Not really, my friend. She is definitely the other woman though; Alek is fairly open about it, so we suspect the wife knows about her. He meets her regularly, at the same restaurant in the centre of Moscow, so he is hardly trying to conceal her. They go for dinner at six p.m. at least two or three times a week – the restaurant is owned by his personal chef I think – and then they go back to her hotel. It's no secret."

"Interesting. Do you know the name of this restaurant by any chance?"

"I'm sure we do, John. Is it not in the files?"

"Not that I could see."

"Leave it with me; I will find out and let you know before you go. Good luck, John. It has been a pleasure to assist you." He offered his hand one last time.

"Thank you, Vlad. See you on the other side," John replied, privately hoping that he would never lay eyes on the man ever again.

"I hope so, John. I certainly hope so."

John caught Dimitri's eye and flicked his head sideways, in a gesture that suggested they should be hitting the road.

"You go ahead, John. I'll meet you at the van." Dimitri answered. "I need to try and sober myself up."

Vlad chuckled. "I will make a quick call about our lady friend, John, and then come and see you off. When are you leaving, Vitali?"

"Forty-five minutes," Vitali replied. "Please don't be late."

"We won't, Vitali, don't worry. I'm going to head back to my room, to pick up my rucksack and check in on the wife. You guys go ahead, I won't be long."

All four men then headed off in their own different directions, and John was certainly pleased to finally escape the intensity of their company and make a couple of last minute preparations for the task that lay ahead.

CHAPTER FORTY FIVE

Back in his temporary accommodation, John pulled out his burner phone, but instead of calling Wendy as he had promised, it was in fact Byrne that he was desperate to speak with. John needed to update him on the new intel he had gained over dinner.

"Listen," he began, the moment Byrne picked up. "I've only got a few minutes to speak, so listen. That girl, the one in the photos…"

"Yes, John?" Byrne just about managed to get out before John carried on.

"She is his mistress; Vlad confirmed as much over dinner. Can you see what you can dig up on her? Vlad said they meet regularly at the same restaurant, usually at the same time. Any intel would be massive."

Byrne agreed to investigate, and again wished John good luck for the trip ahead.

"Thanks. I'm going to get rid of this phone now; Dimitri has a stack of burners with him, so I will destroy this one and replace it. Can't risk having it with me any longer, especially if your guy is logging it at HQ tomorrow."

"Good idea, John. I will await your call then. Stay safe," Byrne added, as he prepared to end the call.

"Oh, Byrne, just one more thing. There is something I need to tell you before you go, my friend, just in case things don't go to plan over there."

"I'm sure that isn't necessary, old boy. You've been in tighter spots than this and still come out of it smelling of roses, this time will be no different I'm sure."

"Yes, yes, whatever! Listen, man, will you? It's the reason I think we are in this mess, Byrne, and if I don't make it back home, you will need this intel, believe me. If the worst happens, do what you feel is right with the information I'm about to tell you, okay?"

"Whatever you say, John."

"I'm not sure that I did the right thing with it, back then. Maybe I should have done more," John said wistfully. "But I do know one thing; if the shit hits the fan, this information might literally be a life saver."

"I'm all ears," Byrne replied, finally feeling like he was fully on the team.

"It's to do with Haditha. You remember that 'off book' operation I told you I found out about? Well, to be honest with you, that op is the reason I left the job in the first place."

John began to tell the story of Haditha all over again, to new and expectant ears. He covered everything: the tip off from Dimitri, the call with Redcalf, the trip up to Rawa, and the night he risked everything to lay eyes on the facility first-hand.

"So, what happened next?" Byrne asked after a few minutes, now completely engrossed in the story unfolding.

"Once the coach left the bunker, it drove for about an hour, with me in the luggage compartment. Eventually, it came to a stop, and I could hear the scientist guys getting off. I waited until the noise died down, jumped out, and hid behind a bush. I then proceeded to watch on as every single person got out at the same stop; it was then that I realised I had just found reliable witnesses who would help me build my case."

"Good result, then. Where were you, John?"

"A hotel, one of the few outside of Baghdad. It was called Ayoub Alenzi, near Albaqhdadi. I later found out that the British secret services were paying for bio-chemical experts from around the world to stay there. Over the next few months, I saw many different people, mostly Brits, but also a few other nationalities. They would check in one night, stay for a few nights and then disappear. They would rotate them regularly, perhaps to limit the knowledge any one person could gain. Anyway, one by one, I researched who they were, and found a way to speak to them about their business there. Security was incredibly tight in the hotel, and armed guards would scan the scientists' credentials before they were allowed out of the hotel and onto the coach. But getting back to the hotel, security was more lax; I guess they didn't expect anyone to hop on the bus at the other end!" John joked.

Byrne gave a murmur of acknowledgement from the other end of the phone, struggling to process the enormity of what John was telling him.

"Instead of going into the hotel, I waited around outside, and in the shops around the complex, picking them off one by one. I would target the scientists in small pockets, and after making initial contact, we would arrange secret meetings, under the pretence that I was an MI6 vetting officer, making sure their presence was verified, which of course, was easy to confirm: I had the ID and experience to back up my story. I also figured that by the time someone blew the whistle, I would have all the evidence I needed, so I wasn't too concerned. At the point, I was definitely all in. Each group that I met gave me a different angle; they were kept very separate inside the bunker, so no one scientist had a complete picture, but slowly, bit-by-bit I managed to piece it all together."

"Chemical weapons?" Byrne breathed.

"More than just chemical weapons, Byrne. The WMD experts I spoke to told me they were testing weapons grade chemicals down there, apparently left over from Saddam's reign, and very dangerous, and the biochemists I spoke to explained that they were working on a vaccine for some super flu; a super flu that previous groups had already created down there in advance of their arrival. It took about three months to collate all the evidence I needed, and by then, it was clear to me that the British government had sanctioned the design and creation of a super virus, which could be used with ballistic weaponry. We were meant to be in Iraq eradicating such materials, but instead, at this facility, the British secret service were stockpiling for themselves. By all accounts, this weapon was so powerful that, if released, it could wipe out an entire city, lock down a country, even."

"Jesus, John, what did you do?"

"I built as compelling a case as I could to take back to my superiors, with copies of documents; photos; recordings of first-hand accounts. It was undeniable. Then, after those three months, I got out of there as quickly as I could, before anyone could twig what I was doing."

"Why not spill the beans though, John, when you got back, I mean? Why did you just leave the job?"

John paused, wrestling with this question himself. "I'm not sure, Byrne, old friend. Like I said, maybe, given that decision again, I would have chosen a different path. But at the time, all I knew was that I was going to confront Redcalf with it all as soon as I got back to London, and that's exactly what I did, in his own office, no less. I stormed in, completely unannounced, and laid it all bare on his desk: the photos, the documents, the personal accounts and everything. It was a perfect storm, Byrne, and he had no choice but to admit the truth to me."

"He didn't try to deny it at all?"

"Like I said, it was undeniable. He sat there in his chair and admitted it all to me, like it was nothing. I was raging, and ready to go to war on it, but he promised me that the operation was over anyway, so there was no gain in whistleblowing. He asked me to remember why I had joined MI6 in the first place, and asked me to leave it buried out there in the desert. He made a good case, Byrne, and I guess I bought it. He offered me early retirement, and the life I was craving. I took the easy option, I suppose. I made sure my family were safe, and threatened to expose it all if I got wind of anything like it happening again in the future. I guess, when it came down to it, I chose my family, much the same as I'm doing now."

"That makes sense, John. Don't beat yourself up about it. You did what you thought was right at the time."

"Thanks, Byrne. I did withhold some documents, just in case I needed the evidence; if anything happens to me out here, ask Wendy about our 'happy place'. She'll know where I mean. Anyway, I've got to go now, they're all waiting in the courtyard for me. We are due in Russia in a few hours."

Byrne bid his farewell, then hung up the phone. He was finally beginning to understand the magnitude of the predicament he had gotten himself into. He thought long into the night about John's decision ten years ago not to blow the whistle, and debated what he would do should John not make it back from Russia. It would not be an easy decision; of that he was certain.

CHAPTER FORTY SIX

"Where the hell have you been, John? Vitali's getting anxious," Dimitri whispered, as he rushed over to confront John.

"Relax, I'm here now. Let's go," John replied not at all interested in Dimitri's apparent paranoia.

"Apologies, Vlad, the wife kept me talking," John announced to the group, feeling the need to placate his hosts. "What's the plan then?"

"No problem, John. We are only a little behind schedule. Maxim here will fill you in on the details."

Maxim was the first average sized man John had come across during his brief stay on the estate, and he was slightly relieved that he would not be facing two super humans; should push come to shove over in Moscow, one would be more than enough. Maxim had short, dark hair, and was wearing a blue uniform with the logo 'Requiem International' embossed on his left breast. Vitali was identically dressed, albeit in a shirt that must have been four times bigger than Maxim's.

"As you can see, we are fully dressed for the occasion," Maxim said, as he opened the back of the van and pulled out one of the two leather body bags laid out inside. "This is what you will be travelling in. It might get a little warm, but see here and here: these are the specially designed air pockets we have added for you."

"Good, good," Dimitri replied, looking slightly green at the prospect of traveling for two hours zipped up in one of those things.

"We have tested them fully ourselves, but feel free to get inside and try it out for yourselves if you prefer."

"No, that won't be necessary," John interjected. "Can we stop somewhere just short of the border, before you zip us up fully? The less time we are inside those things, the better."

Maxim nodded, and Dimitri embraced Vlad, thanking him once again for his hospitality before jumping into the back, handing over his belongings to Maxim in the process. John waited a moment, slowly making his way over to the steps where Vlad was positioned.

"Thank you, Vlad. You have been more than helpful."

"No problem at all, John. Like I say, we are on the same side. Oh, and about the lady friend we discussed. I spoke to my man over there and he knows of her; she is quite the socialite apparently. Her name is Anna Lovaka, and Alek keeps her in that hotel I mentioned, the Hyatt Regency in Petrovsky Park, near Dynamo central station. The restaurant is just around the corner; it's called the YAR and is very grand indeed. Two Michelin stars, and a waiting list as long as your arm. Alek doesn't have any problems getting in though, he owns the place. I trust that will help you in your mission, my friend. Good luck, and goodbye."

John thanked his host for the intel, shook his hand for a final time, and jumped into the back of the van, ready to depart. The doors slammed shut on the two men inside, and John banged hard on the side panel, to signal that they were ready to leave.

CHAPTER FORTY SEVEN

About three hours into the drive, Dimitri was already complaining about his back not holding up with all the potholes in the road.

"We've got another eight hours of this, Dimitri, so quit with the complaining."

"Eight hours! I can't stay inside this box for another eight hours, John. I need a break."

"Well, you are going get your wish shortly, I think. How long have we been going? About three hours?"

"I reckon, yes," Dimitri replied.

"Well we can't be far from the border then, can we? So I guess we will be stopping shortly. Then they are going to zip your face up, so be careful what you wish for. Try to relax, man. We are not in control at the moment."

"I didn't sign up for this, John. Plus I need a piss. Bang the side or something, will you? Get them to stop."

"I told you about the booze, didn't I," John said, laughing at his partner's stupidity and showing zero sympathy for his predicament. In fact, it was helping John pass the time; he was quite enjoying watching Dimitri squirm. "Give it another ten or fifteen minutes, and I reckon we will be stopping anyway. You'll just have to wait."

John was right. A few minutes later, the van pulled off what had seemed like an endlessly long, straight road. The engine settled down to a slow purr and eventually stopped altogether. John heard the front doors open, and Vitali light a cigarette. Eventually, Maxim opened the back doors, to Dimitri's immediate relief.

It was even darker outside the van than inside it, and the night sky offered little in the way of reassurance to either of them. Vitali had clearly pulled up in the most secluded area he could find; there was nobody around for miles, and John could not help but think this was the perfect place to leave two bodies. Two gunshots and that would be the end of it. With this in mind, John braced himself for the worst, but when his eyes finally focused on the two Ukrainian men standing over him, he could only see the spark of Vitali's cigarette, and no sign of a gun in either man's hand. He gave a huge sigh of relief and lifted himself up to a sitting position, ready to crawl out of the van for a break.

"Right, it's time to zip you up I'm afraid," Maxim informed them.

"Can I have a piss first, Maxim? I'm bursting."

John laughed out loud and both the Ukrainians joined in, seeing the funny side.

"Hurry up, Dimitri, and stay close to the van, okay?" Vitali ordered.

Dimitri hopped out and scurried into the woods.

"I might as well take the opportunity to relive myself too," John said to Maxim, as he also made the small jump out of the van and onto solid ground.

After a couple of minutes, both men returned to the

van, Dimitri looking considerably more relaxed. Vitali made some joke about him not holding his liquor, and John chuckled in response as he lay back into his space, resigned to his looming burial, albeit only temporary.

"I'm sorry to have to do this, John, but if all goes to plan, you should not be zipped up any more than a couple of hours."

"Two hours?" Dimitri complained again,

"Yes, I'm afraid so," Maxim replied patiently. "Half an hour to the crossing; an hour to get through, give or take, and then another half an hour to get inland, if that's okay with you, my friend?"

John answered for him. "Yes, yes, let's just get it over with. Zip me up, I'm ready."

Dimitri reluctantly followed suit, muttering something in Russian about the indignity. Maxim zipped him up, slammed the back doors closed, and before long, the hearse was on the road again.

CHAPTER FORTY EIGHT

Vitali glanced down at the digital clock in front of him. Just after midnight. He could see the signs for the border quickly approaching, and banged on the panel separating him from the two breathing corpses in the back. Three bangs: the code the men had arranged to signal they were approaching the border.

John heard the signal first and coughed slightly to check on his partner. He was pleased to hear the return 'cough' almost immediately, and relaxed back into his bag, content in the knowledge that Dimitri was now focused on the task at hand. Those coughs were the last attempt at communication either man undertook, and they both lay back in silence, zipped from head to toe, waiting for what would hopefully be Vitali's all clear on the other side.

Vitali himself was considerably less calm in the front. He was a wanted man in Russia, and knew that if he got caught on Russian soil he would be subjected to the most barbaric forms of interrogation, without any real prospect of ever getting out alive. He was considered a terrorist to the Kremlin, for crimes he had committed in Crimea, the Donbas, and Russia itself. He hated what Putin stood for, and was willing to sacrifice everything in his desperate attempts to protect his country. 'One man's terrorist is another man's freedom fighter', Vlad had always told him, and he was right. Vitali did not consider himself a terrorist; it was Putin who was the terrorist, and he was just doing what he had to do to protect his people.

Maxim was also on the FSB radar, but more for his links to the Ukrainian Nationalists than for any specific acts of terror. Despite this, he knew that, should they be stopped at any point and captured, he would fall victim to the same fate that would befall his comrade: days and nights of torture, followed by a slow and painful death. It was not a very appealing proposition.

"Vitali? You ready?" Maxim asked, trying to ease the tension.

"I think so, Maxim. You?"

"Yes, I'm ready. Remember, stay cool. I will do the talking; if things don't immediately go to plan, don't panic and start shooting like you usually do. Even you won't be able to kill a whole border patrol."

"I know, I know," Vitali responded dismissively.

Vitali had a reputation as a bit of a hot head, to say the least, which was why Maxim had been sent along as well, to do the talking, if needed. Maxim knew that their best chance of getting into Russia was through diplomacy, not violence.

Maxim spotted the signs up ahead. "There it is: E101 border crossing. Remember the plan, Vitali?"

"Yes, don't worry about me. You concentrate on your job," Vitali replied, knowing it would be the last time he would be required to speak for a while.

It was a straight road that led to the crossing, going from the M02 on the Ukrainian side to the M3 on the

Russian side. It was only a small border crossing, with a mere two hundred metres separating the two warring countries. If it were not for the group of border guards holding submachine guns, and the enormous flashlights that almost blinded Maxim on the drive up, they could still be in their homeland.

Maxim wound the window down on the driver's side window, and prepared the necessary paperwork, as he waited for a Russian soldier to head over to the van. With any luck they would just lift the barrier, noticing the signage on the van, and let them through.

Unfortunately for all concerned, that did not happen. They sat there, parked up against the barrier for at least ten minutes, each second seemingly doubling the tension. Eventually, out of the mist, one of the patrolling soldiers slowly made his way up to them.

He crouched down and stuck his head through the window. "Paperwork?" he barked at Maxim, as he looked both passengers up and down several times.

Maxim handed over their forged Russian passports and the relevant commercial paperwork, and the soldier proceeded to look through each document in painstaking detail. Finally, after what seemed like an eternity, he handed back the documents.

"Muscovites, hey? A long journey, god rest their souls," he said, referring to the dead soldiers in the back.

"Yes," Maxim replied, deliberately saying as little as possible, convinced that they would be able to detect a Ukrainian accent if he talked too much.

The soldier stood back and waved at the guy controlling the barrier, signalling for him to let them through. Maxim allowed himself to breathe again, and readied the engine. But as he waited for the barrier to lift, seemingly only seconds from safety, the solider heard a message on his radio transmitter.

"Halt!" he shouted, immediately lifting his hand high into the air, signalling again to the barrier guy. This time, the signal was to stop the barrier.

Every sinew in Maxim's body was telling him to get the hell out of there, and the expression on Vitali's face was not doing anything to calm matters, but somehow, he managed not to push the accelerator. Instead, as calmly as he could, looked out at the solider.

"Problem, comrade?" he asked.

The response was not instant; the solider finished his conversation on the radio, before answering Maxim's question.

"No problem, just a random spot check. Can you both get out of the van, please?"

Maxim looked at Vitali, and Vitali looked straight back at him, neither man knowing what they should do about this unexpected turn of events. Eventually, Maxim made the first move, opening his door and slowly stepping out of the van. Vitali followed suit, after making sure he had stuffed his bag of guns as deep into the foot holes as possible. They both moved to the side of the checkpoint and stood where the solider had directed.

"Can you open the back, please?" the solider said.

Maxim's heart sank, and he felt an overwhelming desire to run or fight, but he did neither, carefully opening the back doors instead, as requested.

"Two dead soldiers, comrade. Taking them back to their families," he said.

"Can you open the bags, please?" the soldier continued.

248

Maxim glimpsed Vitali in the corner of his eye, readying for battle, and quickly interjected. "What? Are you sure you want to do that? Not a pretty sight by all accounts."

The solider hesitated a little, but persisted. "Yes, I need to do a full spot check."

"Come on, they have given their lives for this country. Surely they deserve some respect? We are working for the government, you know, comrade. Our contract is in your hand. I will have to report this, solider. What's your number?"

Again, the solider hesitated, but this time, he did not reply. Instead, he reached for his radio for confirmation. "Wait here, I will be back shortly," he said, as he walked into the adjacent office.

John could hear the commotion, and sensed that something was not right. He had felt the doors open, but knew that both he and Dimitri had no option but to play dead and hope for the best. At least Dimitri could hear what Maxim was saying, and could brace himself if needed; John had no idea what was going on.

A couple of minutes later, the solider returned, giving little away. Maxim walked towards him, hoping to distract from the body bags in the van, and continue their argument away from the breathing corpses.

"You are free to go," the solider relented.

Maxim glanced back at Vitali and gestured with his hand for him to close the back doors and get in the van. "I should think so too," Maxim replied, feeling increasingly confident in his role.

"Apologies for the inconvenience," the soldier offered, keen to calm the situation down a little. "Just doing my job."

"No problem, comrade. I understand," Maxim said, appreciating the young soldier's predicament and not wanting to push his luck. He took back the paperwork, thanked the solider one final time and sat back in the van. They waited again, for what seemed like forever, until the barrier eventually went up, and Maxim put his foot on the accelerator.

"Fuck, fuck, fuck," Maxim breathed as soon as he had driven a few hundred metres into Russia. That had been too close.

Vitali followed suit, shaking off the adrenaline and banging on the panel three times to signify to John and Dimitri that they were safely across the border. The plan had been to wait until they were well inland before he gave the signal, but he could not hide his relief, and the two corpses in the back were certainly not complaining.

CHAPTER FORTY NINE

Nine hours and a few stops later, the van was approaching Moscow. By now, John and Dimitri had been let out of their leather coffins, and Dimitri was communicating with Vitali in the front through the speaker on his mobile phone.

The journey in land had been long but fairly straightforward, and the four men were discussing the final leg of the operation. They had spent the hours reviewing the success of the border crossing, and laughing about how close they had come to getting caught. Gradually, the conversation ran out, and one by one, each man retreated into their own space and inner thoughts, contemplating both their own self fortune, but also the reality that the danger was far from over.

During the last stop, a couple of hours south of Moscow, Vitali had given John a map of the city, with their start and end points already marked. He had also left the back doors unlocked this time, so they could quickly make their exit when the time came, and John began to plot their optimum route to safety, aided by the fresh morning daylight seeping underneath the van doors.

It was not a complicated plan; rush hour had been and

gone, and the two men were due to be dumped at a multistorey car park, right in the centre of Moscow. They had changed into civilian clothes, and were ready to make the relatively short walk. This was the safer option, John had decided, despite Maxim offering to drop them directly at the warehouse. He felt more comfortable approaching the warehouse on his own terms, just in case something went wrong, or the whole thing was a trap.

After John had walked through the plan enough times for Dimitri to sing it off by heart, John finally relaxed. There were no complications left for him to ruminate on, so his mind inevitably drifted back to his wife and kids.

"Dimitri, can I have a new burner from your stash, please? I dumped mine back in Kyiv, to be safe."

"What?" Dimitri queried, and John immediately feared the worst. "Sorry, my friend, I haven't brought them with me. I've only got this one, I'm afraid. Do you want to use it?"

"No, thanks. You really ought to get rid of that now, it's been with us far too long. Leave it in the van, just in case anyone is monitoring your activity."

"Good point. We can always pick fresh ones up before we head over to the warehouse, if you like?"

"No, don't worry. I don't want to risk being picked up on any cameras. It's not important. Just wanted to check in on the family again, you know."

"I'm sorry, John. It must be hard for you, being away from them."

John nodded in appreciation, but clearly did not want to discuss it any further, so Dimitri left him alone, listening out for the three bangs once more: their code, and the signal to complete the extraction.

CHAPTER FIFTY

BANG, BANG, BANG went the panel. It was like a small earthquake had just hit the van; John immediately turned the handle and they jumped out, somewhere in the middle of central Moscow. The van quickly drove back out of the car park, without so much as a goodbye or good luck. That was the last John would see of the Ukrainian Nationalists, or so he hoped. Though grateful for their assistance, he was glad to be back in charge of his own destiny once again.

Maxim had dropped them off in a black spot, in-between the car parks CCTV cameras, so they paused for a moment, stretching their aching bodies and gathering their bearings.

"It's only two miles. Walk alongside me and keep your cap on and your head down," John said, impatient to begin their journey to the safe house.

"I have done this before, you know," came Dimitri's sharp reply, which John chose to ignore. Instead, he set off; he had already memorised the route, and knew where they would need to circumvent the cameras. He had the map tucked away safely in his rucksack in case they needed it.

They walked for about twenty minutes through the

bustling streets, down side alleys that appeared to lead nowhere in particular. Dimitri had already resigned himself to playing follow the leader for the whole journey; the fact that he had been born in this city seemed to matter little to John, though in truth, he was happy to play along. He knew John had it covered; there was no need to complicate matters with a second voice.

The two men skilfully negotiated their way around the city, carefully avoiding as many cameras as possible. John knew it was inevitable that they would be picked up on camera at some stage, but if they could avoid it before entering the warehouse it would at least give them a head start. John did not think anyone would be on the lookout for them right now, but he knew Malakov would have the tools necessary to retrace their steps if, and when, he was made aware of their presence here. If they wanted to maintain the element of surprise, they only had a short window of opportunity.

After another few minutes of walking, the city shops and posh cafés started to be replaced by car parks and garages, and John sensed that they were heading out of the main hub. Dimitri followed as they negotiated a few more streets, until John suddenly raised his hand in the air, signalling the need to stop. It reminded Dimitri of the black ops teams on TV who only communicated with their hands. He duly followed the instruction.

"It's over there, Dimitri. That old grey warehouse to our left."

"They are all old and grey, John. Which one?" Dimitri smirked.

John tutted. This was not the time for pissing about. He pointed to the same target again. "That one there, the one that hasn't got any windows."

"Oh, I see, got it," Dimitri replied, almost apologetically.

"Here's the plan. It looks deserted enough, but just to be safe, you go around the building to the left, and I will approach from the right. I have the keys, so when you find the main door with the lock on, wait there and I will join you."

"What if there is something amiss?"

"If you see any sign of life, or even if something feels off, abort. I will meet you back here, agreed?"

"What if I can't get back?"

"It's a deserted warehouse, not Colditz. Look, if you encounter a small army of Russians, get the hell out of there. I will meet you back at the car park, okay?"

"Okay. Like you say, it looks fairly abandoned to me."

"Exactly. You ready?"

Dimitri nodded.

"Great. See you on the other side."

The two men set off, Dimitri arcing around the warehouse to the right, as instructed, while John headed round the left side. He passed a couple of back street garages, and what seemed like a wood cutting business, before entering the small courtyard that housed three separate buildings. Their warehouse was the centre building, but he first checked the building to his left, to make sure there were no unexpected neighbours. The hanger was open and empty, and John immediately felt a whole lot better about the situation.

Gradually, he made his way in between the buildings to his warehouse, and started to scan the perimeter. It was not a large building: two floors, and almost every window was boarded up. Before long, he had found the main entrance, and saw Dimitri waiting next to it, leaning against the wall. John relaxed a little and nodded his approval, before reaching into his pocket for the key.

"Anything?" he asked, as he tried the lock.

"Nothing, John. This place is deserted; that building on the right is condemned, and there are no other businesses over this side. The only thing I saw was an old Fiat Punto sitting in the street. I'm betting that's our wheels."

"Brilliant," John replied, as the key opened the rusty old lock. "Looks like Vlad has been true to his word."

"I never doubted him, John. He's a good man."

John nodded, begrudgingly accepting Dimitri's judgment of Vlad, as he pushed open the door and cautiously entered their new 'home'.

<u>CHAPTER FIFTY ONE</u>

Byrne was starting to worry. He had not heard from John since last night, and had no way of knowing whether he had made it over the border safely or not. John had said he would phone as soon as he arrived in Russia, so why the delay?

Byrne desperately wanted to call Wendy, just to ask if she had heard anything, but he remembered John expressly telling him not to involve her any further. There was no point worrying her until it was all done; Wendy could not help them now, so there was no need to alarm her unnecessarily. She had enough on her plate.

He thought about his next move for a while, but with no clever ideas springing to mind, he eventually accepted that he had no option but to wait for John to contact him. He would stew for a few more hours before he really started to panic. In truth, if he could not speak to Wendy, and he could not involve his boss, what options did he have left? He would just have to sit tight and sweat it out until he heard from John. He had gone dark before, for a lot longer than this, and always came out the other side. This was the worst part of being a handler, the waiting, and Byrne was terrible at it.

****

The two men were starting to settle into their new surroundings, which were the polar opposite of Vlad's country mansion. John had claimed the only mattress, albeit motheaten and probably lice infested. He had managed to find an old sheet to cover it, and Dimitri had gathered a few pieces of wood to prepare a fire for the long, cold evening ahead.

John sat on the floor in front of the collection of twigs and branches, and was once again going through the intel Vlad had given him. He had laid the pictures and locations out like a jigsaw puzzle, with Alek Malakov at the top; his son, Andrei, marginally lower down, and the rest of the pieces of the puzzle underneath, trying to find the key that would unlock the whole thing.

"What are you thinking, John?" Dimitri asked, as he glanced over.

"Just looking at our options. If we assume the house is a no go, at least for now, how do we get to him, and give ourselves enough time to find out some answers?"

"Maybe we do a bit of reconnaissance of our own?" Dimitri replied, not realising that John's was a rhetorical question. "We go up into the mountains and watch them for a while; see if we can work out any patterns."

John reluctantly accepted that a second voice had now enter the discussion, and replied, "I thought about that, but we haven't got the equipment to stake them out properly, and more importantly, we haven't got the time. It would take days, if not weeks, to spot any patterns in his behaviour, and we just don't have that sort of time. I want to be out of here as quickly as possible, even if it means we take a few extra risks in the process."

Dimitri nodded his head up and down, gathering the last of the dry leaves that he needed to ignite the fire. "What if we go after Andrei, then? Wait for him to leave the house then chase him down; use him as bait?"

"What, in our Fiat Punto?" John laughed. "Can't see that going very well, can you? Besides, where would we take him?"

"Back here?" Dimitri suggested, challenging John's authority.

"No chance. We would be sitting ducks. I don't fancy our chances if Alek brings an army through here, do you?"

"I guess not," Dimitri sighed, busying himself with his fire.

John remained on the floor for a long time, analysing the documents, and Dimitri could not help but watch him work, in awe of his peer. John reminded him of a detective, piecing a case together on the wall of his run down old flat. His diverse skillset was undeniably impressive.

Eventually, John shattered the silence, slamming his palm down on the floor. "She is the key," he said, pointing to the picture of Anna Lovaka. "She is our way in. If Malakov meets her as regularly as Vlad suggested, then we can catch him in the act, so to speak, and take him down there."

"Where, John? You mean at her hotel? That doesn't sound good; it will be swimming with guards."

"No, not the hotel, the restaurant. He won't be expecting us to attack him in a public place, and I guess he won't have as many men around him while he is whispering sweet nothings in her ear. I imagine an armed guard would ruin the ambiance."

Dimi chuckled, pondering the plan that was rapidly formulating in John's head, and decided to challenge him once again. "You think we can just walk in there and ask him if he shot your son?"

"No, you idiot. We take him down there and then bring him back here to ask him the questions."

Dimitri paused, still not convinced by the idea. It was very risky indeed, which was very unlike John. He was famous for his meticulous planning and diplomacy. This seemed way out of character. "It's a bit risky isn't it, John? Anything could go wrong; working in public is never a good idea."

"I would usually agree, Dimitri, but I don't see any other credible options. It's just me, you and a knackered old Punto versus half the Russian mafia. We are going to have to take some risks. The element of surprise is our only advantage, and this way we get him off guard, do what we need to do and vanish before anyone realises we are even in the country."

"I'm not sure, John. Seems reckless to me,"

"We are going to need to take a few extra risks to get Malakov."

Dimitri paused again, before finally nodding in agreement. "If you think it's our best play, then I'm willing to follow your lead. But surely we can stake out the restaurant first? Make sure we know what we're walking into?"

"Agreed. Let's get ourselves over there tonight and see what's what. Vlad said Malakov always meets her at around six p.m., so that gives us a few hours to get over there and work out where's best for us to set up. Just outside, though. I'm not going in and risking everything until it's time to take him out."

Dimitri nodded, relieved at the delay that had just been added to the itinerary, but trying not to show it.

"Good, that's settled then. You go and check out the car, make sure it works and is taxed or whatever. I'll find us some lunch; meet you back here in half an hour to go over some of the finer details."

"Roger that, car keys?"

"Oh yes, that would help wouldn't it," John chuckled, throwing the keys to his partner. "We are getting close, Dimitri. Your revenge will be sweet, my friend."

CHAPTER FIFTY TWO

Dimitri pulled up under a copse of spruce trees, opposite the Hyatt Regency in Petrovsky Park, and waited for John's next instruction. John had eventually conceded that it made more sense for Dimitri to drive, given his knowledge of the city and Russian drivers; besides, he was happy to enjoy the extra leg-room in the passenger seat. It was only 4.15p.m., so they had plenty of time to get to the YAR restaurant, only a couple of blocks south from where they were parked; John wanted a look at the hotel first, just in case they needed to come up with a plan B.

They sat there for ten minutes or so, whilst John debated with himself whether he should go in a check out the layout. Eventually, he decided it was too risky, and not essential to the plan at this stage. Instead, he chose to distract himself with the condition of the car.

"Any problems with the car, Dimitri?" he asked, breaking the now comfortable silence.

"Don't think so. I checked out the engine and it seems in top condition to me. Vlad will have covered all of that for us, I'm sure. He's almost as meticulous as you, John."

John shrugged, trying to look sceptical, but Vlad's

efforts thus far had not gone unnoticed; he had delivered on every detail he had promised, and John was starting to admire him, just a little.

"There's a little surprise for us in the back though, John, underneath the blanket. Take a look."

John's left eyebrow rose slightly, and he stretched into the back to look under the blanket, revealing a large, black sports bag.

"What is it?" John asked.

"Look inside," Dimitri replied, enjoying being in the know for once.

John unzipped the bag and immediately zipped it straight back up again, hastily covering it with the blanket.

"Jesus... there are enough guns in there to take out a small army!"

"One final present from Vlad, I guess."

John was silent for a moment, and Dimitri struggled to identify whether he was pleased or angry.

"Let's just hope we don't have to use them," he finally said, revealing his appreciation. "Come on, let's move. The last thing we need is a cop patrol knocking on our window, especially with that little lot in the back."

****

An hour later, Dimitri parked the car in a side street, just off the square where the famous YAR restaurant resided. He had circled the restaurant a few times and decided this space was the ideal spot for a quick getaway, should it be required.

John was in the park opposite the YAR, having been

dropped off ten minutes previous. He had a good view of the main entrance from his spot – a park bench about two hundred metres across the square – and he was waiting patiently for his partner to arrive. The plan was simple: watch the entrance and wait to see if Alek showed up.

If he did, John would finally be able to answer all the questions that had been swirling around his head since they had come up with this crazy plan: questions were not good they meant risk and risk could get them killed, but it was now clear to John they were risks that they were simply going to have to take. He sat there patiently, his trusty cap concealing his appearance whilst allowing him to see the action unfold in front of him. It was the same cap he had bought from the service station in Switzerland at the beginning of the road trip, and it had served him well.

As he waited for his colleague to join him, the week's events began to replay in his mind like a 'previously' montage on a hit TV show. The time had not gone unnoticed on John. It was almost exactly a week since Malakov had invaded his home and changed their lives forever, and he liked the poetic symmetry of doing the same to Alek exactly a week later; finishing the job with the help of Vlad's little parting gift in the back. But, if he was honest with himself, he knew that was not his style; in any case, it would be suicidal to try and end Malakov so publicly. The element of surprise was their only advantage in this fight; revenge would have to wait another few days. Today was purely about gathering information, assuming they showed at all.

A couple of minutes later, Dimitri's head popped into view, and John watched as he walked into the park and sat down on the bench beside him.

"Quarter to six, John. Anything?"

"No, nothing yet. It looks dead in there to me, only a few tables eating. Maybe Vlad got it wrong? six o'clock seems awfully early to be eating in a Michelin star restaurant."

"Maybe… but he does own the place, remember. I'm sure he's only really interested in dessert anyway, if you know what I mean."

John smirked at his partner. "Is that what you would do then, Dimitri?"

"Unfortunately, John, I've never had a mistress hauled up in a five star hotel to call upon whenever I fancy, so I couldn't tell you. Maybe they just don't do it on Mondays? Vlad said they only meet three or four times a week. Alek must be getting old."

"Not unlike the rest of us…" John mused. "Listen, let's not be too hasty. There is still time; it's only ten past six now. Let's give them a while longer."

Both men sat in almost complete silence, watching on from afar as one or two new guests went in, and one or two came out. But there was still no sign of Alek, or Anna, for that matter, and neither of them were inconspicuous enough to have slipped past them. Tall, slim, blonde and stunningly attractive, Anna was the sort of woman who turned heads everywhere she went, and Alek was six foot three and built like a Russian weightlifter. If either of them had entered the restaurant, everyone would have noticed.

John made them wait in the freezing cold, their hunger growing by the minute; not helped by the magnificent smells emanating from the establishment they were watching. Eventually, just after eight John called it quits.

"Looks like a no show tonight. Let's head back to the hotel for another look before we settle down for the night. We'll try again tomorrow."

CHAPTER FIFTY THREE

It was the early hours of Tuesday morning, and Byrne could not sleep. John had not been in contact for over twenty-four hours now; clearly something was not right. For all Byrne knew, John could be dead in a ditch in Russia, or being subjected to the worst kinds of torture, if he had even made it into the country alive. The Ukrainian Nationalists could have double-crossed him at any time, or the authorities could have picked them up at the border; even Dimitri, his only ally, could not be completely relied upon.

A million possibilities were racing around his head, and none of them ended well for John. He was desperate to assist his friend in any way possible, but felt helpless, sitting there in his pyjamas not even knowing where John was, let alone what condition he was in. The only thing he did know was where he was heading, and even that piece of information was useless to him now. The only people with the skills to extract John from inside Russia where MI6, and they had made it quite clear that they refused to involve themselves.

He needed to think fast; there must be a way for him to help his old friend. In desperation, Byrne opened his laptop, and began to type.

****

John was sleeping like a baby, exhausted from the mental exertions of the day, as Dimitri watched over him, having chosen to take the night shift. He had a gut feeling that tomorrow was the day. Surely Alek would not go another day without seeing his mistress?

Laying back against the wall, Dimitri considered how far they had come since that first meeting at the old lady's funeral. The memories flashed through his mind over the next couple of hours: the shaky start at the casino; John following him back home; the random assassin who had been sent to kill one of them, or perhaps even both; his two dogs whom he might never see again; the road trip across Eastern Europe; Vlad and his army in Kyiv, and last but by no means least, the crazy border crossing into Russia.

The time had passed quickly with John by his side and as he listened to the snores of his comrade, he realised that he had a formed a deep connection with this ex-British spy. Strange how things turn out, he thought, hoping that this particular story would have a happy ending for them both.

After a few hours, John was up and about, and it was Dimitri's turn to get some rest. John went through the picture puzzle on the floor for the hundredth time, collected a new stash of branches for the night's fire, and checked what supplies were left over from the grocery shop run he had made twenty-four hours previously. Fortunately, they had enough food to get them through another day in the warehouse; there was no need to risk another shopping trip just yet.

Time was dragging its feet, and with nothing to occupy his mind, and no one to converse with, his thoughts drifted back to the hospital; back to his wife and son. He was aching inside; not knowing Ethan's current condition was killing him, and every sinew of his body wanted to just bail and get back to him as quickly as possible.

The truth was, he was scared: for his son and for himself. This whole journey had been like some strange nightmare until now, but since the stake out last night, the realisation had hit home. Malakov was finally within his reach, and that terrified him. He had been out of the game for so long; he could not be sure that he still had the skills to extract the information he needed out of Alek, let alone kill the man, if required. He just hoped that autopilot would take over, and if not, that his need to protect his son would push him to do what needed to be done.

John shook his head from side to side, trying to shake off his demons and empty his brain of the facts that had led him to this point. He desperately tried to occupy himself, focusing on the plan for the night ahead. He knew, deep down, that he had everything covered, but at least going over every fine detail again prevented him from ruminating about his boy; anything was better than sitting alone with only his own thoughts and fears for company.

Eventually, after what had felt like an eternity, Dimitri woke up, and John felt like he had been released from his own personal purgatory.

"Thank God you're awake. It's been hell sitting here alone, waiting for the time to pass."

"Tell me about it," Dimitri replied. "At least you had

the daylight to keep you company; it was freezing last night. What time is it?"

"Just after three. Here, have the rest of this bread and cheese. We can think about making tracks once you've eaten."

"I just hope he turns up tonight, John. I'm not sure I can do another night in this place."

"I know what you mean, but you're going to have to. Even if he does show tonight, it's only going to be a surveillance job. It could be a few nights yet before we make our move, so best just to accept the reality."

"I vote we just shoot him through the restaurant window and take our chances. Anything's better than another night in this hell hole."

"Would you prefer a Russian cell? Be serious, Dimitri, you know the whole shoot and run thing wouldn't work in this case. Get some food down you; you're going to need your strength."

CHAPTER FIFTY FOUR

Here we go again, Dimitri thought, as he parked his backside on the park bench opposite the restaurant for the second time in twenty-four hours. He had managed to secure the exact same car parking spot, only this time, John had come with him, and they had both made the short walk over to Petrovsky Park together.

John had been content to head straight to their stake out point this time, rather than going via the hotel, so they had made the trip across Moscow in good time, and were now stationed at the park bench, shortly after five p.m. Luckily for them, it was empty, though that probably had something to do with the freezing temperatures and icy winds driving through the city that late February evening.

"I've got a feeling this is the night, John. If Vlad's intel is correct, he's got to come and see her tonight, surely?"

"You would hope so," John murmured, unable to shake his scepticism.

They sat there for a while, patiently watching as the restaurant began to fill up. It was a lot busier than it had been the previous night, and by ten to six, over half the restaurant was already full. Then, it happened. Both men saw it at the same time. A black Rolls Royce pulled up outside the main entrance, and a mean looking man with a long black overcoat and short, slick black hair got out of the passenger side, before making his way around to the path facing rear door.

John could not quite make out what was happening, but he could guess, and a couple of moments later, his suspicions were confirmed, as Anna stepped out of the car. She was wearing an elegant, backless black dress, quite the contrast to her bodyguard's long overcoat, and her blonde locks flowed in waves down her back.

As the Rolls Royce drove away, Anna and her minder quickly made their way inside, and were promptly greeted by the maître d'. Anna was then shown to her table, nestled into the window with a fantastic view of the kitchen. The minder was not so fortunate, and made his way in the other direction, over to the bar area next to the entrance.

It seemed almost criminal to Dimitri that such a beautiful woman should be made to wait. "Unbelievable," he whispered to John. "Imagine making a girl like that wait for you."

"Shh," John replied. "I don't think she will have to wait long, look."

Dimitri looked back at the restaurant. An almost identical black Rolls Royce had pulled up outside the YAR, only this time, it had come from the opposite direction. Just as before, the passenger door was the first to open, and another of Alek's thugs got out. He did not look as imposing as the Anna's minder, but still looked as though he could handle himself.

"That must be his personal minder. Do you recognise him?" John asked.

273

"No, sorry, John. After my time. He looks a lot fitter and younger than us; must be a new kid on the block."

"Shh," John breathed quietly again, dismissing the fact that he had asked the question in the first place. "Look, he's getting out."

Standing less than two hundred metres from them, acting as though he did not have a care in the world, was the architect of this whole nightmare: Alek Malakov. Every muscle in John's body immediately stiffened, ready for battle, and an overwhelming feeling of nausea came over him as he finally laid eyes on the mastermind behind the attack on his family.

Alek stretched his six foot three frame out of the car and looked around the park, as if scanning for intruders. Dimitri felt a strong desire to duck out of his view, but managed to resist the temptation, trusting instead that their disguises and the distance between them would be sufficient to conceal their presence.

Alek took a second look around, and Dimitri felt sure he was onto them, but Alek simply shrugged and retreated into the restaurant. He was also greeted by the maître d', and escorted to the table where Anna was patiently waiting. The lovers embraced for an age, before eventually sitting down opposite each other and sharing a toast.

Alek's minder made his way over to the bar and spoke to Anna's guard for a moment, apparently relieving him of his duties, Anna's minder quickly made his way out of the restaurant, into the awaiting Rolls Royce, while Alek's man took up his place on the stool at the bar.

"Just one guard," Dimitri whispered excitedly.

"Jesus, this could be it. This is our chance."

"What do you mean John,? I thought we were just watching him tonight?"

"When are we ever going to get this close to him again, with only one bodyguard for protection? This is our chance; we have to act now."

CHAPTER FIFTY FIVE

John talked and Dimitri listened as they went through John's hastily designed plan.

"I don't think they will be in there for too long. You go and get the car, and bring it round to the entrance. Park it exactly where the Rolls pulled up. That will be my cue to walk over to you. Make sure you load two of the handguns from the arsenal in the back; just two, mind, and keep them small. With any luck, we can be in and out without even needing to use them. We don't want to cause mass hysteria in the restaurant, in and out quick, before anyone realises what's happening."

"Roger that, John. Do you want me to stay in the car?"

"No, leave it running outside and follow me in, a couple of paces behind. Make sure you go in separately, so it doesn't appear that we are together. When we get in, I will walk straight up to Alek's table and point the gun in Anna's face,, you go to the bar and sit next to Alek's minder, before he has chance to react. Make sure he knows you are there; stick your gun in his back or something."

"Works for me."

"I will persuade Alek that it is in his and Anna's best

interests to take a walk with me; your job is to make sure the minder is disarmed and on the floor. I will then get in the back with Alek. You leave last, jump straight into the car, and drive us away. Hopefully the whole thing will take less than a couple minutes."

"Where do you want me to head?"

"Straight back to the warehouse. We can talk to him there."

"But I thought you said we would be sitting ducks, John?"

"I know, but this way, we will catch them off guard and hopefully buy ourselves some time. It will take them a while to work out what's happened, and before they even start to think about tracking us down, we can do what we need to do. All we need is enough time to find out the truth, then we can then vanish into the wind. Now, go. The last thing we need is them skipping dessert and leaving early."

"See you inside, John. Good luck."

"Good luck, my friend. This is it, what we have both been waiting for. Let's not mess it up now."

CHAPTER FIFTY SIX

Dimitri drove up to the entrance as instructed, and pulled into the short stay parking zone. He glanced over the road and could see John already making his way towards him, so he wound down his window and readied himself for action. This needed to go exactly to John's plan, otherwise it could easily turn into a blood bath on the streets of Moscow, and create an international incident. A shootout involving an ex-FSB traitor, a British ex-spy and a Russian ex-general turned mafia boss would be global news, and had the potential to dwarf the fallout from even the Salisbury poisonings of 2018.

In theory, it was a simple extraction: one man; no mess; quick and efficient. But Dimitri knew that it would not be that easy. He hated working in public areas, and had enough experience to know that these sorts of operations rarely ran smoothly.

John approached the car a leaned in through the open window. "Ready?" he asked.

"Ready," Dimitri, passing John the P-96 pistol he had just loaded. John calmly placed it into his inside jacket pocket and continued his ascent toward the entrance. As he walked, he noticed that all the waiters were occupied with other tables, and knew this was the optimum time to make his move. Without breaking his stride he opened the glass door and walked across the restaurant, towards Alek's table.

As he drew nearer, he briefly glanced to his right, and saw that Dimitri was already out of the car and approaching the door himself. John calculated the distance that remained between him and his old adversary, and knew that Dimitri had more than enough time to enter the YAR, walk the couple of steps to the bar, sit down, and disable Alek's minder.

Anna was looking straight at John as he approached her table, but she had no idea who he was, or what he was about to do. Alek had his back to John and the rest of the restaurant, and was sniggering at something he had just said to Anna, blissfully ignorant of what was behind him. Now was the moment John had dreamed of almost constantly for over a week, and it momentarily crossed his mind that one squeeze of his trigger would end this nightmare once and for all.

He shook off the temptation; he knew that shooting Alek was not the right play. A public assassination was the last thing he needed to be dealing with; the authorities would be all over the scene in minutes. Making it out of Russia alive was going to be difficult enough; it would be almost impossible with the Russian police involved as well. It was a much better play to take Alek hostage and do the job properly back at the warehouse.

Anna was sitting bolt upright, looking straight into John eyes; it was impossible to tell whether she was frozen in fear or simply confused by his intentions. John was now close enough for Malakov to feel his breath on his neck, and Alek instinctively began to twist his head around in response.

The breath was quickly replaced with a cold sensation: a metal object pressing against the back of his immense neck. In that moment, it dawned on him. Someone had a gun pointing at his back.

John was the first to speak. "Don't even think about it, Alek. Hands on the table."

Anna realised last what was happening to her lover, and began to shriek.

"Shut her up, Alek, or I will do it for you." John responded coldly.

John's icy tone had done the trick without Alek needing to get involved, and Anna immediately fell silent.

"Shh, Anna. It's okay. I will deal with this intrusion," Alek said flippantly, hoping his bodyguard would come to their aid. But he was nowhere to be seen, and after a few more seconds elapsed, with the gun still firmly positioned against his neck, Alek realised he was on his own. He tried to make out the accent but could not quite place whom it belonged to. It must be someone from his past.

"What do you want? Money?" Alek asked, knowing already that this was not a robbery, but trying to flush out his adversary.

"No, Alek. I just need you to answer a few questions. Shall we take a walk?"

"John Steele? Is it really you?" Alek exclaimed softly, delighted to have solved the riddle.

"Yes, Alek. We can deal with the niceties later. Tell Anna you will be back soon, and to stay calm. Everything will be okay if you do as I say."

"Yes, John, of course. Where are we going, may I ask?"

"You will have to wait and see. Now, come on. Don't test me," John warned him, pressing the gun a little harder into Alek's neck.

"Okay, okay I'm getting up. Now, listen, my dear. John here is an old friend from my army days; it appears he would like to reminisce on old times, so don't be frightened. I will be back soon enough. You finish your dinner and go back to the hotel. There's a good girl."

John pressed the pistol deeper into Alek's flesh, as if to highlight the urgency of the situation, and began to push Alek discreetly through the restaurant. As they made their way through the slalom of tables to the main door, Alek could see his minder with both hands spread on the bar, and an apologetic look on his face. The man peering over him seemed vaguely familiar; no wonder his guard had failed to do his job when Alek had needed him most.

John negotiated the main door with his left hand, making sure to keep the gun firmly in Alek's lower back with his right, but Alek was unconcerned. All he could think of was the guy in the bar. He had seen him somewhere before; he knew him, but could not place him. He was not one of John's usual guys, but was obviously working with John now. Still, something didn't quite add up. His face was familiar, but the scenario did not fit. It was driving him mad.

A few seconds later, they were outside the restaurant, and John gestured for Alek to get into the old Punto waiting in front of them.

"Really, John? This piece of shit, isn't it bad enough me being your Zek, heh?"

"Shut up and get in, Alek." John's tone was menacing.

"Okay, as you wish. I just hope I don't get seen in this thing."

Alek was growing in confidence, and felt strangely pleased that John was his captor. He knew he could not be pushed too far, but all the same, John had a certain respect; a decency that many in the business did not. If this had to happen, at least he was working with professionals. He also knew that if John had wanted him dead then he would already be so; as long as he played ball, there was a good chance he would make it out of this alive!

Alek's private moment of reflection did not last long, as only a few more seconds elapsed before the man from the bar, John's assistant, came bursting into the car. He slammed the driver's door shut behind him and sped off, like a rally car driver starting his stint, chucking both men around in the back as he made his getaway.

All three men looked through the rear window in unison, to see if anyone was following, but to John's relief, there was no one.

"Well done, Dimitri," John congratulated his man.

In that moment, Alek realised who the second man was. Dimitri Gregorev. The plot thickens, he thought to himself.

CHAPTER FIFTY SEVEN

What the hell were John Steele and Dimitri Gregorev doing working in tandem, Alek thought as they drove through the streets of Moscow, his mood having changed considerably. His initial confidence had quickly dissipated by the revelation that Dimitri was involved; with John, he knew where he stood, but with Dimitri, things were always murkier.

Of the two, he despised Dimitri far more than John. John was just doing his job; he worked for the opposition, true, but he played by the rules, and Alek felt a degree of professional admiration towards him. Dimitri, on the other hand, was a different proposition entirely: a traitor that could not be trusted. Being held hostage by him had thrown Alek off balance.

"What brings you two unlikely comrades together then?" he asked, trying to appear unruffled. "We thought you had gone on the run, Dimitri, but it appears you have instead been working for the British."

"You, Alek. That's what has brought us together," Dimi replied, as he hurtled around the back streets of Moscow and towards the relative safety of the freeway. "And no, I'm not working for the British. This is a one-time-only deal. John asked me to help him get to you, and I guess it was just too good an opportunity to turn down."

"Why on earth would you want to get to me, John? I heard you retired, no?"

"You know why," Dimitri interrupted. "Now be quiet, Alek. We are the ones asking the questions, and when we get to where we are going, you will have plenty of time to tell us the answers."

"What questions? Where are you taking me, John?" Alek asked, sensing who was in charge of the mission. "Look, I can be reasonable, but you are starting to irritate me a little now. Tell me what has upset you, and I'm sure we can come to some sort of arrangement."

"Shut up, Alek," Dimitri exclaimed. "You are not in control here, so drop the nonsense. We want to ask you a few questions, no more, no less. Now, shut up, or I will let him loose on you, okay?"

Alek glanced at John, who had not said a word, and was shocked by the primal hatred that he saw in his eyes. John was not acting on behalf of MI6; this time, it was personal, and that unnerved Alek. He decided his best bet was to bide his time until he found out what they wanted. Then, perhaps, he could negotiate his way out of this mess.

CHAPTER FIFTY EIGHT

It took Dimitri twenty minutes to make it back to the safe house; he had been careful not to attract any unwanted attention on the way, knowing that they had successfully extracted Alek without his men having time to follow. He had deliberately kept to the speed limit on the freeway, and had parked inside the hanger, off the street, to shield their car from prying eyes. In all reality, their car was probably the only lead Alek's men would have to work from, so keeping it from view was priority number one.

Meanwhile, in the back, John had been busy disorientating his hostage, still not saying a word, preferring instead to focus his efforts on making the trip as uncomfortable as possible. The gag came first, more out of necessity than anything, to give them a rest from Alek's incessant questioning; then later, as they hit the freeway, the blindfold, designed to conceal their intended destination, in case Alek recognised anything on route.

Dimitri was confident that they had not been followed from the restaurant, and by the time he had locked the warehouse back up, Alek had fallen silent, accepting his immediate fate. John grabbed the nearest stool he could find and plunged him down into it, using the rope from the car to tie his feet to the chair legs and bind his wrists. He then removed the gag and blindfold, and waited for Alek to gather his composure.

"This is all a bit over the top, isn't it?" Alek complained almost immediately, still trying to exert some degree of influence over the situation. "Couldn't we have discussed this over dinner, instead of you bringing me here to the middle of god knows where."

John had still not said a word; he looked down at Alek and wondered when he would finally stop persisting with this ridiculous charade. His patience was wearing thin, but he deliberately took his time, keen not to show him his frustrations. Finding himself a stool, he sat himself down opposite Alek.

"Ready?" John finally said, looking squarely into Alek's eyes. "Good," he continued, after receiving a nod of acceptance from his target. "Tell me, Alek, why did you order the hit on my family?"

Alek's bravado evaporated in an instant. No wonder John had that look in his eye. "What are you talking about?" Alek responded, his voice thick with confusion.

"Cut the crap, Alek. My son is lying in an ICU bed as we speak, in a coma, because you ordered four men to come and assassinate me. Now, we can do this the easy way, or the hard way. All I need to know is why, and all this will be over."

"John, listen to me, I have no idea what you are talking about, I swear."

John looked Alek up and down again and got to his feet, glancing over at Dimitri then back again with a resigned, disappointed look on his face. "Okay, Alek. As you wish."

That was Dimitri's cue to walk over, and Alek was all too aware of what that meant.

"No, Dimitri, don't do this. I don't know anything about your family, John, I'm telling the truth. Why would I lie? I know what you are capable of. Please…"

Dimitri ignored Alek and slowly continued his approach. He was going to enjoy this; he wasn't a sadistic man by any means, but the chance to inflict a degree of revenge on the person who had ruined his life made the brutality of his actions feel a little less barbaric.

John walked to the back of the room. He could not afford to become too invested at this point. Besides, the sounds penetrating the hanger were enough to judge the right time to intervene, which eventually he did, calling a halt to proceedings and asking Alek the question for a second time.

"Alek, listen to me. I can make this all stop. Just tell me: why did you order the hit on my family?"

Alek's bloodied and beaten face dropped even further down, and an overwhelming feeling of helplessness consumed him as he finally started to realise the severity of the situation he had found himself in. "I have no idea what you are talking about, John. Please…"

Dimitri set about his victim for a second time, this time with more vigour; he was like a rabid dog, destroying his prey.

Eventually, John called an end to round two, this time walking up to Alek's by now almost unrecognisable face and whispering, "Talk to me, Alek. I'm not playing around this time. You crossed the line when you involved my kids, so believe me, I'm prepared to finish you right here right now myself if that's what it's going to take."

"What do you want to know, John," Alek pleaded, as he spat globules of blood from his mouth. "I understand, honestly I do. I know what it's like to lose a son; you more than anyone know that. I know you are not messing around. What do you want, ask me, and I will tell you?"

"Why did you order the hit, Alek? And were you working alone?"

"No, John, I promise. Why would I? I've only just ended one war with the British, why would I want to start another one now?"

John paused for a second. It was either desperation or honesty in Alek's voice; he could not quite decide which.

"Bullshit," Dimitri interjected. "He's not going to talk, John. Let's just shoot him and get out of here, while we still can."

"No, wait, Dimitri. Let's try this another way. What do you know, Alek? Let's start with how you managed to worm your way out of Belmarsh. That seems like as good a place as any to start."

"That I can tell you. It was Andrei; he managed to negotiate my release."

"As easy as that, was it? What did he offer though, Alek? I can't imagine MI6 were all that receptive to the idea of releasing a known terrorist that they had spent years tracking down in the first place?"

"It all happened by chance, really. Andrei had been digging around ever since my sentence in 2010, trying to find some leverage that he could use to get me home. I never really thought it was going to happen; I told him

288

every time we spoke to forget about me, but he wouldn't have it. He came up with all sorts of ideas, but I never really took much notice, until one day, he came to me and said that a file had fallen on his lap from someone inside the British secret services."

"Haditha," Dimitri exclaimed. "It always comes back to Haditha."

"How do you know about that, Dimitri? Until you mentioned your family, John, I assumed that was the reason you had come over here, to scare me off. But now I haven't got a clue why you're here, and I certainly have no idea about your family, honestly."

"Slow down, Alek. What do you mean, scare you off?"

"I mean, when I got back to Moscow, I rolled the dice again. I threatened them with going public; blackmailed them if you like. I even threatened to involve you, John, in the scandal, but I didn't expect them to take me seriously. Involving you was a complete shot in the dark; looks like I was onto something though."

"Blackmail who? The British government? Why did you think my name would resonate?"

"Yes, your government, and your precious MI6. I knew you were in charge over there at that time, and remembered that Dimitri suspected you were more involved than you let on. So, I tried my hand again, to see if I got lucky; involving you was designed to imply that we had more than we actually did. Looks like it worked."

"So, you actually have nothing on me at all?"

"Just my instincts, and Dimitri's suspicions. You have to understand: that file got me released from a life sentence; I knew we had something big."

"Did they ever bother to check your intelligence?"

"No, it was all smoke and mirrors. The file was the catalyst, and they got seriously jumpy. I added the chemical weapons bit more in hope than expectation, and went for it. By the time they had recovered the original file, I was back in Russia with my family."

"Jesus," Dimitri murmured.

"Keep going, Alek, it's an interesting tale. Still doesn't tell me who shot my son though, does it?"

"Listen, I didn't have anything to do with that. Can I have a drink of water? I told you we could have sorted this back at the restaurant; this way is so old fashioned."

"No water yet. Keep going; then, maybe, you'll get a drink."

Alek sighed. "Andrei had been trying to infiltrate MI6 for years, as had the FSB for that matter, but I never gave him much of a chance. Then, one day, he came across a low-level vetting guy, who had got into a bit of scrape with some of our muscle, running our casino in London. He owed us a lot of money, and Andrei offered him a one-time deal: get us some leverage, and he would dissolve the debt. I really just wanted some creature comforts in my cell; I never dreamed I would get out."

"So, he gave Andrei Haditha, did he?"

"Exactly, though neither Andrei nor the gambler really knew what it was; what it meant. It was just an old, classified file that fitted the period Andrei had asked for. They thought it might buy me a better cell or something, that is, until it fell into my hands of course. I read the file and remembered that Dimitri had been doing some digging about something similar, back in 2008, something about the British and a hidden chemical lab. He went to you with it, as I recall, and you assured him it was bogus. I didn't realise at the time how cosy you two had become, of course, otherwise I might have asked for a second opinion. When I saw the photos of the lab, and everything in the file, I put two and two together and took a punt. The files didn't expressly disclose what the lab was for, but I went for it anyway, and we concocted our own story about chemical weapons being made in Haditha. Turns out we were right."

"Go on, what happened to the vetting guy?"

"We dealt with him; gang incident outside our casino, according to the papers. Andrei arranged to hand over the files, and they flew me back home. It seemed the file alone, along with our version of events, was enough to spook them, and they bought it. I couldn't believe it, to be honest with you."

"Very clever, Alek," Dimitri interrupted. "Until you got greedy, hey?"

"I suppose so, yes. After I got back home, it only took a few weeks for me to realise that there was plenty more to be gained from this particular piece of intel. You see, our business interests in London bring in almost one hundred million pounds a year, but I suspected Haditha was worth a lot more to your government than that. So, I was prepared to risk our diplomatic benefits for one big pay out."

"How much Alek, go on…"

"One billion pounds, to be exact."

"Jesus Christ. You really tried to bribe the British government out of one billion, there is no way in hell they would have that kind of money, let alone pay it to you!"

"You know that and I know that my friend, but what

was the harm in trying, I just used the leverage I had over them to extract the maximum possible result! I had all the cards in this hand particular hand after all my boy."

"But why did you think they would go for the same trick twice, Alek?"

"Ah, that's where you came in, and I suspect why they sent you here now, personally. I added your name into the mix, and it was like dynamite. I'm still not sure why, John, but you seem to be inextricably linked to this Haditha place. I suspect they sent you to me on purpose, to either shut me up or get killed trying; either way, the problem goes away. It seems you are expendable after all, John."

"They didn't send me, Alek. I came off my own back."

"Did you really? It seems you have been played yourself, my friend. Consider, for a moment, that it wasn't me who ordered the hit on you. Who else would have the motive and means to try such a thing? I don't know any details, clearly, but I'm guessing it was Russians that entered your house, am I right?"

"Yes, four of them."

"Do you think I would be so vulgar, John? If I were to attempt to assassinate you, I would hardly use four of my own men. I suspect, John, that you have been led down the garden path, as you British say. Maybe it was in their interest for you to suspect me; you come after me, and do their job for them. Can I ask you a question now, John? In fact, two, if I may?"

"Go on."

"What exactly do you know about Haditha? And would they be willing to kill you to stop what you know coming from out? If I'm right, John, then I suspect you will find your attackers not so far from home after all. Which leads me to my final question; what exactly are you going to do about it?"

CHAPTER FIFTY NINE

John paused the conversation there, having given Alek the floor for long enough. He needed a few moments to digest what he had just heard, and to make sense of the ramifications, if Alek was indeed correct. There were still a couple of things that he wanted to understand before he could completely accept the truth, but his gut was already telling him there was something in Alek's accusations.

"What about the flowers then, Alek?"

"What flowers? I have no idea what you are talking about, John."

"Someone sent a bunch of flowers to the hospital, saying 'thinking of our sons'."

"Not me. Again, I ask you, why would I go to all the trouble of concealing my identity in the first place, only to then signpost you directly to me when the attack failed. It makes no sense, John. I think you are starting to see what I see, aren't you? Sometimes, you just can't see the wood from the trees, especially when it's personal. From the outside looking in, it's a lot clearer."

John was fast running out of objections, and the ugly truth was becoming clear. Someone had simply manipulated him from the beginning; they had indulged his original theory, formulated under intense stress, and had given him little need to look anywhere else. The reality was slowly dawning on him: the multi layered attack, designed with meticulous intent to conceal the real perpetrators; the back up plans, put in place in case the operation was not a success; the subtle intel dropped in here and there, to make sure John stayed on track. It was all the work of professionals, but who?

Once John's course was set, all they had needed to do was sit back and watch the action unfold. It was almost the perfect plan, designed to kill many birds with one stone, and would have worked if not for John's gut instinct, and Alek's ability to talk himself out of trouble!

"Get down now!" Dimitri yelled from the back of the hanger out of the blue.

John leapt to the floor, reacting instinctively to his comrades warning, he quickly stood his mattress on its side and knelt behind it, hoping the thick bedding would offer some cover. Dimitri dived into the back of the old Fiat and started loading weapons, throwing them in John's direction.

"What is it? What have you seen?"

"It will be Andrei," Alek announced calmly, despite looking completely beaten up. "We have access to the city's CCTV, you see. It was only a matter of time before he tracked us down."

"John, what do we do?" yelled Dimitri, his voice laced with panic.

John had barely a chance to respond before the first shots were fired, directed predominantly towards the front door and the two padlocks: the only defence standing between them and Alek's thugs.

In what seemed like a matter of seconds, the locks had been shot off, and the doors flung open, to reveal the enemy out in the courtyard. Alek was right; it was his son, Andrei, and from what Dimitri could see, there were two other hitmen beside him.

"Why the hell has he come in all guns blazing?" John asked rhetorically while still taking cover.

"I'm afraid my son's a bit hot headed my friend, shoot now ask questions later type of attitude! Its always troubled me a bit to be honest." Was Alex's unwelcome response?

For what seemed like hours, the bullets continued to shower down on them, and it was John who took the first hit, deep in his right thigh, enough to take him down. He winched in pain, blood flowing freely from the wound, but he still somehow managed to drag himself up to where Dimitri was holding station. The pair stuck it out for as long as they could, but it was no use; they were overwhelmed, and cornered. It was only a matter of time before they would be over run.

Briefly, the firing paused, as Andrei and his men reloaded their weapons, preparing for another assault on the warehouse.

John saw an opportunity. "Cover me, Dimitri. I'm going to dive over to the hay bales in the courtyard and see if I can get a better angle."

"Roger that, John. Three, two, one, go!"

John leapt out of the warehouse and dived behind one of the bales, taking a couple of air shots in the process. Carefully, he crawled around the other side of the bale and ripped off another round, the last bullet striking one of the hitmen in his left temple, and swiftly exiting through his right.

One down, two to go, Dimitri thought, and instinctively seized the mantel, walking out of the warehouse like someone from a spaghetti western; a submachine gun in both hands, he fired indiscriminately in the general direction of Andrei and his friend, continuing his attack until both weapons were exhausted, and he had nothing left to offer.

In that moment, it dawned on him that he was still standing, and that no one was firing back at him. Were they dead? He quickly checked his limbs for injury, and was delighted to find himself still in one piece.

Then a haunting scream broke the silence. Alek! He had not only just witnessed the death of another son, but with it had also come to the realisation he now had no hope of getting out of this alive. Dimitri looked on at Alek, feeling almost sympathetic to his arch enemies pain, it became clear to him in that moment that killing Alek now would actually be an act of mercy.

But before he dealt with Alek, Dimitri needed to check on John, making sure to first check on the bodies of the three dead intruders. He eventually reached the bale behind which John was hidden, quickly ripped off his shirt and tied it around John's leg, trying to stem the blood that was pouring from his partner's wound.

"How's it look?" John asked weakly, falling in and out of consciousness.

"You'll be fine, John," Dimitri lied; what else could he say? The bullet had clearly hit John's femoral artery, and there was nothing Dimitri could do. He took a moment to assess his options, picked up John's gun, and walked back into the warehouse,

Alek saw him coming, and knew this was the end; he did not even try to stop him. "Do it, Dimitri, please. Put me out of my misery."

Dimitri lifted the handgun, took aim, and fired straight between his adversary's eyes.

"No!" John yelled, his surprise giving him a sudden burst of energy. "He didn't need to die."

"Don't be silly, John, of course he did. He would never have forgiven us for killing his last remaining son; he would have hunted us down like pigs. I had to do it; this way, I've got a chance. Surely you can see that?"

"What about me?" John asked, afraid of the answer.

"I'm sorry, John, I really I am. But another bus full of Alek's men will be here any minute, and I can't take you with me, not with that leg. I'm sorry, my friend, but this is where it ends."

John closed his eyes, resigning himself to his fate. He had always known that Dimitri was only in it for his own ends; besides, he was right. There was no way he was getting out of here with this wound.

As the blood loss caught up with him, he drifted off again, and his family appeared by his side: Ethan, Amy and Wendy. The vision of his family dissolved his pain and anxiety, and all he felt was an overarching feeling of peace and tranquillity. Seconds later, his utopia was disturbed by an engine starting up in the background. He managed to force his eyes open one last time, just long enough to watch Dimitri and the old Fiat Punto, disappear in a wave of dust.

CHAPTER SIXTY

Byrne was relived to be back on solid ground, even if it was foreign ground. The plane had landed on time, and he had made it through customs relatively smoothly. He adjusted his watch – it was just after six p.m. local time – and began to scour the car park for his ride. He felt unashamedly excited to finally be out in the field again, not to mention he was eagerly anticipating his first face-to-face meeting with his Russian asset. He knew what she looked like, and had been in regular communication with her for many years, but all the same, this felt like a momentous occasion.

Yvette was waiting outside Pushkin International airport for her long time handler to make his appearance. After their most recent phone call, she had felt compelled to help him, and the fact that the legendary John Steele was in her city, and in need of support, felt like more than just coincidence. She would not let her country down now.

She watched the 'arrivals' window from the safety of her Lada Vesta, and immediately spotted her man: the ginger hair and long overcoat were unmistakably English. No wonder he had spent his entire career behind a desk; he would not have lasted five minutes undercover.

A brown Lada Vesta approached Byrne, and he assumed the flashing headlights were the sign he had been waiting for. Byrne was slightly frazzled by the whole experience, but decided to roll with it, especially when he noticed it was a woman driving towards him. He took a deep breath and approached the car with caution; this was going to be the most significant twenty-four hours of his career, perhaps even his entire life.

"Yvette?"

"Yes, get in, Colin. I can't stop here."

Byrne hurried to the passenger side and tossed his rucksack in the back, "Pleased to finally meet you, Yvette. Thank you so much for doing this."

Yvette was a Russian citizen who had been recruited straight out of Moscow University, having been flagged as a potential defector by MI6, due to her strong anti-government stance on social media and regular attendance at socialist conventions.

Despite this online persona, she had also been snapped up by the FSB at around the same time, owing to her excellent English and expertise in Western Politics. It appeared to Byrne that she had been deliberately ambiguous in her convictions from the start; she was made for the life, and had clearly justified her adolescent behaviour sufficiently well to convince the powers that be to hire her.

Byrne had to admit that he still had no real idea where she stood politically. He wanted, perhaps needed, to trust her now, more than ever before, and that made things feel a great deal more uncomfortable. If she had been lying low all these years, hiding in plain sight, a double agent all this time, then this sort of operation would be exactly what she had been waiting for. However, he doubted that was the reality, and comforted himself with the memories of her service over the years, and all nuggets of information she had passed his way. Still... she had never given him anything major; anything that would risk giving her away, so to speak. No, his mind was playing tricks on him. She had always come good when he needed her, and had probably saved his job on several occasions, not to mention helped the government stay informed on Putin's latest whims and desires.

Byrne eventually reverted back to his initial conclusion, put it out of his mind, and set to work. "No time to settle in I'm afraid, Yvette. We need to get straight over to John; he has been dark now for nearly two days so I'm getting concerned. Here, can you drive us to this place? It's the warehouse he was meant to be basing his operation from."

Yvette read the postcode off the napkin Byrne had just passed her, plugged it into her satnav, and waited for the response. "No problem. It's over the other side of the city though, Colin, so it will take a while, especially at this time of night. I hope you're ready for a long car ride."

CHAPTER SIXTY ONE

Yvette was right; it took them forever to get through the rush hour traffic, and it was approaching seven thirty p.m. by the time they finally pulled up outside their destination.

"You wait here while I check it out, Yvette, okay?"

"Sure. I will turn the car around and keep the motor running, just in case."

"Good idea," Byrne murmured, as he stepped out of the car, completely out of his depth and not knowing what to expect.

He did not have to wait long to find the answer; the moment he walked around the corner and into the courtyard, the worst of all the scenarios he had imagined on the flight over lay before him.

John was stretched flat on his back in the courtyard, a river of blood flowing around him; his body still and lifeless. Byrne rushed up to the body to check for any signs of life, forgetting for a moment the danger he could be running straight into, though he quickly realised that he had missed all the action. The place was eerily silent, and as he scanned the area, it soon became apparent that something crazy had just gone down. Dead bodies lay splayed all over the floor, and one man sat bolt upright in a chair, having been subjected to what looked like a horrific execution.

Colin checked John's wrist for a pulse. Nothing. He tried again on his neck. This was not the way he had imagined things would play out; all of a sudden, he was missing his comfy chair and walnut standard edition desk.

"Take a deep breath, Colin; slow down; take your time; think," he kept repeating to himself, trying John's neck one more time. Was there something? Something very faint perhaps, or was he just desperately clutching at straws? Either way, he was not going to leave him here.

He rushed back to the roadside and signalled for Yvette to pull the car round quickly, before running back to his friend. He threw one of John's tree trunk arms over his shoulder, and pulled with all his might. After what seemed like an eternity, he made it to the Vesta, opened the back door, and dumped John inside.

"Drive, Yvette! For fucks sake, drive, will you?"

"Shit, is he dead?"

"I don't know; just get us the hell out of here, as fast as you can." Byrne demanded, as he slammed the passenger door shut.

"Where though, Colin?

"You tell me, you live here. Just get us there fast, will you?"

"Okay, okay. I will drive us to my flat, that's the only place I can think of, but it will blow our cover…"

"I don't really give a shit about our cover at the minute, Yvette. We can't leave him here to die. Take us to your place; we will deal with the consequences later."

CHAPTER SIXTY TWO

He opened an eye, trying to adjust his blurry vision. no idea where he was, and no recollection of what had just happened to him. As he looked around, his second eye joining the first, a feeling of complete disorientation overwhelmed him.

He glanced down the bed and saw his right leg bandaged heavily, attached to a pully system above him. His hands were slashed and bloody, but all of his fingers seemed to be working properly. The rest of his body felt nothing but pain; it felt like he had been hit by a bus.

"Nurse? Nurse?" he rasped. He was not sure why he had shouted 'nurse', but he knew he was hurt, so it seemed fitting. As he looked around the room, he noted that it did not look like a typical hospital room. There were no other patients around him for a start; the room dark and dingy; the curtains were closed tight, and only the small lamp in the corner offered any light at all.

The door opened sharply, and a man rushed in. "John, you're awake, thank God!"

"Byrne?" John replied shakily, as he recognised his friend. He was pleased to see a familiar face, but also conscious that Byrne did not fit the scenario he had imagined himself him. He considered, for a moment, that he might be dreaming, or worse. "What… were am I? What's going on?" he finally managed to ask.

"Don't worry for now, John. I'm just pleased you are awake. Just take your time coming around; we'll go through everything later. Yvette, could you fetch John some tea?"

"What are you doing here, Byrne? Where am I? Am I back in England?"

"No, I'm afraid not, John. I will explain everything all in good time. You have been through a lot, my old friend, but you are safe now. You need to rest."

Yvette returned to the room a few minutes later, holding the cup of tea Byrne had requested, plus a couple of biscuits. "Here you go, John."

"First things first, John. This is Yvette; we are in her flat in Moscow. She is one of us; I'm her handler, and have been for years."

"Thank you, Yvette. It's good to meet you."

"When I hadn't heard from you for a second full day, I panicked, I guess. I had almost run out of options, but I wasn't about to abandon you, not after all we have been through. So, I decided I needed to come to Russia and find you. Honestly, John, Yvette was just about the only person alive that I thought might actually be able to help. I phoned her yesterday and told her the whole story. I prayed she would actually give a damn, and luckily for us, she did, otherwise I'm pretty sure you would be dead now, John."

John looked up at Yvette and nodded gratefully.

"I knew she could at least offer us shelter if we needed it," Byrne continued. "She has been stationed here in Moscow for over ten years, the last five of which she had spent working as a secretary inside the FSB.

305

Honestly, John, one day I will tell you the stories; over the last few years, she has almost single handed provided us with all of our intel on Putin. She has been so important in the fight to prevent another Cold War that I had to think long and hard before I decided to involve her in this, and risk blowing her cover. But in the end, I had to. I couldn't leave you to die over here, and I couldn't see any other way of getting you out. It seemed to me that you had bitten off more than even you could chew, and when we lost contact, I decided I wasn't going to sit back and take it lying down."

"Thanks for the vote of confidence, Byrne," John grimaced.

Byrne smiled. "When I finally made the call to her and explained what was happening, she said she was compelled to help us. She organised me a diplomatic Russian passport, and I booked the flight. As soon as I landed, she picked me up and we drove straight to the warehouse; it was the last place you said you were headed before you went dark, so I figured it was as good a place as any to start. We found you just in the nick of time, I reckon. You were in a bad way, my friend, and the scene looked like something from a horror movie."

"I don't remember…"

"It's okay, you will. Your job is to build up your strength so that we can get out of here, okay? Focus on that."

"Where even are we, Byrne?"

"We are in Moscow, John. I told you, this is Yvette's flat; it's the only place we could think of that would buy us some time. We need to get you fit again, and figure out how the hell to get us all back home."

"I don't remember, Colin. I don't even know why

306

I'm in Moscow…"

"Don't worry, John, temporary amnesia following a traumatic experience is normal."

"What traumatic experience, Colin? For fucks sake, what happened to me?"

"All in good time, my friend. Please trust me; you need to rest now. Get some sleep and we'll talk again later. I'll be in the other room if you need me."

John desperately wanted to go against Byrne's advice, but was helpless to resist. He was hooked up to some kind a leg brace contraption for a start; had tubes coming out of every orifice, and felt incredibly drowsy all of a sudden.

Byrne stepped into the kitchen area opposite, where Yvette was busying herself with the dishes.

"He is looking sleepy again, now; I think the tablets have done the trick. Let's see how long he sleeps, and then I will tell him"

"Do you think it's wise, in his condition?"

"I'm not sure we have much choice, Yvette. We need to get out of here, fast. It's only a matter of time before they track us down; when did you say you have to go back into work again?"

"Monday."

"Right. We have three more days to get him ready to move and organise our extraction. Time is definitely ticking."

CHAPTER SIXTY THREE

Over the next few hours, very little happened inside Yvette's one bedroom flat. John slept soundly, and Byrne withdrew from conversation, preferring to sit alone and prepare himself for the days that lay ahead. Outside their bubble, the real world was another matter entirely. It seemed from the news that the whole of Moscow had gone into a state of emergency lockdown, following a terrorist attack in Red Square the night previous.

Although Byrne felt deep sympathy for the hundred or so lives that had been lost, and the thousands of people who had been injured in the attack, he could not help but think that this attack might have just bought them the time they needed. The murder of a well-known Mafia boss and his associates had certainly been knocked from the front pages in the last twenty-four hours; all of Russia seemed to have bigger things to worry about, for now.

Unfortunately, the attack in Red Square had brought with it new problems. The terrorist attack and the murders of Alek and Andrei were not considered connected in the news snippets he had read, but the police had launched a city wide man hunt for any additional culprits still hiding out in the city. The two men who had blown up the van in Red Square had been found, dead at the scene, but this had not quelled the country's thirst for blood, and Byrne was all too aware that it would not look good if the three of them were found, hauled up in Yvette's flat. If only someone would just take credit for organising the attack, then hopefully at least the search of the city might be called off.

It was approaching ten p.m. before John stirred again, and both Colin and Yvette rushed to his side, eager to witness some improvement in his health.

"How are you feeling now, my friend?"

"Okay, Byrne, thanks. Can I have a drink? My mouth is so dry."

"Of course," Yvette replied, rushing off to the kitchen.

John sat up in his bed and gathered his thoughts for a moment. "Right, Byrne. Tell me everything. I need to know what's going on."

"Okay, I will. But you need to take it easy, John. Some of this might be upsetting, and you are not out of the woods yet."

"Hit me."

Byrne paused for a minute, collecting his thoughts, then began to tell the story all over again. "Well, this all started about ten days ago, back in England. Someone attacked you in your home, John."

John stared directly into Byrne's eyes, and Byrne could see the anger raging inside of him.

"I remember that... I remember... Jesus, how's Ethan? How's my son? What the fuck am I doing here? I need to be with him and Wendy—"

"Ethan's doing fine, John, calm down. We are hiding

309

in Moscow, how do you expect us to get back to the UK?"

John seemed to calm down a little. "Shit, I remember now. Malakov, that's why I'm here, isn't it? That's why I left Ethan to come here. Where is he, Byrne? Have you got him? And where's Dimitri?"

Byrne could see John's memory was slowly returning, so refrained from going into any further details for now. Instead, he focused on the task at hand: getting themselves the hell out of Russia. "John, trust me, I'm working on getting us out, and you back to Ethan. I've got all the answers you need, but they are going to have to wait. We need you to focus on building up your strength. As soon as you are strong enough, we can leave, but telling you too much too quickly might set you back, and we haven't got that kind of time."

"What do you mean? Stop talking in riddles, Byrne. Why can't we just fly back home?"

"Not an option now, I'm afraid. A lot has happened in the last couple of days; things are more complicated than you realise, John. I will fill you in, I promise, but first you need to listen. There is something more important I need to tell you; it will help you put it all together."

Yvette popped her head around the corner and could see that she had interrupted at an intense moment. She ducked down under the eye line of the men and handed John a glass of water and a sandwich. Almost apologetically, she took a seat at the end of her own bed, giving Byrne the nod to carry on.

John threw a concerned look over at Byrne.

"It's okay, John. She can be trusted. We are all on the same side here. Now, listen. This may be difficult for

310

you to hear, after everything you have been through. I'm not really sure how to say this, so I'm just going to go for it. I've worked it out, John. It wasn't Malakov who placed the hit on your family."

"Why do you think that, Byrne?"

"The identities of the two paramedic guys who entered your house came back as bogus; they had entered the country from Moscow via Dusseldorf three days previous, as we thought, but they were not sent by Malakov, or any other Russian for that matter. That's just what you were supposed to think. My guy at HQ gave me the heads up before it all got retracted. They weren't Russian at all, just made to look that way so we would suspect Malakov."

"Wait, I know… I know this, Byrne," John tried to contribute, but Byrne was no longer listening, too wrapped up in the enormity of his own discovery.

"Shh, John, listen to me, it's important. There's more…"

"Yes, I know there is more, Byrne. I remember it all now. You are right; it wasn't Malakov at all, he told me as much back at the warehouse when… shit, he's dead isn't he?"

"Yes, John. I'm afraid he is."

"And Dimitri… he left me there to die, fuck, I remember. That treacherous bastard…"

"Now stop right there, John," Yvette demanded. "You can't afford to be getting this wound up. Your blood pressure is too high. You two need to stop now, otherwise you will go back into shock again, John. Here, take these. We will pick this up again in the morning."

"Yvette's right, John. At least we are all on the same page now, and its great news that your memory is back.

Now, lay down and focus on getting stronger. As soon as you're ready, we can start to plan our evac. We need some leverage to convince Redcalf to bring us in; that won't be easy mind, he doesn't even know I'm here yet... but that can all wait, my friend. You rest up, and we will talk tomorrow."

John gazed up at his to accomplices and found he had little energy to argue; those tablets Yvette had given him were making it difficult to keeps his eyes open, let alone focus on a plan of escape.

Yvette noticed the drugs taking effect and quickly ushered Colin out of the bedroom.

"Shh, Colin, he's going again. Let's get into the living room and start to think about a plan of action. We can fill him in when he wakes up."

CHAPTER SIXTY FOUR

On Friday morning, at 8.13 a.m., to be precise, Byrne woke to the sound of Yvette humming the tune of 'I dreamed a dream' from Les Misérables in the kitchen. It was certainly not the worst way to wake up, he had to admit.

"Morning," he called from the living room. It felt strange; he had been alone for so long, it felt strange greeting someone this early.

"Morning," came Yvette's tuneful reply.

"Is he still asleep?"

"Yes, he is," she said, walking into his room and sitting on the end of the sofa where he had been sleeping. "And I have other news. Look, watch this," she added, turning on the TV in the corner of the room.

Colin watched intently as the news presenter went through the stories of the day. He had caught the back end of the main story, but quickly gathered why Yvette was so keen for him to take a look.

"Jesus, Yvette, the Ukrainian Nationalists have claimed credit for the attack. That's massive."

"I know, but how does it affect us? Will they call off the man hunt now, do you think?"

"Better than that, this might just be our ticket out of

here."

"I don't understand... you said the two events were unconnected?"

"Yes, they are, well, almost are. Come on, let's wake John up and I'll fill you both in on the good news at the same time."

"What good news? John is right, you do talk in riddles."

"Perhaps I do, but this will be worth the wait, I assure you. Would you mind making our patient some breakfast? I will go in and wake him up."

Byrne bounced into John's makeshift hospital room and gently informed him that it was time to wake up. He need not have bothered; the creaking of the bedroom door had been more than enough to disturb John's light sleep.

"What do you want, Byrne? Can't you see I'm asleep?"

"Sorry, John, but I have some good news for you, something that will cheer you up. Yvette is making you a spot of breakfast, to build up your strength; when she comes in, I will reveal all."

"Will you stop banging on about building my strength, Byrne? I'm quite strong enough now. What is it?"

"Yvette, are you ready?"

"Yes, coming," came the instant response.

Seconds later, Yvette walked into the room with a plate of poached eggs on toast and a cup of tea for John, along with two more tablets of those painkillers she had been using to knock him out.

Byrne looked on enviously; he could have murdered eggs on toast right now.

"Thank you, Yvette, you're very kind. But I won't be taking any more of those tablets. They send me off into the craziest of sleeps. If we are going to get out of this, you'll need me firing on all cylinders, don't you agree?"

John quickly polished off his breakfast, not leaving so much as a crumb for Byrne. He certainly looked more like his old self now, Colin thought, as he prepared to reveal his latest great revelation.

"So, the Ukrainian Nationalists have claimed credit for the terrorist attack in Red Square, and Vlad has issued some message stating that 'Sevastopol is, and always will be, Ukrainian'."

Yvette was first to speak, as John's brain quickly flashed back to his chapter with Vlad and the Ukrainian Nationalists in Kyiv.

"I don't get it, why is that such good news for us? Can some please tell me?"

John explained. "It's good news, Yvette, because the Ukrainian Nationalists helped me enter the country."

"Exactly, my friend. Vlad and his little army helped John and Dimitri get into Moscow. He and Dimitri entered disguised as corpses, in the back of the same van that went on to blow up half of Red Square."

"I still don't understand," Yvette replied, looking puzzled. "How does that help us? Surely that just implicates John in the attack?"

"I'm sure it would if the Russians still needed to find the perpetrator. But you see, since the terrorists died at the scene, and they now know who was behind the whole thing, they won't be looking anywhere else."

"So, you think Vlad's confession has taken the heat off us? I still don't understand how that helps us get out of Moscow." Yvette sounded frustrated now.

"Yes, Byrne," John chimed in. "How exactly does this help us escape?"

"Don't you see, John? Redcalf is going to get us out."

"What are you talking about? Redcalf refused to involve MI6 when this first broke, long before the terrorist attack, and long before Malakovs death. Why would he help us now? You must have heard of collateral damage, Byrne? That's us, I'm afraid."

"No, John, you're looking at this all wrong. Redcalf is going to send the cavalry in to save us."

"What?"

"Because, if he doesn't, and we do get picked up, it will most probably start World War Three, and Redcalf can't risk that. All it will take is a call from me, telling him that you are linked to the attack, and he will have to get us out. What do you think Putin will do if he finds three British spies stuck inside Moscow, three days after a major terrorist incident in Red Square? Plus, you travelled into the country inside that van, your DNA is going to be all over it. If they get so much as a hint of British involvement, the evidence will be easy to find; it won't end well for us, sure, but it will be even worse for Redcalf, and he won't take that risk."

"Shit, Byrne, you're right. He has no choice but to get us out; he can't run the risk of being exposed."

"Exactly. Now, try and get yourself up and see if you can walk on that leg. I will make the call, give Redcalf the good news."

CHAPTER SIXTY FIVE

"Put me through to Redcalf, please?" Byrne politely asked Sarah, MI6's long serving receptionist.

"I'm afraid he's unavailable at the moment, can I take a message?"

"No message, tell him it's Byrne, and I'm in Moscow with John Cooper. That should get him on the line."

"Okay, please hold, Colin."

Byrne was enjoying himself, soaking in the unexpected power and forgetting his precarious situation for a moment.

After a few moments, Redcalf joined the call. "Byrne, is that you? Where the hell have you been? Are you really in Moscow?"

"Yes, sir. I'm okay, thank you for asking, sir," he replied sarcastically. "I'm in one of our safe houses in Moscow, with John and our Russian asset, Yvette."

"Fucking hell, Byrne, what do you think you are doing? Get out of there, now, it's not safe. Haven't you seen the news?"

"Yes, sir, we have; that's why I'm phoning you. We need you to organise an extraction team. John is badly wounded, so it will need to be an air evac. Oh, and we will also need to bring Yvette back with us."

"Absolutely not, Byrne, are you out of your mind?"

"No, sir, quite the opposite. You see, you really need to help us; if we get picked up in Moscow, it's not going to look good at all."

"Exactly, Byrne, that's why you are on your own, I'm afraid. We can't be seen to be involved in any of this, especially straight after a terror attack in the city. I haven't sent you in; you went of your own accord, and John has been working without our consent all along. I'm sorry, Colin, but you are on your own I'm afraid. Putin is on the warpath at the minute, so try not to get caught. Good luck, Colin. Now, I've got to go. I can't be seen anywhere near this mess."

"But I've got more news, sir, good and bad."

"Quickly, Colin. I really shouldn't be talking to you."

"Malakov and his son are both dead."

"Yes, we know that already. John, I assume? Unfortunately, it doesn't change the reality, does it? We didn't send him, in fact, I expressly forbid him from going into Russia under any circumstances, so I won't come in now and clear up his mess."

"I thought you might be of that mind, sir. That's where the bad news comes in."

"What are you talking about, Colin?"

"If you don't help us, then it's only a matter of time before we get picked up."

"Yes, I appreciate that, Byrne, but as I said…"

"I heard you. The thing is, sir, I don't think you have thought this through properly. When we do get rounded up, it will only be a matter of time before they break us and force us to tell them why we are here, and once Putin finds out John was smuggled into Russia inside the van that the Ukrainian Nationalists used to bomb

Red Square, God only knows what he will do. Like you say, he is on the warpath. He has already attacked Ukraine, who's to say the UK won't be next in the firing line?"

"What are you talking about, man? Have you gone completely insane?"

"No, sir. You see, John's DNA is all over that vehicle; that's how he got into Russia in the first place, in the back of the vehicle that we now know went on to kill hundreds of Russian citizens in Red Square. So, I would say, sir, that it's in all our interests to get out of here before we get caught. Under interrogation, we would eventually have to give up the intel, and that would destroy your 'plausible deniability' defence. With that evidence, Putin would have a field day; the whole world would have no choice but to see it his way: that the British government and the Ukrainian Nationalists have been conspiring to attack Russia."

Colin paused, waiting for the bombshell to fully drop. The silence on the end of the line was encouraging enough, and he knew Redcalf would be frantically running through it all in his mind, desperately searching for a way out.

"Byrne, this is an absolute disaster. I can't tell you how damaging this could be for our country. If we do get you out, and I'm not saying we will, when you get back here, you are still going to have to face the consequences, don't think you won't."

"Yes, sir, I understand," Byrne replied, content that he had landed enough blows for now.

"Sit tight, for now. I will make a few calls, and get back to you on this number. I assume it's secure? Please tell me that, at least?"

"Yes, sir, it's clean. I look forward to hearing back from you soon."

Byrne put down the handset, removed the jamming device Yvette had given him, and walked back into the bedroom, the smile on his face telling John and Yvette all they needed to know.

CHAPTER SIXTY SIX

For the next few hours, the atmosphere in Yvette's flat resembled what it must have been like in the last few minutes before the World War One soldiers finally got the order to go 'over the top'. They all withdrew to their own spaces within the flat, busying themselves in different ways; trying to ignore the precarious nature of their situation.

Sure, Byrne had played his hand well on the call to Redcalf, but there was still no guarantee that he would play ball. Given what they now knew about their long serving boss, he was obviously capable of anything, and was ruthless in his pursuit of his objectives. They all realised he could double cross them at any moment, but he was their only chance of getting out of Russia alive, a fact they were all painfully aware of.

John was in the bedroom, testing out his wounded leg. Yvette had already explained to him that the bullet had lodged next to his femur, and that if it had gone straight through the muscle and artery, he would have bled out in minutes. He had been lucky. She had removed the offending item on the first night back at the flat, and had left it in a pot on the side of John's bed, as some sort of macabre souvenir.

Byrne was in the living room, trying to pass the time by watching terrible Russian TV. The most nervous of the three, he regularly shouted into the kitchen for an update on the time from Yvette, despite having a perfectly adequate watch strapped to his left wrist.

Yvette was the most practical of their little group, and had spent the time preparing herself an overnight bag of sorts. It had not taken long; most of it had been packed since she had moved into the flat, and had sat on top of her wardrobe, just in case she needed to move at a moment's notice. It included all the essentials: foreign passports, a handgun, and a few wads of cash, in a variety of different currencies. She added to it her toiletries and a couple of days' worth of clothes, before doing the same for John and Colin.

The day passed slowly, and John eventually succumbed to his fatigue, drifting back to sleep on the bed. Yvette also eventually slowed down, settling into her favourite armchair and drifting off to the sound of Colin flicking from channel to channel. Byrne had no desire to sleep, not that he could have even if he wanted to. Having never experienced the realities of being on the front line, he did not know how to cope with this sort of suspense, so had instead taken it upon himself to guard the phone, and be on hand to answer it the moment it decided to ring.

Eventually, shortly before six p.m., Byrne's prayers were answered, though ironically they were all awake when it rang, eating the supper that Yvette had prepared for them.

Byrne leapt up and rushed to the phone, making sure to add the jamming device onto the side before lifting the handset.

"Hello," he said.

"Have you got a pen?" came the response from an unknown voice, definitely not Redcalf's.

Colin looked around and frantically signed to Yvette the need for a pen and paper. She quickly rushed into the kitchen and came back almost instantly with the requested materials.

"Yes, go ahead," Byrne barked.

"This is the message from Redcalf; I will only say this once. Your extraction will take place tonight at three a.m. We have a team flying into Minsk now; they will be there shortly. They will wait on the Belarusian side of the border until they get your signal. You need to get to Yartsevo, and call this number when you arrive."

Byrne quickly scribbled down the information on the notepad Yvette had supplied, and awaited the next instructions.

"Okay?" the voice asked.

"Yes, yes. Carry on."

"Once you are there, and have made contact, the evac team will fly over the border and collect you. Still three passengers, yes?"

"Yes, that's correct. Who am I speaking to?"

"That is not important. Once you have made the call, destroy the phone you used and wait for the evac team to collect you. They should be no more than ten minutes. Once they have safely negotiated the border crossing, they will drop you near Minsk, where there will be a Beta team waiting to escort you back to London. Any questions?"

"No, I don't think so."

"Okay. Good luck."

Byrne turned to the living room, his eyebrows

323

slightly raised. "We need to be in Yartsevo by three a.m., where the hell is that?"

"It's near the Belarus border," Yvette informed him. "Looks like we are going on another road trip. If we leave in the next few minutes, we should make it."

"Then what, Byrne?"

"Then we are getting out of here. Redcalf has organised a helicopter team to get us out; looks like he has come through for us after all. This is it, John, the home straight now. Hang in there, my friend. You will be home with your family again soon."

CHAPTER SIXTY SEVEN

Yvette, as a soon-to-be former member of the FSB, still had the correct paperwork and credentials to get them through any remaining roadblocks in the city, and Colin still had the diplomatic pass that Yvette had created to sneak him into the country, so Yvette thought it unlikely that anyone would question them.

"I suggest we leave to the north of the city, and make out that we are driving up to St Petersburg to meet the Security Council regarding the attack. They won't question that, especially with the airports still being closed off to internal flights. It will mean a slight detour, but once we are through the city barrier, we can make up the time on the other side."

"Sounds like a good plan, Yvette," Colin smiled approvingly.

"What about me?" John interjected. "There's no way they'll let me through."

"You'll have to go in the boot, John. You must be used to that by now," Byrne chuckled. "At least we're not threatening to zip you up in a body bag."

****

The three escapees made their way down to Yvette's trusty old Vesta in the parking lot. Luckily for them, it was already dark, so at least they had some cover whilst they attempted to carry John down the steps. He was a big man, and even with their combined strength, Yvette and Byrne were struggling to shift him.

In the end, John took it upon himself to hop the rest of the way, wincing in pain with every step. Yvette opened the boot and moved a few things around a little, trying to make it look as appealing as possible, but John was still not impressed, muttering something incoherent as he fell back into the tiny space.

"Jesus, this isn't big enough to fit a small child, let alone a grown man."

"Shh, John, people might be listening!" Byrne warned him, as he slammed the boot shut.

Yvette took the wheel, and was pleased to see she still had three quarters of a tank of petrol left from picking up Colin on Tuesday. "We have enough petrol to get us where we're heading, so we won't have to stop. All we need to do is get through the city roadblock; it will be plain sailing from there. The next ten minutes might just define how this story ends," she whispered barely loud enough for her passenger in the boot to hear.

****

Those next ten minutes felt like an eternity, but although John clearly had the bum end of the deal in the boot, at least he did not have to witness the eerie atmosphere that had befallen the Moscow streets since the Red Square the attack. The city was all but empty, and the deep fog made it feel like they were stuck in a scene from an old

Cold War television saga. The fast approaching curfew meant their brown Lada was anything but inconspicuous.

"A couple more corners and we hit the freeway, John. I'm guessing that's where the roadblock will be, so stay quiet."

John turned over to get a bit more comfortable and felt a strange sense of déjà vu. His fate was once again out of his own hands, and all he could do was pray one last time that he would make it home to see his family.

"Papers," John heard from outside the car, as the engine slowed to a halt.

"Here you go, officer," Yvette replied in Russian, and both Colin and John felt their heartbeats pause as they awaited the soldier's response. The solider in question looked about fourteen, but in reality must have been in his early twenties, and he seemed thoroughly unhappy about the assignment he had be given on this freezing winter's night.

"Thank you, you can go through. Safe trip," the boy said, in his thick muscovite accent.

"Thank you, officer."

Yvette casually moved through the gears as she went through the gap his colleagues had created, and accelerated onto the freeway.

"Is that it, Yvette? What did he say?"

"Yes, that's it, we are through. He just said have a safe trip."

Byrne's face lit up and called to the back to tell his friend the good news. "We are through, John, we are through. It looks like you might just get your happy ending after all."

CHAPTER SIXTY EIGHT

About an hour into the trip, Yvette pulled over to release John from his misery.

"Quick, John, hop into the back seat. You should be safe now; I doubt there will be anyone around on these roads in the middle of the night."

"Really, Yvette, I would have left him in the boot, just to be on the safe side. It's the 'last leg' of the journey, if you'll excuse the pun."

John stared at his partner with a look that told him that he still could, and would, beat the living daylights out of him, regardless of his damaged leg. The look was unsurprisingly sufficient to shut Byrne up.

It was just as uncomfortable in the back as it had been in the boot, and John must have attempted a thousand different positions before he finally found one that made the pain in his leg just about bearable.

Yvette, meanwhile, used the time in the driver's seat to contemplate what might be on the other side of the border, not in terms of danger, but in terms of her own future. She was leaving her life behind, the only life she had ever really known. It might have been a lie, but it was still her life, and moving to the UK filled her with fear. John was coming back to a hero's welcome, and a family that needed him. Colin? She was not so sure; he had told her very little about his private life. But he had been a good friend to her over the years, and she hoped that, maybe, he might keep in touch, and help her to settle into her new, as yet unknown life.

"Nine miles left, guys. Do you know where you're going to stop, Yvette?"

"I think so. There is plenty of space for the helicopter to land; we just need to make sure we give them a location that makes the extraction as painless as possible."

****

"I'm going to call it in," Byrne announced, when Yvette had stopped and she duly gave him a nod of acceptance.

Dialling the number carefully, he anxiously awaited the response on the other end. The line connected, but no one said a word.

"We're here," Byrne finally blurted out.

"What is your exact location, sir?"

"Err, where exactly are we, Yvette?"

"Here, give me the phone," she said, snatching it out of Colin's hands. "Latitude: 55.06667. Longitude: 32.69639."

"Roger that, ten minutes to evac."

"Jesus, Yvette, how did you know that?"

"It's on the Sat Nav, dummy."

The whole car broke into laughter, all of them giddy at the prospect of their imminent rescue.

****

Less than an hour later, they had been shuffled into the back of a black Mercedes in Minsk, and were now on their way to the airport, heading for Heathrow. The extraction had gone like a dream, and the evac team had been scarily efficient. The pilot had managed to land the helicopter in almost pitch black darkness, and within the blink of an eye, they had been extracted out of Russia.

The three British spies sat in the back of the Merc in silence. There was no need to speak. What they had just been through had formed a bond that would inextricably link them together for the rest of their lives.

CHAPTER SIXTY NINE

Almost exactly twelve hours after their successful escape from Russia, John was sitting in the secretary's room next to Redcalf's office, impatiently waiting for Byrne to make his appearance so they could get the formalities over and done with and he could be reunited with Wendy and his kids.

It had been too long since he had spoken to Wendy, and he knew he owed her a lot. He had been forbidden from calling her until after he had completed this final debrief, and could only imagine the strain she had been under these last few days whilst he had been missing in action. He was holding onto the knowledge that Ethan was now out of his coma and progressing well, but until he saw him and held him, he knew he would not be able to rest.

He had already booked his train ticket back; the next train left in just under two hours from Euston station, and he intended to be on it. If all went to plan, he would be back in the hospital by seven p.m., seven thirty p.m. at the latest.

Byrne was late, which was not unusual in John's experience. They had been split up as soon as they had arrived back in England, forced to complete their interviews separately, though they had received a hot meal and the chance to have a shower, so it had not been all bad. John wondered what was keeping him… surely they were not still interrogating him?

He couldn't stop fixating on Wendy; he needed to let her know that he was back and safe. It seemed cruel to make her suffer these extra few hours. What harm could it do? His decision made, he stood up from his leather chair and began to approach Redcalf's secretary, who was pretending not to take any notice of him.

"Hello? Sarah, isn't it?"

"Yes, that's right. So pleased that you made it back safely. Is there anything I can do for you?"

"Yes, actually, there is one thing…"

****

Colin was frantically making his way to level five, trying to decide whether he was more afraid of being late for Redcalf or John. Definitely John, he concluded, as he burst through the doors.

"Byrne, finally you made it. What kept you? I've been here for ages."

"Sorry, my friend. The debrief took forever. I'm here now. Do you know what this is about?"

"I suspect it's just one final interrogation from the boss before we are free men again, just to make sure they haven't missed anything. We might even get a pat on the back, you never know. Don't worry, I've got it all figured out. Let me do the talking; I know exactly what I'm going to say."

"Sir Steven will see you now, gentlemen."

"Thank you, Sarah, you have been most helpful.

After you, Byrne."

The two men entered Redcalf's office one after the other, and remained standing as he greeted them.

"Cooper and Byrne. What an unlikely double act," Redcalf opened. "So, first things first. The PM sends his apologies that he could not be here in person to welcome you home, but he has other pressing matters to attend to unfortunately. He asked me to express his sincere appreciation for the risks you have both taken this past week, even if not all of your choices have been 100% by the book. The ends justifies the means in this case, wouldn't you say?"

"Thank you, sir" John interrupted. "Will that be all?"

"Not quite, John. I do need to run a few final things by you both before you go; I appreciate that you must want to get back to your families, but this simply cannot wait."

"What sort of things, exactly?"

"Well, to be candid, what happens next? I assume we can't tempt you out of retirement, John?"

"No, sir, afraid not. This little adventure was more than enough for me, thank you."

"In that case, I trust we can rely on you not to divulge any of the more sensitive aspects of this operation. I should not need to remind you that you are still at liberty to honour the Official Secrets Act that you both signed, all those years ago."

"Don't worry about me, sir. You know I will take my secrets to the grave with me, don't you?"

"Quite, John. And you, Colin? I assume you understand your obligations too?"

"Absolutely, sir. I was rather hoping you could grant me a period of leave though, if possible. My retirement is still a few months away, but I'm not sure I'm of the right mind to see out my notice."

"Of course, Colin, that's no problem at all. I will ask Sarah to arrange it for you straight away. There is one thing in particular, though, that I must stress is particularly sensitive."

"Malakov, by any chance?" John interjected.

"Yes, John, exactly. The fact that he is no longer around is not just a relief to you and your family, but also to the country you serve. You see, he was—'

"Yes, sir, we know. He told me everything just before he died. I know the whole story: the reason he was released, and the attempted blackmail. He certainly was a crazy bastard."

"Yes, quite. You realise then how embarrassing this would be should it reach the public domain, especially considering the files in question?"

"Absolutely, sir. Haditha rearing its ugly head again. It won't seem to go away, will it? You can trust us, though. Like I said all those years ago, as long as I'm left in peace, there won't be any problems in that regard. I was good to my word then, wasn't I, sir?"

"You were, John, yes, you were. Very good. It seems we have everything in order here. I suspect you are both quite keen to get out of this place now?"

"Correct, sir, but there is just one other thing I would like to discuss first, if I may?"

"Of course, John. What is it, old chap?"

"Nothing really, it's just that, while I was waiting with Sarah, I took the liberty of asking her to send Wendy some flowers for me, you know, 'I will back very soon, stay strong, love John'. That sort of thing."

"Of course, I understand. You don't want her to

334

suffer any more than she needs to. I'm sure Sarah has it all in hand. If that will be all…"

"Not quite, sir. You see, you are right. She was most obliging; apparently, she often does the honours for you, when required."

"Quite right, a female job if ever there was one…"

"Something caught my attention, though. You see, when I asked her if she wanted the hospital address to send them to, she said 'no need', she would just use the address you gave her when you sent us flowers just after the attack."

"Seems like par for the course to me…"

"Except, when I quizzed her on it a little more, she said that you specifically asked to write the card that time, not delegating it to her as you usually do. And the thing is, we only received one bunch of flowers in the first few days; it was particularly memorable, because the note on it read: 'thinking of you and our sons'. Most odd, don't you think? In fact, it was that card that convinced me that Malakov was behind the attack, and encouraged me to travel halfway across Europe to track him down. I assumed Malakov had sent them, but he couldn't have, could he, if you also sent a bunch? Two into one just doesn't go."

"I'm not sure what you are getting at here, John, but I don't appreciate your tone."

"Let me spell it out for you then, sir. It wasn't Malakov who sent the flowers, just like it wasn't Malakov who ordered the hit on my family. It was you, wasn't it, sir?"

Redcalf paused for a moment, his face a mask of surprise.

"That's a hefty assumption to make from a bunch of

flowers, John. I mean, you may need a little thing called evidence before you start shouting that around town. Now if you will excuse me, I've got things to do."

"Not so fast, Steven. Byrne, cover the door. I haven't finished yet."

Byrne looked over at John, and could see the rage in his eyes. What the hell was he talking about? Yes, Malakov had not been responsible for all this, but blaming Redcalf? That was a pretty big leap.

"Are you out of your mind, John?" Redcalf exclaimed, outraged.

"Not at all, now sit down. The flowers were just the cherry on the cake. I was coming for you today anyway.

I'd pretty much come to this conclusion the moment I recovered consciousness, and then when Byrne added to the body of evidence, by confirming that the paramedics were fakes, I was sure. You see, the truth dawned on me when Dimitri was beating the living shit out Malakov back in Moscow; he told us a few things that made a lot of sense."

"Well, of course he would, he would say anything to save his skin."

"A bit like you now, then? No, he was speaking the truth. It wasn't him. Why would he want to stir the pot again so soon after getting out of prison? And why would he send us flowers after the attack failed, just to signpost his involvement? He just wouldn't. I can't believe I didn't see it before, but like he said, it's a lot clearer from the outside."

"So, he convinced you it wasn't him, I get it. But why vent all your anger at me? The flowers don't mean a thing, John."

"But who else has the motive and resources to

organise such an elaborate attack? You just made it look like it was Malakov to cover your tracks, in case your plan failed, which of course it did. It was very clever, making sure the hitmen had flown into the country from Moscow, via Dusseldorf; organising two different teams, with initial intruders to make it look like a robbery and then paramedics, complete with an ambulance, to come in if I got the better of the first two. I must admit, I didn't suspect the paramedics at all, it was pure fortune that they missed me and hit Ethan, well, depending on which way you look at it I suppose."

"Do you really think so little of me, John?"

"Well, I didn't, if I'm honest. That's why I didn't see it straight away. But then I didn't know what you were up against, did I?"

"Up against?"

"I had no clue that Malakov had such a big hold on you, and when I found out that the files he had were the Haditha files, it became obvious. People will do funny things when their own neck is on the line, sir, twenty years in the field taught me that."

"I didn't send you over there to kill him, John, you went of your own accord. I expressly told you not to, remember that?"

"Genius, sir, truly. You led him to believe it was Malakov," Byrne chipped in, becoming increasingly empowered. "Didn't you? And me, for that matter. You gave me the tools that would give him a suspect, and all you had to do was sit back and watch it play out."

"Exactly, Byrne. He got you to point me towards Malakov, and knew that, if I took the bait, he would come out on top either way. If I were to find him and kill him, then the blackmailer would be no more, and if

Malakov ended up killing me, then Malakov would lose any leverage he had in the first place. Either way, Redcalf, you would save the PM a fortune; avoid any awkward conversations about Haditha, and to top it all off, the one skeleton left in your cupboard, i.e. me, gets swept away in the process."

"Interesting theory, John, but like I said before, you have no evidence. The flowers don't mean a thing."

"That's true, I don't, but then again, I don't need any, do I? You forget, we have been here before, haven't we? Do you remember our little chat ten years ago, in this very room? Ring any bells? You see, Byrne, to catch you up, just before I retired, the boss and I had a very similar conversation to this one about Haditha, but what he doesn't know is that I kept a couple of nuggets back for a rainy day, and today, it's pouring down. Remember I told you about those files you would need, if I didn't make it back alive?"

"I do, John. Were they about Haditha, then?"

"Yes, Byrne. You see, Redcalf, that I can prove. I'm sure the PM would be interested in finding out how you covered all that up, and it's also a pretty solid motive to start another investigation into you now, sir. Like I said, I worked out the flowers in no time, imagine what an investigation team would uncover? I expect it would ruin your 'hero's retirement', sir. In fact, you would be looking at some serious jail time; you might never get out of there, sir. Think about that."

"What do you want, John?"

"Me? Nothing, sir, just the same as before. Leave my family and me well alone, and let us live our lives. Do that, and we will take this sordid tale to our graves."

"Will we?" Colin said, turning to his friend.

"Yes, we will. But listen, Redcalf. If either of us so much as gets a hint that you might be coming after us, we will dig up those files and post them to every newspaper outlet in the world, not to mention send a personal copy directly to the PM himself. Go off into the sunset, sir, and enjoy your retirement. There is no point in coming after either of us, it won't end well, I can assure you. Oh, and on the subject of retirement, Byrne would like the same little package you have organised for yourself, and a nice big golden handshake to boot. I'm sure Sarah can organise that for you as well, can't she?"

"Yes, John, I'm sure she can. You win. I will do as you ask, and organise your pay-outs."

"Good. Now, I'm going to go and see my family, but if I ever, ever hear that you have wriggled your way back into politics, well, I might just have to go to plan B. Goodbye, Steven. I hope your retirement gives you many hours to ponder and reflect on the decisions you have made in your career. I'm sure those gremlins will offer more than enough punishment for the path you chose to take."

CHAPTER SEVENTY

Byrne pulled the car around for his partner one more time, and opened the passenger door.

"Thanks, Byrne."

"No problem. You were immense in there, John. Well done, my friend. There is one question I have, though?"

"What is it?"

"Why not bury him, John? Why let him sail off into the sunset? We could find the proof we need; he has admitted to it. You said yourself, I'm sure he left a trail."

John paused, and turned to his friend. "No need. Sometimes, knowing the truth is more important than proving it."

"I don't get it, John."

"I guess you have to ask yourself, is it really in the public's interest to know what actually goes on in the name of keeping them safe, while they are all busy dealing with life? We are still secret service men, Byrne, and we signed the security act in good faith. We can't go changing the rules just to suit us now."

"I suppose," Byrne nodded

"Anyway, looks like you will come out of it smelling of roses. What will you do now, my friend?"

"Yes, thanks for that. You didn't need to, but all the same, thanks, John. To be honest, I quite fancy booking myself a break somewhere… south of France, maybe? What do you think?"

"Sounds good to me. You deserve it. You really came through for me, and I will never forget that."

"Thanks for the memories, old chap. Now, go and catch your train. Your family are waiting."

BV - #0062 - 280422 - C0 - 197/132/20 - PB - 9781803780399 - Matt Lamination